K-
Journey

By Sharolyn L. Sievert
Illustrated by Emily B. Boote

For the love
of dogs!

Sharolyn L Sievert
2013

K-9 Search:
Journey through the Storm

By Sharolyn L. Sievert
Illustrated by Emily B. Boote

ISBN-13: 978-1481889070
ISBN-10: 1481889079

1. Search and Rescue operations – fiction
2. Search dogs – fiction

Published by: K9 Search Books

www.K9SearchBooks.com

Printed in the United States of America.

Thank You

Some years are harder to live through – sometimes the storms of life seem overwhelming. When those times come, we need people in our lives that support us, keep us going and buoy us back up.

While I can't list them all – my family comes first:

My mom Sherry and my siblings, Linda, Sheldon, and Curt, as well as their families who support them when they've come to my aid.

And my dear friend Carma (you'll always be "Auntie" to my furry kids!).

Thank you to all of you
- Ariel, Gus and Jael – and of course me!
I'd love to hear from you –
email & we can swap some "dog tails"!

sharolyn_k9503@yahoo.com

Be Not Anxious

Consider the lilies of the field, how they grow; they toil not, neither do they spin, and yet I say to you that even Solomon, in all his glory, was not arrayed like one of these.

Matthew 6:28-29

Prologue

Holding on with a death grip, I wondered why I had ever agreed to go out today. I also briefly wondered if my hand was actually frozen to the pole or if it was self-preservation that held it there. I glanced over at Karen and saw she had a duplicate grip on the other end of the pole that curved up and over our heads. I wasn't the only one anxious which did make me feel a shade better. Why would anyone in their right mind agree to get on a boat in November with winds cresting the waves into six foot rollers? I suppose it was the reassurance by our hosts that the boat, a Boston Whaler, was designed to be stable no matter what Mother Nature threw at it. Mother Nature took on the challenge with gusto.

We had been on this same boat a few days before checking a different location on the lake but it had been relatively calm then. It was calm when I left home this morning too, but during the two hour drive to the search area conditions had changed. I wondered as I drove why Sheriff Tvrdik would choose such a day for a water recovery search as the wind threatened to blow my truck off the road.

The reason became clear during the briefing. Apparently, he had arranged for underwater equipment from agencies across the state to come tomorrow. Or more accurately, he asked and was told the equipment was available only tomorrow. We all knew its usefulness greatly depended on one thing. A small, well-defined search area.

Our search on Wednesday had eliminated a small section of what would need to be checked today. The problem was the rest of the lake still remained. It definitely put the pressure on our dog teams.

I personally didn't think the goal was achievable. I believed in the dogs as a tool in helping to find drowning victims, yet I also knew they had their limitations. High winds and waves, in my humble opinion, weren't the best conditions in which to use them.

As we left the protected anchorage of the dock, my dog raced to the front of the boat, the love of the search obvious. Within minutes, I found myself hanging on for dear life and watched in horror as my dog was literally lifted up off the deck. He slammed back down as the boat crashed into the first roller. He landed not unlike Bambi on ice - four legs splayed out - and I heard his teeth snap as his jaw hit. With a shrug and a shake, he tried once again to approach the bow of the boat only to hit the white plastic deck again as another watery wall hammered the boat. I settled myself as best I could on the bow and held tighter onto my dog. My other hand latched firmly onto the rail and I thanked God for a good personal flotation device, or PFD, for both my dog and myself.

Within minutes, I realized my position wasn't tenable. Making the decision to move during the short lull while the boat hung suspended between the waves, I scrambled quickly with my dog at my side. I reached the captain's console and skittered behind it, feeling the boat lifting for the next roller. As the bow of the boat came out of the water, it met the next wave. The resulting crash of boat hull meeting the wave jolted us all. Of course the how and why didn't matter as much as making a frantic grab for the pole which was now my life line.

In the back of my mind, behind the fear of drowning and the possible loss of my dog, was the nagging doubt that I didn't see how we could possibly work this search. My dog was staying behind the console and apparently had no intentions of doing anything more than standing there. I didn't blame him. I didn't want to let go of the metal pole that held the law enforcement light bar over my head. Karen yelled over the crashing icy waves, "Something to tell your grandkids about, when you have some!" The sheriff, who had decided to join us on the adventure, just laughed. My own laugh was shaky by comparison.

We went on, heading north and directly into the teeth of the cold wind. Every time the bow went down between waves, a cascade of icy water sprayed over us. Another look at Karen and I knew we were both thinking the same thing; protect the dog at all costs. She held onto the boat with one hand and kept one hand free to make a frantic grab if he went sailing. My death grip on the pole was matched only by my death grip on his leash.

Peering through the watery mists around our heads, I saw that a small peninsula of an island was coming up on our left. As we came around the tip of it, the sheriff dutifully informed me that we were now in the middle of the lake, some two miles long, and at its deepest point. Nodding, I realized a moment too late he was warning me. Suddenly the wind, released from the protection of the island, became a gale. To get around the island, the boat would have to turn its port side to that wind. Instinctively I knew this was the most dangerous part of our boat ride. As the boat turned, I could feel the props spinning freely out of the water and something deep inside me shuddered. As I looked across the vast lake, I noticed for the first time we were alone out there. If something should happen, who would rescue us? The relief of everyone on board was almost tangible as the propellers finally caught and pushed the boat forward again.

Shaking off the fear, or at least pretending to, I resolutely looked out and decided to trust the sheriff and undersheriff not to risk our necks or their own without good reason.

Privately, I wondered again why I had let myself be talked into this search. And the answer came in the form of my search management instructor, Barbara Jennings. I could see her leaning against the beat-up table in front of a bunch of young, eager students, explaining about searches. These kids, for they hardly seemed like adults, hadn't yet experienced that adrenaline rush when the pager goes off. They hadn't been mired in mud or rain-soaked in the middle of the woods. They hadn't held on for dear life, as I was now, on a patrol boat. But they all understood the message she said so simply, "Search is a classic mystery, one we all want to solve if we possibly can."

And that is why I was on this boat, why I was risking my life. I really wanted to find out what happened. Looking at the Sheriff, I knew he did as well. This search had gone on too long, covered too much territory, and had too much invested in it for him to let it go. He glanced at me and gave a slight nod as if reading my thoughts, confirming them.

Turning to look at wind and waves, I let my mind drift over what I knew about the case. It had begun shortly after Pop McCaffrey's funeral when my unit, Elk Ridge Search and Rescue had been called in for a missing person search. A young man had gone camping and didn't come home on time. There was nothing different from many other searches to which we had responded. Nothing to arouse suspicion or cause anyone to be concerned; it had all seemed normal.

As time had gone on however, one irregularity followed another. Vagaries were followed by contradictions. And almost two years after the 9-1-1 phone call from the family, Sheriff Tvrdik knew he had a problem. The possibility of foul play was rising to the top of probabilities while the straightforward "lost and presumed deceased" slid to the bottom. That is when he called us again, hoping the dogs could help provide a break in his case.

After all, while the clues had gone cold and witness memories faded, there is one thing that doesn't die away, the scent of death.

Chapter 1

Pop McCaffrey's death seemed to be the saddest bit of good news I was ever given that I could recall. I'd felt the loss more than I'd expected, but it was softened by the fact I knew he had made his peace with God before he died. Pop had given me the chance at a new beginning some years ago and I was thankful for it. I also knew I would miss him.

Of course, I couldn't deny that I was also grateful his estate was in order before he died. So in order, in fact, his son Charles hadn't made any effort to contest his final wishes. Charles had been my nemesis ever since I came to Elk Ridge and I prayed the death of his father would finally end the feud. So far, it appeared it had.

Pop's carefully ordered affairs included the building I now stood in, known as "The McCaffrey House". A bed and breakfast for people with disabilities, McCaffrey House provided not only my employment but my home as well.

So while the loss of a dear friend was hard, the news McCaffrey House would remain as a functioning business was a blessing. Pop had planned well for its continuance. Things would change as they always do, I knew that. I would work with new owners and an advisory board instead of Pop and our lawyers. What I hadn't expected was that Pop would name me as one of those new owners. He owed me nothing; I hadn't expected anything. In a way, I guess I knew it was his way of saying thank you.

Most of the other owners I knew well and saw daily. Martha and Margaret Thwaite had taken care of Pop's wife Virginia over the last years of her life. Adam Drahota, raised by Pop and Virginia after his own parents died, was the man who introduced me to Pop and had the idea of starting the business of McCaffrey House.

The final new owner I had never met, and apparently no one else had either. All anyone seemed to know was that he was a friend of Pop's from the war years. We hoped he would be a good man and have the same goals the rest of us did for McCaffrey House.

Pop, or as it stated on all the legal documents, Jason Charles McCaffrey, made his wealth through investments. With that wealth, he built a home, which was really more like a mountain lodge in the heart of the north woods of Minnesota. Situated on 200 acres of timber, prairies blooming with wildflowers, lakes and even a few swamps, it had everything anyone who loves the outdoors could want.

To accommodate his wife's mobility issues, Pop built trails through the land and they went out every day, weather permitting. One of the last photos taken of them had captured them on one of those walks. Virginia was gazing up at Pop; it was a look that I thought of as reflected love, because the look he was giving her was the same. They sat so naturally, his arm around her slender shoulders, her hand caught in his. The lake behind them shimmered and the trees stood tall around them. It looked like an engagement photo and I often wondered who took it.

That photo sat on my desk. Somehow it said more than I could about this place and the love that built it. It also reflected what I hoped to have someday for myself; a man who could look beyond my failings and love me anyway.

These thoughts cascaded through my head as I finished my morning shower, brushed my teeth, and got dressed. I put my hair in a ponytail and pulled on my coat and boots. All the while, Gus was bounding about, clearing an easy three feet off the ground from a standing position. Ari just tried to avoid the sixty-five pound Basset cross whom we affectionately called his "little" brother. Gus, realizing the moment was almost there, dashed under Ari's tummy to get to the door first.

Bending down, I nudged him back a step so I could open the door of our two-room apartment. Situated over the garage of McCaffrey, it let me manage the everyday affairs of the business yet have a place of privacy as well. Of course, privacy is a relative term as I lived with my mother. I'd learned over the years that she often knew more about my life than I think I did. At times, I wished she didn't, but life is what it is.

As I left, I could hear her in our small kitchenette, likely preparing her simple breakfast. I had started my coffee and could hear it dripping into the pot as the door slid shut behind me. Taking the dogs down the stairs and out through the garage, I waved to our maintenance man, Harold.

He waved back and thankfully didn't stop for small talk as he often did. Usually I didn't mind, but today I had a long list of things I needed to do, which included catching up the McCaffrey House accounts which had been sadly neglected since Pop's funeral.

Harold patted the dogs as they raced up to greet him. He leaned against a snow shovel as he watched them head for the small patch of woods we kept specifically for their use. Harold was our maintenance man and chauffeur for McCaffrey House, and I knew he was the local community's handy-man extraordinaire as well.

Because Harold was here, I knew Margaret and Martha were also. He brought them in Lolly, the McCaffrey House's handicap van. Each morning he picked them up, each evening took them home again; and anytime in between, anywhere else they needed to go.

Plowing through a new drifting of snow, I did my morning mental check list. Lately I'd noticed that I was starting to forget things and wondered if I shouldn't start writing them down. I hoped the forgetfulness was from information overload and not old age, but one can never be too sure. I was, after all, on the far side of forty now.

The dogs bounded through the snow, sending clumps flying as they ran. It was a giant playground to them. Normally I would have strapped on my snowshoes, but today I was in a hurry. I also hadn't realized the winds the night before would make such large drifts to deal with. Harold wasn't expected to clear the path to the dog's area, but there were days I wondered if I shouldn't ask him to anyway. The dogs didn't seem to mind, but my knee certainly did.

Finishing their business in record time, Gus plowed around me through the snow, his short legs and round barrel body not slowing him down a bit. In the deeper drifts, he looked like a Mack truck, pushing snow ahead of his big chest until his chin rested on the snow that inevitably piled up. He'd back up and go around the pile, starting a new track. We laughingly called him "The Snowplow" as Gus navigated his way around in the winter. He cheerfully nudged my leg, got a pat, and took off again.

Ari on the other hand gracefully bounded like a deer through the snow, his body moving easily, even though his age was starting to catch up to him. I didn't know how much more time he had left in him to work in search and rescue. I also knew it would take at least a year to get another dog ready for when he retired.

I had a hard time accepting my dog was aging. The first time he stumbled for no visible reason, I wrote it off. Then came the cold mornings he got up slower than usual, or remained standing instead of lying down because it was easier. I also began to see that he sat more carefully and every few seconds would shift his weight to ease the strain on joints.

I put him on supplements, prayed hard and began a concerted effort to find a puppy to train. The day of Pop's funeral brought the call I had been waiting for; a breeder on the East Coast was willing to donate a puppy to me. While the news was wonderful, deep down, I was hurting.

Ari was special to me. I wanted him to be like Peter Pan, never growing old. I wanted him to be able to work at least for the rest of my lifetime, although I knew it wouldn't happen. Even with the glucosamine, chondroitin, and whatever else I could find, he still had moments of discomfort. I understood. I was aging and felt it too. But Ari was my first SAR partner. He lived through my mistakes and conquered when many thought we would fail. He knew what I was thinking and I knew what he was thinking. I couldn't imagine finding another dog whose heartbeat matched mine like his did.

My best friend and K-9 mentor once tried to tell me about the relationship I would develop with my SAR dogs. At the time I hadn't understood. I did now.

"Rebekkah," Bev had said, "Your dog is different than a pet. You will know your dog better than you know your family, your kids, even your spouse. You will read each other's thoughts. When you lose your first, it will be like someone ripped your heart out and stomped on it for good measure. You'll pick up the pieces, but you'll never get them all. Some remain behind so you never get over it completely. People don't really understand, although they think they do. They are more than a family member, they ARE your heart."

I thought of Bev as I watched my dogs. Today Ari was running circles around Gus and myself, age a forgotten thing. He suddenly stopped and a performed a play-bow in front of me, asking me to respond with his favorite winter game. It was exactly as if he knew I needed to be pulled from the edge of a very sad cliff.

Scooping up a handful of snow, I lobbed the snowball in his direction, knowing I had the world's worst aim. It didn't matter. Ari leaped gracefully up and snagged the snow out of the air, landing in stride and running off, Gus hot on his tail hoping to get some of the special snow.

Gus, for all his loveable traits and abilities, was near-sighted. He wasn't very good at catching balls or anything thrown his way. But he still liked to try, so I called his name and waited until he turned to look before throwing the next snowball.

As it arched toward him, I knew what would happen next. It always did and I knew the feeling. I had tried out for softball as a child and, while now I could laugh, at the time I was traumatized. Every time I was at bat I had done exactly what Gus did. I shut my eyes and flinched backwards. I could never hit the ball because I was expecting the ball to hit ME. It wasn't until I was an adult and someone stepped behind me and talked me through the sequence that I hit a ball. It grounded out at the pitcher's mound and I was tagged out easily. I didn't care though. I had actually hit a ball and hadn't closed my eyes or flinched. I didn't play another game of softball after that. I figured it was better to quit while I was ahead.

I hoped someday Gus would have his breakthrough too. Today wasn't it, however, as he waited to the last second and flinched, the snowball hitting the ground in front of him. Applauding anyway, I was glad he had a better constitution for humiliation than I did. He jumped up and down like a kindergartner being told he was getting an ice cream cone for trying.

"OK guys, we need to head back. Mom's got a lot to do today, including setting up problems for training tomorrow, ok?" I started back toward McCaffrey, knowing they would come as they always did. Breakfast awaited and while Ariel was somewhat indifferent towards it, Gus was a food hound.

Feeding the dogs was easy; feeding the guests of McCaffrey House took precision and skill. I entered the kitchen and awaited my orders from the two women who reigned supreme there.

Margaret Thwaite was whippet-thin and serious. She could also appear to be vacuous, inattentive and possibly a little slow on the uptake. But appearances in her case were somewhat deceiving. She was focused, but her focus didn't include really anyone except her sister Martha. She was an amazing chef, although she never went to any culinary school to earn the title.

She could create meals out of apparently nothing, and remember all the details to write down later.

Martha was shorter and much rounder, very much rounder, than Margaret. She also had an interesting wardrobe that consisted mainly of reds. When I first met her I thought of Mrs. Claus, and while the visual remained, Martha was sharp and opinionated. Not qualities I've ever equated with Santa's wife. Martha was the business end of the cooking team. She made sure what they made was quality controlled, met the dietary requirements, and above all, made sure Margaret wrote her recipes down for later.

These two women had become my friends and in many ways, my life mentors. They'd periodically make a comment, usually off hand, that stuck with me. I even had one of their statements tacked to the wall by my work computer, "It is only a moment, not your entire life." That quote got me through some dark moments. Although, Martha is also the one who liked to say that the light at the end of the tunnel was usually the oncoming train.

"Rebekkah, stop standing there in a daze and get moving. The meats there need to go into the chafing dish and you know where to put the breads."

Martha's strident voice cut through my reverie and reminded me to get to work. Scooping up platters of steaming food, I distributed them as ordered, returning to gather the different breakfast breads they made fresh every day. I also did my own quality check as I toted things, snitching a bite here and there. Very irregular, but it was how I got my breakfast every morning.

By 6:30, breakfast was in place. People came as they wanted, knowing it was over by 9:00 and they would have to wait until tomorrow for another go at the buffet. Watching people as they came into the room, many drawn by their noses, was always immensely satisfying to me. This was one part of running a bed and breakfast I loved.

My part in the process was simply to set up and serve. My mom usually sat down with the guests and chatted with them. She told me from the beginning she felt so uncomfortable, yet I was impressed with how well she played the hostess day after day. She listened and asked pertinent questions, leading conversations to include others at the table. I often wondered if I would have been able to do this without her.

As my guests departed, I helped clear the table with Megan and Agnes, my right and left hand helpers. Martha and Margaret had done their part in cooking the feast; we got the task of cleaning up after them. Leftovers were delivered into the kitchen and, depending on what they were, could end up in other dishes for us later. Margaret always managed to elevate leftovers to more than just the normal Minnesota hotdish of cream of mushroom soup and tater tots.

Finishing the kitchen chores, I went to my little office just down the hall from the kitchen. As I had told my dogs earlier, the accounting books were calling and I had to answer.

I felt a bit out of sorts as I printed the last report. Normally I would have emailed them to Pop and the lawyers, Perry and Bill. Today however, I wasn't sure what I should do. Pulling out the documents I had received from Pop's attorney after the funeral, I read them through again. Nothing told me what to do; it was all resting with the advisory board apparently.

Bill Carlton, my attorney, had gone through the entire thing with me. I knew that besides the five owners, the advisory board consisted of Dr. Gary Sheffield, Pastor Dave Michaels, and Terrence O'Reilly, an attorney only known to me by name. Bill said they were currently reviewing the state of the business and would make recommendations to us, the owners. Until that time, things were being run as they had been prior to Pop's death. Except of course, I still didn't know who should get my weekly reports.

As I started to close the folder, the name of our fifth owner jumped out of the page at me. Jeremiah Hedstrom wasn't exactly a name a person would forget easily; at least the Jeremiah part. The Hedstrom name itself was fairly common here in Minnesota.

Adam used to sit at Pop's side as he went through his trunk of memorabilia, telling stories and letting Adam read his journals from the war. We all assumed that if anyone would know who Mr. Hedstrom was, it would be Adam. We were apparently wrong because he claimed no knowledge of the name.

As if Bill had been leaning over my shoulder, my cell phone vibrated and then progressed to the ring tone I had set for calls from my attorney. Pulling it from the case, I flipped it open, happy to talk to the man who not only represented me legally, but was also my best friend and, for lack of a more mature term, my boyfriend.

"Morning Bill. How are things in the big city?" I imagined him in his own environment, which was a large office with warm woods, old books and comfortable chairs. It was a place to relax and talk about all your worries, knowing the person across from you cared.

"Morning back. Fine, it appears that everything is just about complete with Pop's estate. He was a smart man, dealing with his properties as he did. Have you gotten used to the idea of owning part of McCaffrey House yet?" I allowed myself a moment of enjoyment, listening to his baritone voice.

"Not yet, it doesn't seem real. Everything still seems to be going along like it always has." I paused as I fingered the documents in front of me, "Do you have some sort of camera set up in my office? I was just rereading this stuff."

"Now that is an interesting idea. Much better than the still photo sitting on my desk... but alas, no I haven't. Maybe we are just starting to think alike?"

"Do you really want to think like I do? Don't forget I have a rather morbid sense of humor, stemming no doubt from the fact I work dogs trained to find cadavers."

"Ugh, you would have to bring that up. But I'm a lawyer; I'm used to just about everything now."

I smiled into the phone, knowing he was right. "Bill, has anyone heard from Mr. Hedstrom yet?"

"Everyone keeps asking me that. No, he'd likely contact Terry first. Terrance, you know." I knew he meant Terrance O'Reilly. He laughed then, and I thought of how much over the last few weeks our relationship had changed.

Through my own misunderstanding, I had pushed him away. It was in nearly losing Bill that I realized I loved him. We were now slowly testing the waters of a real relationship. We had taken care not to broadcast it, something I was happy about. I just wasn't sure I was ready to handle it. What the "it" was, I wasn't even sure yet. I hadn't even told my own mother, although I believed she had her suspicions.

"The real reason I called, besides to hear your voice again, was to let you know that it is okay if people want to get the things that were left to them by Pop. I wasn't sure if you knew or not."

I knew that several people had received specific bequests that were here in McCaffrey House. A china tea service to the Thwaites, the trunk of Pop's military memorabilia to Adam, and some theology books from the library to Pastor Michaels. The balance of the library he had given to me, which still felt illusory. That if I ever left McCaffrey House, the books would go with me didn't seem real. He also left me the piles of boxes, trunks and what-not in the attic. I had no idea what was in them and had not even considered checking yet. Perhaps when Adam came for his trunk I'd look.

"I'll let them know. Martha and Margaret seem more content to know the china belongs to them then actively interested in moving it from its location in the large hutch in the main room. I'll have to think of something to replace it when they do take it. It will leave a big hole there."

There was a brief moment of silence, and in the background I heard the murmur of voices. I waited, knowing it was likely Tracy, his confidential secretary, making sure he actually was doing the work he was paid to do.

"Yes, ok, sorry…had to sign a few things. I'd like to come up this weekend. I asked Adam if I could use their spare room and he said it wouldn't be a problem. Got the impression he'd like it actually. Are you going to be around before I finalize with him?"

"Bill, you can stay here, you know that. We usually have at least one room available, although I'd have to check for sure. Megan is doing almost all of the reservations now."

"I know the last time you put me up at the House, but there is always the worry about space, plus of course we don't want any speculation."

It took me a full moment to realize what he meant about speculation. He was thinking of my respectability, or maybe his own. It didn't really matter whose, I guess. I had never considered it an issue the last time he stayed at McCaffrey House, but then he had been just my lawyer. He hadn't kissed me yet and we hadn't started dating. Much had changed, even if no one else knew it.

"It makes perfect sense to me, and yes, unless we get a search, I do plan to be here."

"Good. I'll arrive on Friday around supper time. Can I take you out to dinner? I checked and about twenty miles north there is a place on Lake Andersen that sounds good."

I knew of the place, had heard great reviews on their restaurant from a number of locals and immediately agreed. I noted it on my calendar and wished him a good week and a safe drive up.

Hanging up, I found my mom standing in front of me with that "enquiring minds want to know" look on her face. She didn't say a word, but I knew she had heard enough to wonder why Bill wouldn't stay with us, and why he was taking me out to dinner instead of eating with us here.

"Bill's coming up for the weekend and will stay with Adam and Amy. Sounds like Adam really could use some masculine company, and Bill said he's never sure when we'll have space. Anyway, he's taking me to that new place on Lake Andersen for dinner on Friday. Any questions?"

"Only one. When are you going to admit you like him? I won't say love because I'm not sure you know that yet, but you do want more than a lawyer – client relationship with him. Maybe you should let him know. I believe he feels the same."

"Let it go mother. I do like Bill and yes, he likes me, but that is as far it goes right now." I turned and only heard the last part of her response, which went something like, "much further than that if you had any sense."

Flinching, I wondered why everyone wanted me in a relationship. The one area in my life I kept private was my love life, not that I really had one yet. But what I did have I wanted to stay private, even from my mom.

Returning to my work, I realized I had forgotten to ask Bill who I should send the reports to. Debating with myself, I finally decided not to call, to wait for the weekend and ask then. If anyone needed a report, they could always ask. I was just glad to have them done.

After lunch I actually remembered I had to call a woman who was asking about volunteering for Elk Ridge SAR. It was a good sign my mind wasn't completely failing me.

"Evelyn, I'll pick you up in about thirty minutes. Please dress warm, although you'll be walking today and creating your own heat. Tomorrow you'll be hunkered down and hiding, so it is really important to dress in several layers and make sure your outer layer is waterproof if possible. I'll have something for you to sit on, but your heat will melt snow, so best if you are protected."

"Yes, I have your list of things. No problem. Do I bring the scent article today or tomorrow?"

The scent article, the item of clothing or object handled exclusively by our "missing person", would be what Powder, our unit's tracking dog, would use to know which person she needed to find. Otherwise Powder could potentially follow anyone she pleased and be right.

"Bring it tomorrow. You said your son will be coming tomorrow, if he touches or handles it, then we'll need him to be present when Amos starts Powder so that she knows to ignore him. Does that make sense?"

"Yes, but I think, if it is ok, he would like to walk along when Powder works the trail anyway. He is the one that wants to learn, I just want to volunteer to help."

Evelyn's son, who I knew was around 17 years of age, had an interest in search and rescue. Having been around for a number of years now, I hated to burst Evelyn's bubble about Eric. The likelihood was he would probably not stick with it for very long. He might prove me wrong. I actually hoped he would. The problem was, SAR training requires so much time and commitment, the majority of young people gave up quickly, finding other things far more fun and interesting. Either that or they go off to school and start lives elsewhere. Sometimes they go back to it, but more often, people in their mid to late thirties discover it for the first time. They have established lives and children old enough to handle longer absences from their parents. They usually have enough time in their jobs to ensure vacation. Simply put, they can commit the time and resources. Most often, however, it is older married couples or single women with no real attachments except to their jobs and their dogs. Like me.

Hanging up, I had the dogs go to their woods for a quick potty break before loading them to go with me. I also loaded up a cooler that contained training aids for my human remains detection dogs. Although not something we talk about a lot, I knew that inside the cooler were things that most people would find offensive, or a term I was used to hearing, "Yucky". But to train dogs to find deceased persons, the aids are needed. When someone donates a tooth they had extracted, we willingly accept it. If someone gets a nosebleed, we keep the tissues. Our unit even purchased some bleached human bones online recently. I hadn't been kidding when I teased Bill about it.

We were meeting Marge Lee, one of my fellow unit members. Marge was setting up the training for the following day. As our training area was so remote however, it was far easier to bring our new hider to her, than give directions to Evelyn.

As I drove, Evelyn peppered me with questions and I was beginning to think she was more interested in SAR than she realized. I didn't push, but wondered if we might not be able to encourage her to join some day. Arriving an hour later, she eagerly jumped out, greeting Marge with a hearty "Here I am, where do you want me to go?"

Marge, a very straight-forward person who could create some tricky training scenarios, simply told her to wait a moment and told me if I wanted to run my problems blind, I'd have to wait at the truck, or take the dogs to the south and let them run. Nodding, I pulled out my snowshoes and unloaded Gus and Ari, telling them to come with me, not Marge.

"Marge, the items you requested are in the cooler. I left the keys in the console in case you need to move my truck or anything." As I strapped on the shoes, I could hear Marge explaining what she meant by working problems "blind".

"We don't really blindfold her. What we mean is, sometimes handlers need to know where their target is. That way they can work on specific steps of the training. If the dog and handler are strong or preparing for a test, they want to work the problem blind. That means they don't want to know anything."

"You mean, like a real search?" Evelyn impressed me with a concise synopsis of Marge's explanation. I could see Marge smile and knew she liked Evelyn too.

Leaving her in Marge's capable hands, I struck off to the south for a leisurely hike through Marge's woods with my dogs. She and her husband Martin owned some 400 acres that no one in their right mind would buy, but their intent wasn't to buy it for pleasure, but to protect it from development. I had to admit, being able to walk through it like this, I appreciated their efforts.

An hour later, I came tromping back to my truck and found Marge smiling and Evelyn looking totally worn out. I'm sure I had a similar look as snowshoeing is actually harder than it looks, and the snow was deep out there.

"How did it go? Still want to be a hider for us?"

Evelyn looked up from unhooking the snowshoes and flashed a smile of total exuberance. Pulling one foot free, she nearly toppled over, showing how tired she really was. Balancing on one foot, she responded, "I've never had so much fun in my life. I can't wait to come tomorrow. I hear we're supposed to get a little snow which will hide my tracks, right Marge?"

Marge nodded and gave her a shoulder to hold onto as she pulled her other foot free. "You're going to have a challenge tomorrow Rebekkah. You did ask for one, didn't you?" The laugh that followed hinted at her deviousness.

"Yes, I want a challenge for Gus. Ari needs to work hard too, but I don't want him plowing through all that snow tomorrow. He followed in my tracks today, but he's still feeling it. Gus never has figured out that it is easier to follow my snowshoes. He likes to break his own trail."

We all looked at the two dogs. Ari was standing tall, not panting at all, but I watched as he shifted from one foot to the other, his joints giving away his pain. Gus on the other hand was panting heavily, but the expression on his face was beauteous.

17

Happy, cheerful and tired were all wrapped up in that goofy countenance.

Opening the truck, I loaded the dogs and made sure the heat was turned on for Ari. Evelyn helped load our gear, while Marge kept the cooler. She didn't want me to know what she had used from it. Lovely. She was being very wily.

As we drove home, Evelyn watched Ari as he lay on his bed behind my seat and I could see her wanting to ask, but not sure what or how to ask it.

"Ari is eight this year. As he is a German Shepherd, his working life isn't much longer unless we're really blessed. He's currently certified for scent specific air scent, also called area search, trailing, as well as land and water cadaver. The problem is, he's starting to feel his age. SAR dogs live a pretty hard life. They are asked to perform like top athletes often on the spur of the moment, or in the middle of the night after driving for hours in a truck. It is hard on them. Ari is doing pretty well, but I've noticed recently he's been showing aches and pains he never used to have. I don't know if I'll get another 160 acre air scent search out of him."

Evelyn reached over the seat and gave him a gentle rub. He didn't move except to flick his ear at her and open one eye. He was tired, more tired than even I expected. I suddenly wondered if something else was wrong and determined to get him checked over and soon.

Chapter 2

What you will eat or what you will drink

S now was falling as I moved through the woods. I loved the snow, but right now, I knew from the feel of the air and the stillness that we were in for a big storm this time. Gus was ranging out ahead of me, his body periodically disappearing behind trees and brush as he sought the odor he was trained to find. Today was unit training day and as Marge had promised, she set up a tough problem. I suspected we'd be out for a little while.

I had asked for a challenge and the challenge presented was a thirty acre section of land, thick woods in spots, thick swamp grass in other areas; and I was working it as a double blind. Which of course means that not only did I not know where the training aid Marge hid was, neither did my field support walking with me. They couldn't cue me, even unconsciously as so many did. No leading remarks, no slowing down as the dog got close, or speeding up when the dog got distracted. Not even the sudden lapse into silence when the dog moved in to the source of the odor. We had to completely rely on Gus to do his job.

He bounded through the snow, his blue harness standing out against the whiteness. When Al gave a soft cough behind me, Gus turned to study him, his motion frozen for a moment.

"Rebekkah, I need to use the facilities. We've already worked that brush area over there, I'll use it." I nodded and told Gus to wait, something he generally doesn't do well. And of course he didn't. He continued to work a perimeter around me. Pulling out my little camera, I decided, since we were waiting, I'd get a photo of him in the falling snow. As I got him in frame, he suddenly went into a point.

Those that have seen Gus, know that the question of his parentage is highly suspect. His beautiful face, golden in color had deep dark brown eyes well set apart. They were perfectly triangular to his dark nose. His ears flapped over but set so the triangular folds made his forehead seem even broader. It was a clean cut and happy face. Based on that, many assumed he was a Yellow Labrador. But he seemed to retain no Lab instincts, and from there back, he didn't resemble one at all. Only about seventeen inches high, he could easily slither under Ari's belly and often did so to get someplace faster. His chest, massive and deep set, filled the gap between his front legs. His front legs, while longer than a normal Basset Hound, still retained the knobby kneed look of the breed. His broad front paws, which as a puppy did a double-hit as he walked, finished the look.

But then he changed. His long back had a strange striping down the length and we often joked he was part thirteen-stripe gopher. However the big muscled shoulders belied that idea. Someone suggested his shoulders should sport a tattoo that said "SARGE" with muscles flaunted in a sleeveless T-shirt. Gus however, had his petite side, becoming quite slender behind his girth. He had a neat tucked-up waist, rather slim hips with trim and tidy hindquarters.

But it was his tail that humored us. When carried out behind, it stuck straight out, then curved dramatically, looking very much like a scimitar. And where the tail "broke", a dark patch of black fur rested. Just like Shelties and Collies have on the middle of their tails. When we first got him, we thought it was a patch of oil or dirt and tried to wash it off. It never came off and was just another part of his uniqueness.

So when he went to a point, as he was doing now, the whole image changed to a working bird dog, his left paw pulled up tight under his large chest, his head outstretched, and his tail as straight as he could make it go. I snapped the photo and turned to see that he was watching Al come back.

Gus's poor eyesight made him study things and it took a minute before he recognized Al. Knowing he was upwind of my dog, Al let out a hearty greeting and welcomed Gus as he bounded over to greet him like an old long-lost friend.

"Good boy Gus! I'm done doing my business, are you ready to get back to yours?" Al leaned over from his height of somewhere around 6'2" and gave Gus a resounding slap on his side. Gus responded by hopping up into Al's face to repay the favor with a wet kiss.

"Get to work Gus, we don't have all day. At the rate this snow is coming down, we're going to have a fun drive home." Gus spun and raced off, his work ethic far exceeding his desire for affection, which was great.

About fifteen minutes, and I was sure another half inch of snow later, Gus turned so fast he nearly rolled. I glanced at Al and told him to mark the spot on the GPS. Gus slowed down and began sniffing deeply into the snow, tracking slowly along and I realized almost as soon as Gus did he wasn't searching for human remains. He had heard a mouse or small critter under the snow and was following it.

"GUS! Leave it! Get back to work." My drill sergeant voice was one that got his attention back to task.

"Let me guess, we lose that last waypoint?" Al was tapping into the GPS to delete it when I hesitated. The first stop looked spot on to Gus's normal behaviors when he was on the target odor. I wondered if he had it but got sidetracked by the critter.

"Gus, check back." A simple command, but Gus knew what it meant and scurried back. Both Al and I saw the change, same as the first time. He stopped short and turned toward the same tree. He worked around and around it, this time no distraction evident.

Calling him away, I worked him in basically a small perimeter around the tree. I wondered if the odor was clinging at that tree but in reality the source of the odor was further away. I could see nothing on or around the base of the tree except snow. Gus finally threw himself onto the ground in his normal dramatic fashion and demanded his reward with a sharp bark.

"Can you touch it boy?" Gus looked around, stood up and threw himself back onto the ground, but touched nothing. "Shoot. OK, either it is above his head line, but he's not put his head up at all... a burial? This close to the base of a tree? Too many roots." I paused and looked at Al, his cheeks as red as his nose

"Rebekkah, I can't help you, but you know your dog. Is this solid enough? Do you call it in and have them download the coordinates? Or do you keep working? If it was a real search what would you do?"

Laughing, I listened to the man who at one time was my student. He was now reminding me of what I taught him. "Ok, call it in and we'll move on."

I half-listened to their conversation as I gave Gus a few treats for finding something I couldn't see or smell. He gobbled them up and was as excited as if he had just started searching instead of being at it for nearly an hour. A flick of my hand and he bounded off again to keep working.

We finished the area with no other alerts and reported back to base. I noted that since we had been out, another inch of snow had piled up on my truck.

"K-9 Echo reporting back to base, permission to turn our radio off please," Al in reality was turning it off anyway. He handed off the GPS to Karen who was handling base from the driver's seat of her Ford Aerostar van. I loaded Gus and gave him extra goodies, passing some along to Ari who had worked a smaller section earlier.

Seeing Evelyn and her son nearby, I stopped and asked how it went. Her son was obviously not as enthralled with his afternoon as Evelyn was. She was, in a word, gushing. I knew if she could afford it, we had a new member for E.R. SAR. We stopped chatting as Marge whistled for everyone's attention.

"Guys, we have definite weather issues here, we all need to get on the road home. I hear our neighboring county has pulled their plows off because they can't keep up and it is getting dangerous. Rebekkah, you were the last out and have the furthest to drive, but just so you know, Gus located the murder scene. A combination of blood and bodily fluid from April Johansson's surgery was poured on the ground at the base of that tree. Good job."

Cheering, we all broke base down quickly and hit the road home. Turning on the auto four wheel drive, I brushed the snow off the truck while it warmed up. I was happy with our training today. Ari had run his problem first, locating the weapon used in the "murder" scenario Marge had set up. Then Chris's Onyx, her red-gold Yellow Lab ran next, finding the "victim" of the crime, really a mannequin filled with training aids to mimic a body. Amos and Powder had run a trail that was assumed to be that of the victim and ended up being a witness (Evelyn) who could corroborate the clues coming in for Marge's imaginary story. After Ari had located the weapon, Karen and Chief also worked the problem, locating the hammer Marge had dipped in April's donated fluids. All in all, it was a busy day of training and all the dogs worked their problems well. I drove out of the woods feeling pretty good about the day.

Within minutes however, the euphoria died as I found myself on a secondary road that was covered first in ice and now the heavy snow that was gaining momentum. Praying hard that the trip would be uneventful, I tried not to be concerned. Seeing the road was hard through the flurries and the windshield wiper was barely keeping up with the thickly falling flakes. Had I been driving anywhere but home, I'd have turned around and parked for the night. Slowing further, I turned on my radio to see if there were any road closings that might affect my travel plans. I had an hour drive to get home on normal roads, but at less than thirty miles an hour, my drive time had increased by almost another hour.

Ten minutes later I found I had to let go of the wheel to flex my fingers out. I had been gripping so tight it was hurting. I rolled first one shoulder, then the other, hoping to loosen my neck muscles as well. Visibility had dropped to only about ten feet in front of my truck and I had reduced speed to almost a crawl.

As the wind picked up, the snow began swirling and I considered pulling over and just stopping. I could call and let everyone know where I was. I had enough gear in the truck to last me three days, just as everyone in E.R. SAR carried in their vehicles. Things like a sleeping bag that would keep me warm and winter jackets for the dogs. I even carried a little pot that could melt snow using the cigarette lighter socket in my truck.

The thought had me starting to apply the brakes when I felt the vibration of my cell phone on my hip, the prelude to the boring ring tone that came next. Stopping completely, I promised myself when I could scrape the money together I'd buy a hands-free headset for the phone. Pushing the seat belt out of the way, shoving my stadium-length coat up, burrowing under my secondary jacket under that, I finally found the phone and pulled it loose.

"Elk Ridge SAR, Rebekkah speaking, how can we assist you?"

"Rebekkah, thank God. I was getting worried. Where are you? Marge called to see if you were home and you aren't. Are you ok? They've closed most of the roads now; this storm is the worst in years, at least that is what Marge said."

And Marge would know, having lived here her entire life. Once mom paused to take a breath, I jumped in, "Mom, I'm ok right now, but driving is horrible, I'm probably thirty miles away yet, and I was creeping along but can hardly see the road. I'll keep going and hopefully will see a place to stay soon. I'm pretty sure there are some homes coming up. If not, I may stay put and wait for it to clear. Before you panic, remember I'm well stocked with gear. I even have my snowshoes with me."

"I don't know what to tell you, but if you are still on 15, it is actually considered closed from what the news reports are saying. Please be careful and let me know what you decide so I don't worry, ok?"

I pictured her, already worried, wondering if she should do something. She'd do the best thing she could, and that was pray of course. I wasn't in dire straits; I could still navigate or choose to stop. I only hoped if I found a home or cabin out here, they'd be congenial about two large dogs too.

Choosing to continue on, I changed the setting from auto to full-time four wheel and put it back into drive. Creeping along, I was thankful my headlights were catching on the roadway markers to keep me between the ditches. I didn't even attempt to stay on the right side of the road, but instead picked the middle of the road as I could see it.

Sometime later I pulled through Elk Ridge and never felt so fantastic as when I saw the lights of McCaffrey House through the whirling snow. Pulling into my garage, I was completely exhausted and after clenching the steering wheel for so long, my hands were actually shaking. Sliding out of the truck, I unloaded both dogs and stood for a long moment to let my body relax. I took the steps up to the apartment slowly as my legs were trembling as I walked.

Pushing open the door, the dogs rushed merrily in, knowing dinner was on the way and clueless that they were ever in danger. All I wanted to was to climb into bed and sleep for a week.

My mom's greeting was fair warning that I was in trouble. The phone was in her hand and I realized I hadn't bothered to call her back. I should have and I knew it. It was unfair. She put the phone back to her ear said, "It is ok, she's here now. Yes, I'll let her know not to ever do that again. If I could, I'd ground her for a couple of weeks."

"Benjamin?" I asked quietly. Of course she would call the Sheriff's office, and of course the sheriff himself would be the one on duty to take her call. Thankfully she didn't call 911 which would have gone through the dispatchers.

"Yes, and he said he agrees, you should be grounded for putting me through that. What were you thinking?" My mom's knuckles were white, gripping the phone. Walking over, I put my arms around her and gave her a hug. She held on tighter than she normally did and I heard a muffled sob into my shoulder. "I was so scared Rebekkah. If anything should happen to you, what would I do?"

Suddenly, she pulled herself together and put space between us, finishing with, "You'd better call Bill and let him know you're safe too."

"You called Bill too? Why on earth? Holy cow mom, why?" Shrugging out of my many layers, I found my cell phone and hit Bill's speed dial number. I didn't laugh when she replied, "Because misery loves company."

"Rebekkah, are you ok? Your mom called all worried – you weren't answering your phone. I told her to call the Sheriff and let him know. She said they pulled all the plows off and she was afraid you were in a ditch someplace. Thank God you're alright."

"Bill, I'm fine. My phone never rang – maybe service was bad. I should have at least tried to call her, but it was hard to drive and make a call at the same time. And of course if she couldn't reach me…" I left the thought hanging that I wouldn't have been able to reach her. In hopes of changing the subject, I continued, "I'm guessing this storm will prevent you from coming up though, unless it clears off soon. I got through because the snow is still really soft, but once the wind hits it, it will become as hard as rock."

"Yes, I suspect it will. We'll plan for the following weekend instead – mark it down so you don't forget and plan something else. And Rebekkah, don't ever do that again. I really care about you and I don't want to lose you, ok?"

Hanging up, I apologized to my mom again. Looking out the window, I knew we would be shut down for a few days and instead of changing as I normally did, I went out to the main room of the House to let our guests know about the changing conditions. Most weren't expected to leave until Sunday or Monday, but at this point, I wasn't sure when roads would be plowed and cleared for travel.

I suddenly wondered if my whole spring would be like this. I loved snow, but not everyone would be as enthusiastic at being snowed in.

Thankfully, our guests enjoyed the snow and were able to go home on time in spite of it. The new guests arrived on schedule, and I was grateful that I could let the staff manage it. I was in the midst of a trial of my own.

Knowing I was getting a puppy was not the same as having the puppy in my arms. Arrangements had to be made, flights checked, finances budgeted to bring her home from Connecticut to Minnesota.

"Yes, I understand that a dog, especially a young puppy, can't ride in cargo this time of year. Isn't there any sort of escort service that your airline could provide? I guess you don't quite understand the problem. The puppy has been donated to me. I'm not in a position to afford airline tickets to fly clear across the country right now. But I do need to get the pup here to Minnesota." I closed my eyes, frustrated and edging towards angry. Who I was angry at I hadn't decided yet.

I hung up the phone thirty minutes later, feeling utterly defeated. I had tried every airline, every cargo service I could find over the past several days. I was nowhere close to figuring out how to get the puppy to Minnesota. You wouldn't think it would be that hard, but apparently, it was.

My hand was still resting on the phone when it rang again, causing me to jump. Answering, I listened to the Northeastern accent and tried to imagine what Judith might look like.

"Rebekkah! So good to talk to you again. How are your flight arrangements coming? I can't wait to meet you and see how you interact with Roxey." During her pause, I realized that

28

not only did the airline have no intention of allowing my pup to fly home without me, Judith fully expected me to escort her as well.

"Judith, I'm checking with airlines and she can't fly in cargo in the winter. I'm not sure what to do actually. That and flights are bit more expensive than I expected."

"I really want you to have Roxey, but I think you can understand that I want to meet you first and see you with her before sending her off to live with you. She's going to be a service dog; can't she fly in cabin with you?"

I took a deep breath, praying that God would fill the silence that encompassed my soul. It wasn't a peaceful or calm silence. It was a crushing empty silence. I had been studying the photos of Roxey for days now, wondering about her, imagining her personality and her intelligence. Claiming her as my own was still hard, but it had been getting easier until this moment.

Words unbidden came out of my mouth, "Well, God will provide Judith. I'm still working on it, don't worry. I've become rather attached to her photo now you know!" I felt guilty for saying something that I didn't believe to be true anymore. I was starting to doubt God really had intended this pup for me. That it was all just a big joke to someone.

We talked a while longer about what training Judith had been working with her on. From potty training to basic obedience to socializing, Roxey was getting a good start. As the conversation ended, I felt the familiar depression welling up inside, a feeling that something I really wanted would be yanked away at the last minute. My hand lowered and began to rub Ari's ears, comforted in the familiar feel.

Hanging up, I began another round of calls, hoping to find grant money, or a service dog escort service. While technically not a service dog in the federal sense, I knew some airlines did work with SAR dogs and figured I'd keep calling until I found something.

By the end of the day, I was tired, crabby and generally unpleasant to everyone around me. I allowed myself to dwell there, hating the feeling, but I couldn't seem to pull myself out of it.

It was the dogs that finally forced me out of my chair and into my snowshoes. Their method of guilt was the melting brown eyes and slowly escalating whines and it usually worked. Taking the walk in the growing darkness somehow seemed to fit my mood.

My mom at least knew the reason for my attitude, but my dogs didn't. I tossed a few snowballs and apologized by letting them have my focused attention for the next hour. As we returned home, I found at least some of my good humor back.

Helping with dinner, I continued to think of places to check for money for an airline ticket. A few months previously I might have actually asked Pop to lend it to me, but that option wasn't available anymore. I considered calling Bill, but deep down, I didn't want to admit I was broke. Bill knew it; he knew all of my financial business. I just hated the thought of admitting it. It was that and the feeling that I was always relying on others to bail me out. My mom would have, correctly, said it was my ego that held me back.

I slept little, periodically getting up to stare out the window and pray. It was all that was left to me by then. I had no other place to go.

"God, you know the situation. I'm really tired, I'm broke and I can't seem to shake the feeling that I'm failing somehow. I really thought you provided her for me. Here it is, I don't know how to say it, but I give her to you. I've been trying so hard to find a way and nothing has worked. If she is meant to be mine, you'll provide. If not, I pray she gets a good home."

I went back to bed, hoping to sleep but of course I didn't. Telling God I was giving my dream to Him isn't quite the same as actually doing it. At least I tried though. As I finally dozed off, I heard the winds pick up and knew we'd be snowed in again.

Chapter 3
Nor yet for your body, what you shall put on.

I don't know what time, but the sound of my phone pulled me from sleep. Groggy, I only said "Lo?" but the next words shook me awake.

"Rebekkah, we need you. We have a bad accident west of town and we need some medics. You are still a First Responder aren't you? No one else can get there," there was a pause and I blurrily said "how are you going to get me there?"

"Snowmobile, Ron and I both have ours here and there is a rescue pod hooked to mine."

I pulled myself out of bed and wondered if I were dreaming. Shaking my head, which was of course a mistake, I stretched and reached for my clothes.

Dressing in my warmest gear, I told the boys to stay home, they weren't needed this time. Pulling on my snow pants, I put my heavy fleece-lined E.R. SAR coat over that. My boots were quality, designed for hiking through the woods in all kinds of weather, not sitting still on a snowmobile, but I didn't have many other options.

Climbing on the sled behind Ron, I wrapped my arms around his waist and held on, my helmet periodically bouncing off of his as we hit drifts. Benjamin was behind us with the rescue pod and all the medical supplies. I mentally prepared myself, wondering how bad it could possibly be. People shouldn't be driving in this weather anyway, and those that were, were likely driving slow. I forgot my own rule of preparing for the worst.

There were three vehicles involved and one could see that someone had lost control and likely had spun several times before

33

hitting the second vehicle, which was forced into the path of the semi. The poor semi driver, while going slow, was part of a much larger force than the car. It ended up wrapped around the front of his Freightliner.

Climbing off, I saw that at least one person was out walking around, another was sitting in the vehicle that was in the ditch and one was lying in the snow, the pool of blood around them looking black in the unnatural light of headlights reflecting off the blowing snow. Grabbing the medical bag, I raced to the person down, unsure if she had been thrown during the impact or pulled out by someone. Yanking off my helmet, I heard Ron, his voice husky now with concern, asking what I needed.

"Triage the scene Ron. Check on the person in the vehicle over there and find out about the semi driver. Is there anyone still in the vehicle stuck on the front of that truck? What we need to determine now is who needs the most help first." I paused and grabbed his sleeve, "Ron, don't forget to put on protective gloves; there is blood everywhere." —

I had put my nitrile gloves on under my heavy leather mittens before we left. Pulling a mitten off, I felt for a pulse on the woman in the snow. Someplace on the pod was an AED, but I hadn't seen it when I grabbed the medical bag. I hoped Benjamin would. I thought I felt a pulse but pressing my hand against her chest, I wasn't sure. Calling over my shoulder for the AED and some help, I positioned a C-collar and waited, simply holding C-spine until I felt Benjamin kneel next to me. He easily fit the collar on and as soon the last Velcro was in place, he too checked for a heartbeat. Shaking his head, he immediately started CPR, letting me set up the AED and bag-valve-mask or BVM.

At that point I was incredibly happy Benjamin was still a certified paramedic. With a quick motion, the woman's shirt was opened and an expressive, if unrepeatable word, exploded out of his mouth. Benjamin was letting the world know what he thought of underwire bras. Cutting through them is often hard, but necessary for the AED. Otherwise it could arc and cause burns.

While I set the pads in place, he continued the respirations with the BVM. I heard Ron, his voice sounding normal again, tell us the person in the car was in pain, but appeared to be from injuries to their knees, the air bag likely saving her life. There wasn't anyone else in the severely damaged car; the others said she was thrown clear on impact.

Sighing, I checked the victim's neck angle and had Ron come down into the snow beside me and perform a jaw thrust. Even with the c-collar on, I could see the air wasn't going in to the right place. When the AED was ready, we cleared, everyone moving back from the woman to allow the automated external defibrillator to do its work. We all watched the AED intently. It ran through its series and gave the necessary shock, then told us to continue compressions. Benjamin, his intensity tangible, started them again, going through count cycle before we tried again with the AED.

Ron thankfully was doing a good job of keeping the others out of the way even while holding the victim's jaw. I kept hearing them asking if the woman was going to be okay and Ron answering in proper form that we were doing everything we could. He also murmured to us that he had radioed for support, which apparently would take time.

Rechecking the AED, this time it didn't give a shock and notified us to continue compressions and I felt a glimmer of hope that it had detected a normal heart rhythm, but just as quickly as my hope had risen it was dashed as Benjamin checked for a pulse at her carotid and then again by placing his hand flat against her chest. While he started compressions again, Ron and I both knew he hadn't felt anything. She was gone, this young woman lying in the snow. A vibrant life was gone in an instant, passing from life to death without any warning.

Benjamin nudged me and said softly "We'll keep at it, but we need to call this in, see what they want us to do," and turning to Ron, he continued, "Call it in, but quietly. See what they want us to do. We can't stop CPR now that we've started until someone with higher medical authority tells us to."

With Benjamin visibly tiring, we attempted the AED again with the same unhelpful result. I took over compressions while he handled the BVM. It felt so strange, this thing we were doing in the dark cold swirling night. Everything around me seemed dim; my only focus was the timing of the compressions and the backs of my hands.

We received word from the medical community hundreds of miles away. They didn't see the scene as we saw it, didn't see the poor woman lying so vulnerable in the snow, but the result was the same. Discontinue resuscitation efforts.

I glanced around for the first time since I'd initially sized up the scene and saw clothes were scattered around, papers blowing in the wind, swirling around and down. It was as though her whole life had been thrown out of the vehicle at the same time her life was. Looking back at the young woman, I realized her chest was naked for everyone to see and felt my stomach tighten. We had to leave the AED pads in place until the medical examiner came to confirm death, but we didn't have to leave her so exposed.

"Benjamin, can you find a towel or blanket?" I tried in vain to recover her with the remains of her bra and shirt, but they wouldn't stay in place. He immediately realized what I was trying to do and moved over to some of the clothes scattered around to find something while I held the cut edges in place, my hand resting softly on her, my prayers for her relatives, wherever they were. Benjamin came back holding not only a large blanket from the rescue pod, but a strong flashlight.

In placing the blanket, we bumped the BVM from her face and I was startled to see in the light that both ears had drainage, the type of drainage that indicated severe head trauma. It didn't make any difference now, but I knew that while we had done what we could, we likely couldn't have saved her. Tears formed in my eyes, and a few trickled down, freezing on my cheeks. I realized then that I was cold; really cold.

Ron and Benjamin between them managed to assist the injured woman from the passenger seat of her vehicle and put her in the rescue pod. I pulled the blankets around her and rechecked her vitals as they secured her in. As we worked, several more snowmobiles showed up. One of the new arrivals switched from his sled to the one with the injured woman and left quickly for the hospital. A moment later, her husband was bundled into a heavy coat and spare helmet for a cold trip to join his wife there. The semi-driver was fine and remained in his cab, communicating the situation to his parent company and wondering what he would do with his truck.

I wondered the same thing, but it wasn't really my worry. Poor Benjamin and Ron would be dealing with the scatter of vehicles locked together and starting to be covered by the blowing snow. The woman under the blanket wasn't my worry anymore either, but I felt such an infinite sadness I could never explain to anyone. One moment you are alive, the next, without fanfare or notice, you are gone. I felt my eyes being drawn to the shrouded figure more than once.

I was so focused that Benjamin startled me when put his arm around my shoulder and ordered me home. I glanced around at the scene and saw that our small ranks had been supplemented with two state troopers and some firemen. I wondered for a moment if they could spare a snowmobile and driver to get me back. As long as I had lived in the snowy state of Minnesota, I had never driven a sled and didn't plan to start now.

Benjamin must have seen my hesitancy and flagged one of the firemen who had arrived and I could hear them discussing the best way to get me back home. My feet, while wearing two pairs of socks and my good boots, were starting to get seriously cold.

Finally an agreement was struck and a fireman was assigned to take me home. Whoever he was, he wasn't keen on leaving a scene like this to drive some woman back to safety. If I had needed medical assistance it likely would have been a quick sell, but as it was, I was now superfluous to the scene. My predicament was cutting in on his adrenaline rush to do something.

I climbed on behind him and found his size wasn't just due to his snowmobile suit. I couldn't wrap my arms around his waist and he none-to-gently shook me off his back anyway and said to grab the handles, his sled was equipped for a passenger. Smiling, I thankfully grabbed the handles and leaned into the seat as he hit the gas and we shot off at a much faster clip than we probably should have. That was ok with me; I wanted to get back and let this man go back to being a hero, if only according to his own conception of what that might be.

Long years of being part of a volunteer fire department, I had learned about these kind of fireman. They were the ones that didn't show up to training. They only responded when they knew it was a "big one" and something they could tell the boys about down at the VFW. They liked to carry a radio so they could listen in on calls and took an odd sort of ego boost in being known as a fireman.

The vast majority of firemen also love the adrenaline rush of the work they do. The difference, however, is they also take their tasks seriously. They train consistently and show up even if it is a call that has no potential of a pat on the back later. They do the menial tasks as well as the mighty ones without question. They are the real heroes, although they would never let you call them that.

I arrived home unscathed, dumped my outside garments in a messy heap in the garage, and went straight back to bed, completely exhausted.

Amazingly, my mom didn't wake me. She took my dogs out, fed them, and filled in for me at breakfast. When I finally woke up, it was because I could hear our apartment phone ringing incessantly. Crawling out of bed, pushing dogs out of the way, I groggily answered, "Hello?"

"Rebekkah, are you still in bed? Did I wake you up? OH – are you SICK?" My sister Sarah's voice seemed to echo in my head and I wondered briefly if I was ill. I wasn't, I was just not awake yet.

"No, Sarah, not sick at all. I didn't sleep well last night. Mom must have let me sleep in. What's up?" Sarah didn't call often, but when she did, it was usually something important.

"Sis, mom told me about your situation. I have some frequent flyer miles and I want you to use them to go get your dog. You'll fly Northwest out of Minneapolis to Hartford. Can you go this weekend?"

"What? Sarah, what are you talking about?" In the haze of my mind, I thought mom had made plans for us to visit Sarah that she forgot to tell me about.

"Don't you need to go to Connecticut to get your puppy? Mom said you did…"

Light finally dawned through my sleepy fog. Sarah was offering to give me my dream.

"Sarah, are you sure? Weren't you saving up for a trip to Hawaii or someplace like that?" My eyes suddenly blurred over, tears coming and there wasn't anything I could do to stop them.

Sarah ignored my question, instead going on about the flight, "Sis, I just need some details in order to make sure it all goes ok. You'll have to do some calling too. Remember the dog has to have all its shots and stuff. You'll want bulkhead seating; and Rebekkah, someone told me to tell you to bring clean-up supplies and piddle pads."

It was this last thought, domestic and mundane, that finally broke my silence. I started to laugh.

"Yes, I'll do that. You said I need to make calls, can you walk me through it?" My sister had sacrificed her vacation for me. I didn't understand why, but was so very thankful. In a few hours she had everything arranged, leaving me feeling somewhat like I was hit by a tsunami.

My call to Bill to explain that, yet again, we'd have to postpone his visit was actually harder than I expected.

"Rebekkah, I completely understand, really." I listened to the timbre of his voice and sensed something inconsistent with the words.

"Bill, I didn't plan it this way, it just happened. Sarah made the arrangements…." I trailed off, knowing Sarah had asked me if the weekend would work and I had agreed.

Momentary silence met my answer, and feeling a guilt I didn't even understand, I filled the silence with nonsense. I knew it was nonsense, but I wasn't sure how to stop myself.

"Rebekkah – please stop. You are babbling and that is something I don't think I've ever heard you do before. When I say I understand, I understand. I will tell you that I wish you had asked me first, knowing I had planned to come up."

"I'm sorry, I should have I guess. But you can come the following weekend and meet the new arrival!"

Again silence met my answer. He wasn't happy, which made no sense to me. He should be happy for me, but he wasn't. I only wished I understood why. Bill finally said, so softly I almost couldn't hear him, "I pray you'll have a safe trip and please call me when you get home again."

When a storm comes, sometimes there is very little warning. So it was for me. I was so wrapped up in my own little world, I wasn't even aware of those first few drops of rain. I simply brushed them off and went on planning my trip.

I drove to my friend Bev's home on Friday, excited and worried at the same time. My life was about to change again and while I couldn't wait to get Roxey, I worried about every single step of the process. The flight arrangements were still not finalized for the trip home. I had printed out the clause from the airline's website about "Service Dogs in Training" to present if there were problems, but that didn't stop me from worrying.

I hadn't seen Bev in what seemed like years. We had been keeping our friendship up via email, but it wasn't the same. I happily left my truck at her place and accepted a ride to the airport. As she drove, I knew I was talking non-stop. Glancing over at her, I fully expected she would be happy to get rid of me. Then I realized she was as excited as I was about my new puppy.

"Rebekkah, go through your bag. Do you have everything? You don't want to get to Hartford and find you forgot a leash or something important. You brought a backpack carry on? Good thought, you don't want to be dragging a puppy and a suitcase through the airport."

She smiled as she came across a little folded up dog vest in the bag. It was blaze orange and Paula, the wife of one my members in E.R. SAR, had carefully sewn "In Training" on both sides. It would hang like a tent on a puppy, but it was Gus's first search vest and it seemed right to use it for my new puppy. Bev knew it was Gus's; she helped me train him. Brushing her fingers over the fabric, she folded it back up and tucked it inside.

"It will be too big, but at least she'll be clearly identified." Giving Bev a hug, I went into the airport and departed on my adventure.

As I sat on the tarmac waiting for my flight to clear for takeoff, my unit back home received a call for an overdue camper. The details were sketchy, as they often are on the initial call from an agency's dispatcher. A young man went out to do some snowshoeing and camping in the Boundary Waters over spring break. His vehicle was found where he had planned to park it, his gear was gone. Everything appeared as if he had taken his camping trip as planned. Except that he failed to return on time.

I learned about the search when I called home that night to let Mom know I had arrived safely. How she found out I didn't ask, but I didn't think too much about it anyway. I had only a flicker of jealousy when I heard the teams were flown in by the Civil Air Patrol. While Ari had made training flights, neither of my dogs had ever been actually flown to a search yet.

I was focused on meeting my new pup, not on a search hundreds of miles away. After all, I was here in Hartford because I knew Ari was aging and couldn't handle those heavy duty searches anymore. A Boundary Waters search would be extreme duty. I had seen the devastation caused by the massive straight line windstorm, or derecho, that went through there in 1999. That storm had destroyed millions of trees covering hundreds of thousands of acres. It was the storm of a century for Minnesota and areas like that required young strong dogs like Chief and Onyx. I knew it was well beyond Ari's capabilities now.

So I put the search out of my mind other than to whisper a prayer for the K-9 teams and focused on Roxey. Meeting her, I found Judith to be as open and friendly as she had seemed on the phone.

From her photos, I could see Roxey had her mother's sable coloring but was built like her dad. Watching Wolf move was like watching my own Ari. Smooth, graceful and strong. With such beautiful parents who showed confidence and character, I knew Roxey would be something special. However, upon entering the puppy room I had my first twinge of concern. Roxey sat quietly in a corner, watching me while her siblings tumbled over to meet me. She made no overtures toward the stranger in the room. I mentally wrote it off to the fact it was nearly midnight and we had awakened them with my arrival.

By the time I went to bed that night, my concern had lessened and I was dreaming only of starting this new puppy with her SAR training. I never even gave a thought to the search which was already in full swing.

My unit would tell me later that the man in charge, a man I hadn't met yet, was Sheriff Matthew Tvrdik. From what they saw, he was learning about managing a search as he went, but his instincts were good. I myself would learn later he was as stubborn

43

as they come. But all that came much later. That night I dreamt of sable puppies with giant ears.

In the morning, I once again spent time with my new pup, watching her play with her siblings. I was happy to see that Judith had her dogs well socialized. Wolf was baby monitor much of the time. He watched with benign interest as they clambered around some puppy-sized agility equipment in the yard, only reprimanding one pup as she tried to clamber over the top of him instead.

Once again, however, the warning flags surfaced as I was greeted several times by the other puppies, but Roxey simply watched me. Judith, as if sensing my concern, called her over and introduced us. I crouched down and waited as the puppy sniffed me over. She seemed not so much afraid as cautious.

"Rebekkah, Roxey needs her rabies before she can fly out, I've got appointments for her and Ginger this morning." She called the puppies in as I waited on the living room couch, an Italian Greyhound on one side of me and a cat on the other. As the puppies came running in, I felt a moment of pure pleasure as Roxey bypassed Judith and came to my side.

I hardly dared to breathe, but Judith just smiled and said, "I guess she has chosen you."

We gathered up the two pups and drove to the clinic. I periodically turned to look at them; Ginger was alert, excited and playful. Roxey on the other hand was quiet and watchful. Again I worried.

Judith chatted as we drove, but I honestly don't remember what about. My thoughts were churning. Is this really the right dog? Physically she was perfect; strong, square, and well put together. She just seemed so timorous, shy or possibly even afraid. Was this trip for nothing?

Arriving at the clinic, I watched Judith take a very confident Ginger through the sliding glass door and I followed with a pup that appeared very nervous of the strange reflection that moved. I waited with patience as she sniffed and looked at it, finally helping to nudge her through. Feeling my concerns getting deeper and stronger, I walked her slowly into the clinic. She quietly greeted Ginger, ignoring her sister's attempts to play. I looked up to find Judith watching me, and I realized she knew I was having second thoughts.

I smiled and looked for positives. She greeted other dogs in the room with appropriate responses of a well socialized pack animal. She didn't bark or whine. She didn't seem to get thrown into a panic. She just didn't seem to have the ability to handle change.

After her shot, I finally heard her whine. It was the first sound she had made since we left the house earlier. Glancing at Judith, I asked if that was a good sign she needed a potty break. She nodded and I headed for the door with Roxey in tow. She came along quite well now that we were leaving. At the glass door she hesitated only a moment and then walked through.

As we crossed the parking lot, I suddenly felt my heart flip.

Roxey's motion slowed, her head dropped a bit, then went up, then down as her nose twitched and her breathing changed. Studying the line of the wind, I saw what she had smelled. Judith's truck was three cars away, and the little pup was working the scent as naturally as I'd ever seen a dog do. Tipping her head to follow it first under a truck, then the head came up as the wind shifted and carried the scent over a car.

Praising her, I sighed in relief and chalked one more thing into the positive column. She could do scent work. But I still worried about her courage. Turning back to the clinic, she trotted up to the door, watched it slide open, trotted in and dropped her head to the floor and sniffed. I let her lead me, watching as she gave a sniff in each row. She kept moving until she suddenly turned down one aisle and trotted happily to the end, greeting Ginger with a poke.

"Judith, I just saw this little pup use her nose like a pro. She figured out the door and had no qualms once she figured it out. I think she's just the type of dog that needs to have time to observe and learn. I was worried, but I'm not now."

Judith laughed and gave me a hug as she said, "I could see you were worried. I was too, but not because of Roxey. I was worried you wouldn't see what she has to offer the right handler. Abbey, my daughter, said you were the one the minute you walked in the house. I didn't tell you, but she had taken to hiding Roxey when people came to see the pups. She'd watch them and if she didn't think they would be right for her, Roxey would remain out of sight. She didn't hide her from you."

"Really? Wow. I hope I live up to that! By the way, we need to put her forever name on the paperwork today. I'd like to call her Jael."

"Why do you want to call her Jail? I didn't think SAR dogs did apprehension work." Judith asked, looking clearly stumped at my choice of names.

"Jael – J.A.E.L. really it should be pronounced Ya'el" I smiled at Roxey who suddenly seemed to look more like a partner than a shy puppy. "Ariel, my older male Shepherd's name means 'Lion of God' in Hebrew. Jael has a couple of meaning variations, including 'to ascend to a high place' and 'to be helpful'. I felt it was a good choice for a K-9 who would have to be agile and helpful." I let the puppy sniff my hand and gently touched her huge bat-like ears before continuing, "Besides, Jael is a Biblical name. Jael of the Bible was praised for saving the Israelite people by killing the captain of the enemy forces. The historic Jael was brave." I finished as I gave the pup a look that said she, too, would need to be brave.

48

Chapter 4

Is not the life more than food

and the body more than clothes?

While I encouraged Jael to be brave, back home my unit members and many others were bravely battling the Boundary Waters Canoe Area Wilderness. The BWCAW, a vast place covering over a million acres of wilderness, allows no mechanized conveyances. While the searchers were flown in by a U.S. Forestry Service de Havilland Beaver, the balance of the trip was on their own two feet and paddling in canoes. Their dogs were challenged with hours of transportation some hadn't been in before, and then asked to begin searching in terrain that had broken many an experienced woodsmen.

Many times over the years I've been amazed at the ability of our K-9 partners to adapt and give their entire being when asked by their handlers. More often than not on real searches they find nothing, but every time they are asked, they willingly go again.

That is the dog I needed for search and rescue and I prayed fervently that Jael would prove to be that partner for me. After all, God had provided her to me and He knew best. Or at least I hoped it was His direction and not my own headstrong desire to get the pup.

The following morning I carefully repacked my bags, making sure all the puppy supplies were on the top of my backpack. Today Jael was coming home. We had completed the paperwork the night before, and in my bag I had the transfer of ownership, copies of her shot records, my own SAR resume and a note from my unit showing me as her trainer. I had contacted the airline the night before as my sister had recommended. After an hour of talking to several people, I still wasn't sure they would allow my puppy on the plane.

I smiled as I realized I was thinking of Jael as 'my puppy'. It was the first time I'd claimed her. Smiling down at her, I pulled the orange vest from my pack and slipped it over her head. Snugging the strap as tight as it would go, I watched it slip sideways. As predicted, it hung like a tent on her.

Jael stood still for a photograph and we all got into Judith's truck for the trip to the airport. Abbey sat in the back, her arms around Jael, holding her for the last time. I felt tears creep into my eyes, knowing what it must feel like for her. My Jael would always be Roxey to her. Reaching into the back seat, I gently touched her hand.

"Thank you for keeping her safe for me Abbey."

"She's a special dog Rebekkah. I know you'll make a great team. Send pictures, ok?"

I nodded and the truck fell silent as we arrived at the airport. This was it. Goodbye for them, and for me, the anxiety of not being sure if they would let Jael on the plane with me. Glancing at Judith, I gave her what I hoped was a confident smile.

"Be brave like your Jael, Rebekkah. All will be well."

Approaching the counter, I handed my ticket in and started the long explanation of my traveling companion. The woman behind the counter smiled and held up a hand.

"I've got you booked with your SAR dog in training in a bulkhead seat. We are completely ready for you. When you get to the gate, just let them know, they'll help you. She's adorable by the way."

50

I turned to see my puppy sitting perfectly quiet next to Judith. She looked like a dog ready to serve her master. Smiling back, I said only, "This is my first time traveling with a puppy and I can't thank you enough for making check in so easy."

Turning, I pulled on my backpack and took Jael's leash in my hand. As we started toward the security gates, I felt a little surprised as the puppy walked along with me. I could see Judith and Abbey shadowing us on the outside of the lanes channeling us ever closer to the x-ray machines. I felt so strange taking the pup from them.

Arriving at security, I carefully placed the backpack in the bin, slipped off my shoes and patted the pup as I did so. As I stood back up, holding a leash in one hand and shoes in the other, I realized something was wrong. A TSA agent stood blocking my way.

"Ma'am, the dog should be shipped cargo."

"Actually, she can't, she's too young and it gets too cold in cargo. She's cleared by the airline to fly with me in cabin." Sounding more confident than I felt, I placed my shoes in a bin to send it on its way. The agent stood for a moment and then stepped back. I walked forward with my puppy in tow. As we passed under the scanner, alarms went off and I wondered if the agent was actually calling in reinforcements. My brain recognized a moment later that it was the metal detector and my heart settled back into a normal rhythm.

I checked my pockets while Jael patiently waited. Nothing in any pockets. As I stood there, one of the security people said softly, "Try the collar and leash."

Scooping my puppy up in my arms, we slid the collar off and dropped it with the still-attached leash into a bin. Holding my

51

breath, I stepped through the scanner once more. Silence; I glanced up to see that our entrance had brought several more security.

"Must have been the collar and leash; thank you for thinking of that. Is everything else ok?"

"That is the quietest puppy I've ever seen. Isn't she precious?" One of the female guards slipped the collar back over Jael's head and gently scratched her cheek. Several others stepped over to ask permission to greet my puppy and with a slightly embarrassed glance over my shoulder, I waved goodbye to Judith and Abbey. I smiled as I realized they were laughing at my odd predicament.

Placing my pup back on her four paws, I pulled on my shoes, grabbed my backpack and started the slow walk to our gate. Periodically Jael would stop cold as things caught her attention. I'd stop, let her look for a moment and then encourage her to walk with me again. Each time she toddled along beside me as if she had known me all her life, not just 24 hours.

Arriving at the gate, I felt a sense of relief. Here I could sit and not worry about missing my flight. Checking in, it was pretty obvious I was the person they were waiting for.

"Do you want to load first or last?"

"I think last, then we won't be waiting quite as long on the plane."

"That's fine. She's a wonderful looking dog and so well behaved already!"

Smiling, I thanked him and explained I could take no credit for her good behavior. Leading her over to the chairs, I sat down and placed my pack on the floor and met her liquid brown eyes.

Realizing she was feeling frightened, even if no one else could tell, I leaned over and picked her up. She nestled down into my lap and in silence watched the world go by.

Jael's little orange vest kept sliding sideways and yet she didn't fidget or fuss about it. Brushing the strange colored variations of her fur, I thanked God for getting us this far without a problem.

Loading into the plane, my pup only hesitated once as we went down the walkway. She caught a glimpse of the world outside, a breath of fresh air blowing through the gap between the plane and the walkway. Jael stopped to peek out; seeing nothing but air, she calmly stepped back and followed me onto the plane.

I pushed my pack under the seat and spread out a piddle pad on the floor where I planned for her to stay. Feeling a hand on my shoulder, I looked up to find the flight attendant explaining it would be best to have the puppy in my arms for takeoff.

Scooping Jael up one more time, she curled up in my arms and I sat back to listen to the safety briefing. It was halfway through the presentation when I realized that no one else was watching the attendants however. Everyone else was watching Jael, including the attendants themselves.

Looking down at my dog, I saw her watch the attendant in first class for a moment, then turn and watch the attendant standing just a foot away from us. Then she turned and watched the first class attendant again, returning her gaze in a moment back to our attendant. The person sitting behind me finally voiced what everyone else was thinking.

"She's comparing them! That is just so funny! Don't you wonder what she is thinking?"

The attendants started to giggle too as their safety briefing came to an end. Jael, if no one else, had watched the entire thing, which was probably a good thing. At least she'd know what to do if the plane suddenly lost altitude.

Takeoff went smoothly and after we had leveled off, I slid my pup to the floor. She didn't move, just continued to watch the world around her. She gave our attendant a start however as she came by with the beverage cart and Jael touched her ankle with a cold nose.

I'm not sure what cued me in, but I realized she was thirsty. She gave no outward sign, made no noise, but she had fastened those brown eyes on my face with a purpose.

"Excuse me, but could I get just a cup of ice cubes for the puppy? I don't really want her drinking a lot of water, but I think she's thirsty."

"Of course, here is your 7-Up and some extra ice. I can't believe how good your pup is being. I mean, she's so young, yet she acts like she's done this many times. Has she flown before?"

"No. This is her first time and I have to admit I'm amazed myself. She's a trooper, that's for sure. Thank you so much."

Picking an ice cube out of the cup, I held it out to Jael, who sniffed it and then took it and laid it on the floor between her feet. Glad for the piddle pads, I watched her as she licked the cube. Finishing, she looked for another, which I gratefully gave her. After three small cubes, she was done.

The rest of the flight she quietly stayed on the floor and I began to think Judith must have had her bark box removed or something. She was just too quiet! She didn't move around, she didn't have any accidents. I kept waiting for something to go wrong.

Arriving at Minneapolis, I was thankful that I could scoop up the unused and still dry piddle pads and stuff them into my pack. Waiting for everyone else to exit the plane, we were the last to leave. Thanking the flight crew, I departed with Jael walking beside me in a perfect puppy heel.

Checking a map board, I had a faint moment of fear. I either had to walk for ages to get across the airport or take the light rail. I wondered if my little trooper-in-tow could handle yet another odd conveyance.

"Jael, we have a decision to make. I don't know about you, but I need to use the facilities. The bathroom is right here and you'll need to come with me. So far you've been an angel. Please don't fail me now." Entering the bathroom, I took her into the stall with me and she simply stood and waited. After washing my hands, I looked down at her and asked with complete seriousness, "Are you really a puppy or an old dog in a puppy body?"

Her serious dark eyes stared back at me. It reminded me how my mom always said Ari was born old. I wondered if Jael, too, had been born old.

I could tell Jael was starting to feel the strain of the day as our stops became more frequent. I used the time to call Bev and let her know I was in town with my puppy; she could leave for the airport anytime. Restarting, we arrived at a moving walkway with no apparent way around it. Taking a risk, I carefully walked onto it and stopped, checking Jael as I did so. She walked on and stopped moving when I did. I felt rather proud as we rode the moving walkway together.

I did question this strange little dog that walked along with me. Was she real? I had never been around a puppy like this. She just kept trudging along, never seeming to question. She had so much thrown at her so fast, and yet she hadn't shut down, had an accident, hadn't cried, whined or barked. Crouching down, I snuggled her up and told her what a good dog she was being.

Arriving at the light rail station, I took a deep breath and waited while the doors slid open. Helping her step over the gap, we entered and once again were the center of attention. Smiles developed quickly and someone asked me what she was in training for, pointing at her oversized vest.

"She's in training for search and rescue. Her breeder donated her to me and we just flew in from back east." I leaned down and rubbed her neck, loving the incredible softness of her fur.

"I'm impressed. My dog wouldn't be this good and he's like five years old now!"

"I'll be honest; I keep asking her if she's really a puppy or just faking it. I've never seen a dog this young act this mature before myself."

I answered more questions as we made our way to the other terminal where Bev would meet us. Helping Jael out of the light rail, I patted her and told her just a little further. As if understanding completely, she perked up and trotted with me to the doors which took us out of the terminal and into the fresh cold air of a dark Minnesota night. Breathing deeply, I wondered if my puppy needed to go potty yet. Apparently not as she merely sniffed and moved on as we walked toward the curb.

I breathed a prayer of thanks as I saw Bev's truck pull up as if she had been nearby watching for us. Throwing my pack in the back seat, I lifted Jael into my arms and climbed into the cab. Buckling up, I started talking about the trip before the door was even shut.

All the way to her house I chattered until, as we pulled into the driveway, I finally paused to say, "I hope this wasn't too much trouble for you. I really appreciate it!"

"Just so you know, my mom is very worried your German Shepherd is going to eat one of her little dogs. Let's take it slow about bringing her in. I do assume you're staying for the night and not trying to drive all the way home this late?"

"Eat her dogs? She's hardly big enough to…. Well, I guess your mom's dogs are pretty small. Don't worry, she's got good social manners. My guess is, she'll submit and move away. But first I really want to see if she'll go potty. She hasn't done anything since early this morning."

Opening the door, I lowered her to the ground and climbed out after her. She showed her first hesitation as an explosion of barking came from Bev's home.

"It's okay baby girl. We'll walk right past them to the gate there and you'll be in a big back yard with plenty of places to take a potty break. I hope." Walking tentatively beside me, I could feel her stress about the barking. I realized then that I hadn't noticed much barking at Judith's.

Entering the back gate, I unclipped the leash so she could wander on her own. She didn't. She hung close to my leg. Sighing, I trooped through the snow toward where I could see marks of other dogs.

Jael padded along beside me and then trotted ahead. She carefully detoured around the already used area and pushed through the snow toward a clean place and crouched. Relief flooded through me as she relieved herself. It took a full two minutes for her to finish and I praised her for going "business" the entire time. She trotted back to me and I rubbed her face, brushing snow off.

"Can mom let Micala and the dogs out?" Bev asked.

Micala, Bev's little British Labrador, came racing out and just as she reached my diminutive little puppy, she slid to stop and rolled on her back. Jael looked at her with what appeared to be concern. Then two little white dogs with coal black eyes and noses raced up to her, barking as they came. Jael ducked her head and turned away, just as I had predicted. Avoiding the confrontation, giving way, and agreeing the other dog had control of the space. She then tried to jump into my arms. I was to find over time this was her defense mechanism for stress.

She did not, however, submit. Smiling, I watched as she sniffed Micala and then the two seemed to accept each other. My new little pup had dignity and some self assurance. That was good. She'd need it when she got home to her brothers-to-be.

That night I took Jael outside at least six times, worried she'd have an accident in my friend's home. She didn't. She didn't have any business at all outside. Morning came much too early for me, but with it, Jael finally utilized the dog bathroom area to its fullest extent.

Feeding her some of the kibble her breeder had sent along, I loaded her into my truck and parted with my K-9 mentor and best friend.

"Good luck Rebekkah. She looks like she'll be a good dog with some patient training. Don't let her sit back at home, get her out and about as much as you can."

"Expect lots of emails Bev. I'm sure I'll be asking lots of questions!"

Driving away, I was on the road for an hour when I started to once again worry about the complete silence in the crate in the back. Trying to push down a growing anxiety, I couldn't do it. Pulling off the highway onto an exit ramp, I stopped and went to the back of my truck and peaked in.

Jael lifted her little head, her ears so large she looked rather like a bat. Feeling a tad stupid, I murmured something about if she had water and closed the door again.

The rest of the trip was silent except my singing along to the radio to help keep myself awake. Turning into the driveway of McCaffrey House, I said to my silent companion, "We're home Jael. You get to meet your brothers and my mom!"

Backing carefully into the garage, I slid out and stretched before going to get Jael out. The snow hadn't disappeared while I was gone, but it had melted some, which I was glad to see.

Hooking the leash to the matching purple collar, I lowered my new family member to the ground and led her outside to the potty area. She sniffed around and relieved herself. Returning to look up at me, I praised her profusely. Pulling out my cell phone, I called my mom to bring Gus and Ari out to meet their new sister in the great outdoors instead of our small apartment.

I waited until I heard the garage door open and then I dropped Jael's leash. I wanted her to feel able to get away if either dog overwhelmed her. I was actually worried more about Ari as his social skills had always been severely lacking. A fault of mine, not his. I had spent so much time socializing him with people, I had forgotten to have him spend time with other dogs and it showed.

Gus on the other hand appeared to like other dogs - especially female dogs. Gus was something of a Canine Casanova. As my boys came racing over, both slowed at the sight of the puppy and for her part, Jael immediately tried to launch herself into my arms.

Deflecting the clawing pup, I gently assured her the boys wouldn't hurt her and reminded them to "be gentle".   Ari approached her from the rear to give a sniff while Gus raced up to her face.   She deferred to him, turning her head, ducking her shoulder and then once again tried to launch into my arms.

Crouching down, I gave Gus a rub while I patted Jael, "Nice Gus. Be nice to your sister. This is Jael. Ari? You okay boy?"

Ari had come up and as soon as he approached her shoulder, she suddenly submitted.   It was the first and only time I would ever see her submit to another dog.   Ari nudged her hard with his muzzle and she remained still until he turned.   As she started to stand, he wheeled around and pushed her back into the snow.

"ARI! Gentle. Go slow boy."   He barely glanced at me and waited patiently as Jael lay under his muzzle, waiting for him to move.   It was then I realized that while her body said "submit", her eyes were still saying "I will not."

Trying to be patient, I walked a few steps away and watched as Gus ran over to where Jael had relieved herself and sniffed it over.   Whatever happened between Jael and Ari in that moment, I was to never find out.   When I looked back, he had allowed her to stand.   With her head low, she leaned out and sniffed him. Turning, he walked away and marked over her spot in the snow.

Jael ran for me and in a clumsy puppy bound, nearly made it into my arms.   Pushing her back down, I said softly, "Jael, you will need to learn to deal with this stuff on your own.   I won't always be able to hold you like this."   I let her stay there however, holding her soft body in my arms.   I almost wished I could hold her all the time.   Ever since I was a small child, I'd wanted a dog to cuddle with but so far I had never had one. Feeling her snuggle into my arms, I wondered suddenly if she might be the one.

The next few days and weeks were challenging for everyone. My new puppy that came without a voice discovered it eight days after her arrival. A sharp, piercing bark that rang through our small apartment. I was thankful to learn it didn't seem to penetrate into the main part of the House. It was hard to believe because it felt like it punctured our eardrums every time she sounded off.

In addition to the newly found barking, Jael had forgotten all she ever learned about potty training in the short flight from Connecticut to Minnesota. My mom had always claimed Ari was the most backward dog she had ever seen in the potty training department. Jael quickly proved her wrong. No matter what method we tried, she struggled to understand that urinating in the apartment was against the rules. I spent many hours on my knees with a brush, paper towels, vinegar and carpet cleaner in my hands.

The bright side to her arrival was her acceptance into the family by Gus and Ari; Gus more so than Ari, as he fell "in love" as only Gus could. He took time each morning to clean her eyes and ears, holding her down with his short stubby legs. He also instigated play with a happy bow which sent both dogs into a headlong game of joyful chase.

Ari simply avoided the activity and I once again wondered if something were wrong with him. A few days after I returned home, I finally made a decision to bring him to a vet. I noticed him limping during one of our walks, and as I bent over to check his leg, I realized heat was radiating from his body.

My luck with veterinarians in the area had been less than stellar, but a few calls to my unit members helped. Al had heard that a new vet had opened a clinic about an hour west of Elk Ridge. It seemed a rather lonely place to set up practice, but I was willing to at least meet him and determine if he could handle the health needs of my working dogs.

Arriving at his small clinic a few days later, I liked the exterior immediately. It wasn't a clinic, it was a home. Or was a home prior to becoming a clinic. Inside, it was apparent it was actually a home and a clinic.

Ari had always been good for vets and never got upset or stressed. He was to be my barometer to gauge the new man. Ari never warmed up to the last vet we used. I also quickly learned he hadn't known much about working dogs or their ailments.

Entering, I watched as Ari kept his feet firmly on the carpet squares thrown about the room and noticed he could go from one to another without touching the glossy hardwood beneath. Chalk one up for the new man. Ari hated slippery floors.

Crossing to a small desk, I found sitting behind it a man some years older than I was. He was scowling at the computer in front of him and without missing a beat, said in a surprisingly friendly voice, "Do you know anything about computers?"

"A little. What is the problem?" I leaned over to look at the screen. It was completely blank. It didn't even look like the monitor was on.

"I don't know. Nancy always starts it up when she comes in, but she called in sick today. I pushed the button down there on the box and nothing happens. I can hear it whirring around, but blank screen." With a blunt finger, he tapped at the screen.

"Is the monitor on? Push the little button in the lower right corner."

As if by magic, an image appeared on the screen. A large up close and personal shot of a smoke gray Great Dane. With uncropped ears.

"Wow, that is a great photo. What a beautiful Dane!" I studied the photo hoping to see if it was one of those commercially produced ones people steal off the internet, but instead the man behind the desk glanced up proudly and said, "That's Bongo."

"Your dog?"

"Yes. He's in the other room, likely fast asleep on my couch with the remote pinned under his jaw. Full of drool. You know, most people don't realize from the photo that he's a Dane."

"With that face, what else could he be? By the way, I'm Rebekkah James. I have an appointment with Dr. Mikkelson. Are you him?"

"Good guess on that one too. You have a German Shepherd who is not appearing to act normally. Let's take a look. Isn't Ariel a girl's name?" I flinched as I heard him pronounce the name as it had become popular after the Disney movie about the mermaid – airy-el.

"Ari-el. Means Lion of God in Hebrew. We call him Ari for short." I walked around the desk, leading Ari who took care to make sure every paw landed on a carpet square.

"Ah – nice name when you know the meaning. He's a good sized dog. Let's get a weight on him."

"74 to 75 pounds usually, but he hasn't been weighed in a year or more now."

Stepping onto the rubber matted-scale, Ari stood perfectly still as the scale's digital readout settled at 75. "OK boy, off you go." Easing off, he walked purposefully to Dr. Mikkelson and placed his muzzle into his lap.

"Hard to enter things into the computer with your head in my lap big guy, but that's ok."

Rubbing my dog's head, he pulled an opthalmoscope from his lab coat. Holding Ari's head with one hand, he studied his eyes. Ari once again held still and was a perfect patient.

"How is he about having his mouth handled?"

"Ari – show teeth buddy." I lifted his upper lips and Ari promptly opened his mouth fully for the vet to check. Next came his ears, then a manual check of the rest of Ari's body, my dog clearly enjoying the attention.

"He's going to hate getting his temp taken you know," Ari merely tightened as the thermometer was inserted. A calmer patient you couldn't wish to see.

Looking at the thermometer, I finally saw a reaction from the good doctor.

"Has he been lethargic and tired? Showing any signs of lameness at all?"

"Yes to both actually."

"I'd like to do a blood test for tick-related problems, but it is likely just a little infection as everything else seems normal."

I stared at him, feeling a bit stupid. Of course he was right; it could be just a tick-borne disease.

The snap test took only minutes, during which we chatted about dogs and his reason for coming to this remote corner of our county.

"My daughter Nan moved here with her husband a few years ago. He runs sled dogs and while they live on nothing, she's been happy. I decided to retire and endured a year of doing nothing. That is really tiring, doing nothing, so I asked if they thought a vet could make a small living up here. Work shorter hours, spend time doing what I want to do but still keep my hand in. Moving here, I realized my daughter needed a little extra income, so I hired her to be my vet tech."

"Here we go. Doesn't take long thankfully. Nothing. Not even borderline. No shadow at all. He probably has a small infection. A low dose antibiotic should take care of it."

He looked Ari over once more and I saw the dog finally begin to fidget, his joints were hurting from standing so long.

"You should see some improvement in a day or two. If not, let me know, ok?" He disappeared through a door and I sat down in a chair and waited. I realized that we never actually went into an examination room. I wondered if he had one, but as he came out, I could see a table in the room behind him.

"Here you go. Again, if he doesn't improve, please call me. I am just not certain I believe the test. Do you have other dogs? Are they showing any signs?"

"I have two other dogs. Gus is a mixed breed that appears to never get sick and my new puppy is a German Shepherd who is three... no four months old now. All of them are search and rescue dogs. Although the pup is of course just in training. That's why this guy is so important."

"Not because you love him so much?" He smiled at me and I couldn't help but smile back. He was right. Ari was important because I loved him.

"Thanks doc. I'll let you know how it goes. He has to recertify for cadaver in a month, so he can't be getting sick now!"

"How often does he have to test in order to deploy on searches? Can he take the test at a later date?" He rubbed Ari's ears as he spoke.

"It depends on the certifying organization, but most require annual tests to make sure the dogs are still working properly. The tests are often hard to get set up, so missing this one could put us off the call-out roster for another year."

On the drive home, my cell went off and I found myself diverting to a search. Calling my mom, I let her know and asked her to tell my staff my change of plans. I then began the task of contacting searchers through our calling tree for the unit.

"Hey we have a search over in Tower Hills. Subject was supposed to be picked up by a family member at the clinic, but it appears he walked away before they arrived. Definite dementia and, with this cold, we need to move fast. Ari's just been diagnosed with a possible low grade infection. If Chief, Onyx and Powder are good to go, great. I've got Ari with me, but I hate to work him if he doesn't have to."

In rapid succession, I had a roster in my head, if not on paper, of who was arriving and when. I knew the town of Tower Hills, but not the immediate area around the clinic. I was glad I had the computer still in the truck. At least I could print out maps if needed.

Arriving on scene, I quickly set up our radio base and computer, using a small corner of the county's emergency response trailer. Karen and Chief arrived first, although I had hoped for our tracking dog Powder first to get a direction of travel. Most people with dementia tend to walk in a straight line, so if we could get the direction, we could send Chief leap-frogging ahead for searching the larger sections of land.

"Do you think he could pick up the scent and get a trail?" Karen shrugged and merely said she could try it.

Letting her go to collect the scent article, I went over the Lost Person Questionnaire and map with the deputy assigned as our liaison. As we worked, I mentally calculated how long before Amos and Powder would arrive. I had contacted other units, but their ETA was even later than the members of Elk Ridge SAR. I really wanted a trailing team to start the search, not our air scent dog. Kenny had been missing only six hours and every hour that passed only made scent work harder.

Karen stuck her head into the trailer and said she was geared and ready to go. Was there anyone who could be her support in the field?

"Deputy, do you know of any firemen or other deputies who could be a field tech for Karen on her search? She'll be busy watching her dog so she needs another set of eyes and ears. They just need to handle the radio, watch for traffic and hazards, fend off people who want to know what is going on. Karen is trained for keeping track of her location and carries a GPS."

He nodded and disappeared out of the trailer as I went over the map with Karen. It was her call how to work her dog, but it was my job to give her the assignment on where to go. In this case, I had no idea what the highest probability area would be. It would be like throwing a dart at the map to decide where to send them first.

"Karen, don't take it personally, but I had hoped to get a direction of travel with Powder, but Amos was out in the back woods when we called, he won't be here for another hour or so.

I'd like you to start at the PLS, see if Chief can pick up anything. He's scent specific. I know you haven't tried what some call off-leash trailing, but it would be worth a try. If you get nothing, please stop and come back in, we'll reassess."

"Rebekkah, Ari is still certified with trailing, why not at least see if he can get a direction for us? He wouldn't have to go far."

I shrugged, uncertain if my dog could actually work. The vet had noticed his nostrils were dried out, which is typical of a dog with a fever. Could he do his scent work?

"No Karen, I don't think so." Still, I glanced at the map noting the area wasn't rugged or difficult. Maybe he could handle it.

"It wouldn't hurt to try, and he's a better option to pick up a trail than Chief is, you know that."

Nodding, I made the decision and put Karen in charge at base until Al showed up to take over.

Chapter 5

Behold the fowls of the air;
for they don't sow or reap or gather

Gathering my gear and the scent article Karen had collected, I waved the deputy over and explained the change in plans. Pulling Ari out of the truck, we went through our normal routine before I scented him. I walked him around the point last seen, letting him sniff and check on a relaxed line, then returned to where I had left the scent article and his harness. Slipping the latter onto him, I normally felt my dog begin to strain at the leash, anxious to get started. Today however he remained quiet. Pushing concerns to the back of my mind, I scented my dog and gave him his working command.

"Track Ari," I stood quietly and fed out his long line as he casted around the PLS for the subject's trail. It took much longer than normal and I knew he was struggling. Was this the right area? Had our subject actually been here? Then Ari began to move, his strides picking up and while he still wasn't his normal self, he appeared to be working a track.

Settling back into a fast walk, I noticed a pair of sunglasses on the ground. Ari stopped and sniffed them, glancing back at me. This again wasn't normal behavior for him. If the glasses were the subject's, my dog would have told me by sitting or touching them with his paw. And if they weren't Kenny's, then Ari would have ignored them.

"Deputy, you might get these glasses checked. The dog located them, but he didn't give me a normal indication that they are the subject's. Best to log them."

Ari continued on, but with an abnormal amount of drifting side to side. It was when we reached the bottom of a hollow which protected a perfect track trap I realized we had a problem.

69

Track traps are those wonderful areas that preserve footprints just by design of nature. In this case, it was an area where the recent snow melt had left a smooth surface of clean mud. And not a single track.

Pulling my dog in, I felt a sort of internal panic. The dog I had learned to trust for eight years had led me down the proverbial garden path. With my gut rolling, I turned to the deputy accompanying me.

"He's off track. I'm not sure where he lost it either. Let's head back to base and see if our other tracking dog has arrived yet."

"Are you sure? We've come about quarter of a mile, hate to stop if there is any chance at all." He sucked air through his teeth and held it a moment. As he released it, he made a peculiar whistle which eventually petered out. When the sound stopped, I thought it about covered the way I felt at that exact moment.

"Yes, I'm sure. My dog isn't having a good day and we need to head back." I mentally berated myself over and over as we walked back. I should have known better than to try and work a dog that was just prescribed antibiotics for an infection. What was I thinking? Was it pride? Maybe it was.

Loading Ari back into the truck, I gave him water and a treat for trying. We had radioed ahead that we didn't get a track, and I was happy to see that Amos had arrived with Powder. I could see her through the windows of Amos's truck, a young, healthy, strong dog, ready to tackle whatever came. For some inexplicable reason, I suddenly felt jealous.

Shaking the troubled thoughts from my head, I entered the trailer and waited for my unit member to check in and get his briefing before heading out with his dog. Al had arrived as well and Karen was clearly getting ready to deploy too.

"Rebekkah! What happened?" While Al's question wasn't accusatory, in my present state, it felt like it was.

"Nothing. Absolutely nothing. I shouldn't have taken him out of the truck Al. What, three hours ago he was prescribed antibiotics because he's running a temp and doesn't feel good. What was I thinking?" Handing in my GPS, I continued, "I wouldn't use this for planning where to search other than I don't think our subject is in there. Ari wasn't on track, I don't know if he ever actually got one or was just trying to please me. But I do believe if he had air scented Kenny, I'd have seen him alert."

"Rebekkah, Karen told me you didn't want to go out at first. You're right, you shouldn't have. But thankfully you pulled in when you realized it was going wrong. Can you field tech for Amos or Karen? I'd understand if you want to get your dog home."

"No, I'll tech, who is going out first?" Shrugging my pack back up onto my shoulders, I reminded myself of the adage I used for every person interested in joining E.R. SAR – we are searchers first, handlers second.

"Amos. Why don't you go with him? He needs someone who can handle radio and the GPS. Karen can at least carry her own GPS."

Nodding, I waited while Al finished dumping my GPS onto his computer and returned it to me. Clearing the data, I headed out the door and met Amos as he unloaded Powder. I admired the beautiful Bloodhound. She was so light-colored and in amazing shape for her age. Amos pulled a small golf-style terry cloth from a box labeled "drool rags" and hooked it to the dog's harness. That was one thing I didn't need for my dogs at least.

Within a few minutes, Amos had his dog harnessed and ready to go. I reset my GPS to turn on the track log and watched quietly from the side as he let Powder cast out around the point last seen. Something akin to depression set in as I watched her with swift decision turn and move ninety degrees away from the direction my dog had taken me. I knew then without a doubt that my dog had taken me for a walk. Knowing someone's life was depending on us to get it right only deepened my gloom.

Powder moved swiftly and surely straight east, her muzzle almost touching the ground as she went. Periodically I could hear her take in a great draft of air and blow it out again. Amos called it her "Miss Piggy" imitation as it did sound like a hog snorting.

"K-9 Bravo to base." I released the mic key and waited for Al to answer.

"Go ahead Bravo."

"Base, we have started our search and are heading due EAST toward the Old Mill Road."

"Bravo, started search, heading east toward Old Mill Road, 1725."

I glanced at my watch as I listened to the time given for our radio communication. 1725, or nearly 5:30 pm in normal human terms, and I should have fed Ari some food before I left base. I had no idea how much time had passed since I left the vet clinic earlier.

"K-9....Bravo...clear." The last transmission was given in short bursts as Powder had decided to speed up and I was jogging as best as I could behind them.

"Base to Bravo, Base to K-9 Bravo."

"Go ahead Base, this is Bravo." My breathing was getting ragged and I really wanted Amos to slow his dog down so I could catch my breath.

"Bravo, can we send a dog ahead of you to work the area? We want to work Sector A2 on your map."

"Amos – did you hear that?"

"Yeah – where is A2?"

"Amos, I can't show you and run at the same time…can you slow down for a moment?"

"Powder! Easy girl – take a breather." Amos pulled her in and I felt rather inadequate standing next to the two super-athletes. Pulling my little map case out of my thigh pocket, I pointed at Sector A2, wishing I had air enough to actually speak.

"Yeah, tell them that's fine. She's really running hot Rebekkah. One thing about dementias – they don't make a hard trail until they hit vegetation."

Nodding, I put the map away, took a deep breath, and thanked God for oxygen. I keyed my mic to let base know to send the other dog team to our east while Amos restarted his dog.

Powder hit her stride in about ten feet and I reminded myself I not only needed to lose some weight, I needed to start exercising. I know I sounded like a steam engine puffing behind them, but I couldn't help it.

I wasn't sure how much further we had gone when Powder suddenly began to drift right then left. Amos eased her up and glanced back at me, a look of concentration on his face.

73

"She missed a turn or something. I know she had it when we crossed by that last tamarack tree line. But it is also possible the scent had drifted there and our subject angled away to the south. We need to go back, sorry."

"OK, really ok. At least your dog is working a real track." Selfishly thankful for the respite from the speed, I gulped air and took some needed water from my hydration pack. What had felt like a cold day hours before now felt like a sauna inside my jacket. Unzipping it part way, I let out some of the heat.

We walked back to the line of tamarack trees, their new spring growth making them look more like large ferns than actual trees. I loved the tamaracks. While people not familiar with them often thought they were evergreens, they are really deciduous trees that produce pine cones. As we passed them, I touched their feather-like new growth of needles, enjoying the softness.

Reaching the point Amos felt sure Powder still had a track, he restarted her, letting her cast out and search for the odor Kenny left behind. Normally we call out to subjects, but typical of dementias, we knew he wouldn't answer. In fact, he might actually attempt to avoid us if he knew we were searching for him. So we remained quiet other than our own conversation.

Powder circled a few times, her focus somewhat broken. Then she finally appeared to make a decision. Turning south, she angled across the open field just as Amos had described earlier.

"Base to K-9 Charlie" My radio crackled to life and actually made me jump. Karen must have deployed now and she was given the next team letter designator of 'C'.

"Go ahead Base, this is Charlie," A voice I didn't recognize answered and I wondered who was teching for Karen.

"Charlie, we didn't get a radio check after you left and want to make sure we have communication."

"Affirmative Base, we have you loud and clear, Charlie clear."

"1805, Charlie," another half an hour had passed. I knew the next call would be to us to verify our location and status.

"Base to K-9 Bravo."

"Go ahead Base, this is Bravo," I responded and suddenly realized that Powder had slowed enough so I could actually talk somewhat normally again.

"Status check, how are you and where is your current location?"

"Base, status good, location is about half a mile southeast of Old Mill Road, heading due south toward," I flipped open my map and, after my eyes adjusted to the print, I finished, "Tower Hills Wilderness Area."

My heart sank and my mind went into a knot. Wilderness Areas are exactly what their name describes. They are areas that have no one living there and usually are not managed in any way. They have full growth vegetation and no roads. There are often trails, but just as often there are more swamps and bogs, all thick with thorny bushes. Once lost, it is a very real possibility a person will never be found.

"Repeat Bravo, did you say 'Tower Hills Wilderness Area?"

"Affirmative Base. Do you want to reassign Charlie from Sector A2?" Amos had finally glanced back at me and I saw the worry on his face. I'm sure mine reflected his.

"Thank you Bravo, we'll update the maps before we make that call." I realized immediately I shouldn't have questioned base. They had likely more information than I did and it was definitely their call to make. I'd be apologizing to Al when we got back.

"Rebekkah, Powder is slowing down, but she's still on trail. I truly believe she is. How far are we from the Area?"

"I'd say half a mile or more. Maybe our subject will angle off again?" But looking at the map, I didn't see anywhere that would make sense for a person walking in a mental straight line to deviate anymore. After the meadow we had just passed through, it was trees. There was a road coming up, but we both knew Kenny wouldn't realize it was a road, he'd only see what was in his mind's eye. And of course, we had no idea what that was.

Ten minutes later we heard Base telling Charlie to stay in Sector A2, another K-9 team had arrived and would be sent to leap frog ahead of us to the Wilderness Area.

"Powder! Easy girl – we both need a break." Amos gently pulled in the big dog, holding out a bottle of water and foldable water dish. Pouring water in, he let his hound slobber happily in the dish as he fueled himself up with water and a snack bar.

"I don't know how much longer we'll be able to go. The dog's doing alright, but I'm wearing down and fast." Amos crouched down to stretch out tired back and shoulder muscles. I did the same, twisting slightly side to side and with some satisfaction heard a small click in my lower back.

Powder, her break done, stood tall into her harness. She actually leaned forward, her muzzle working the air as she waited impatiently for Amos.

"Wow. Did you see that?" Amos pointed at Powder, who was doing a little happy dance with her front feet. "That's a proximity alert if I ever saw one. But she's air scenting, not a ground trail."

Amos stood up and, with more verve than I had, pepped Powder with some encouraging words in her massively long and droopy ears.

Responding to him, she lunged forward and within seconds was at the end of the twenty foot line Amos typically used. She didn't stop there but literally yanked Amos forward. Her front paws kept up the odd happy dance even as she moved forward and twice she swung her great head back and forth, sending strings of drool flying.

Amos had gone from a jog to a full blown run behind his hound with me straggling along, trying to keep up. My damaged left knee screamed at every slamming step, but I felt the adrenaline rush just like the other two did.

Clearing through a small patch of scrub brush, we crossed the road I had seen on my map and in the blur of running, I saw them. Footprints in a track trap on the side of the road. The soft dirt had frozen them in time and even at a glance, I knew they were fresh. Were they Kenny's? I didn't know for sure, but Powder did.

She continued her head-long dash over the road, down the ditch on the other side and cruised hundred or more feet into the woods. Amos was getting thrashed by the branches and I ducked as they swung back toward me.

With a suddenness that brought me crashing into Amos, Powder stopped.

"Oh dear God." Amos's whispered words were definitely a prayer, not a curse. With dread, I peeked over his shoulder and silently said the same thing.

We had found Kenny.

"Bravo to Base," I said while backing away, as training had taught us to do. Amos, after giving Powder her favorite reward toy of a stuffed bunny for finding her subject, had also backed away, taking Powder a distance from the scene and I could hear him playing happily with his dog.

"Go ahead Bravo, this is Base,"

"Base, we have a POD of one hundred percent." My stomach felt a bit off center as I gave this vital piece of information to base. POD or the probability of detection; a simple acronym used by search managers everywhere. In our area of the country, POD coupled with one hundred percent means that the subject has been found deceased. It was a clean way to notify base without telling the entire listening world, which often included the family sitting at base, that we had found a body.

"Thank you Bravo. Do you have coordinates?" I dutifully read them off of my GPS. I would remain here with Kenny until officials from the county arrived. We would never leave our subject until we could transfer the scene. It wasn't easy, performing a death watch. Had it been my loved one, however, I would want to know someone was with them; and if I were law enforcement, I'd want my scene secured by someone trained to do it. I don't know why, but a memory came into my mind, a shrouded figure covered in blowing snow. I had thought of her often lately, even waking up to the realization I'd been dreaming of her.

Crouching down, I leaned my back against a tree, my pack mercifully off and on the ground next to me. I couldn't help feeling depressed. Amos and I both agreed it didn't appear to be a crime scene. It looked very much like an accidental death. Kenny, in his need to continue walking toward his unseen goal, had stepped into a deep rocky creek and had gone down, tangling himself up. Both legs were at unnatural angles and worse, his head was tipped grossly to one side. I was very grateful to Amos that he had checked for signs of life when he went in to reward Powder.

Sitting there, I tried to work out the time frame. How long had Kenny been here? Was he deceased before we arrived on scene today? Or had my stupidity in trying to work a dog I knew wasn't up to par contributed to his death? Sick with worry, exhausted from the long track, I began to seriously question why I was still in search and rescue. Why did I go to such effort to get a new puppy? Was all this worth it?

I jumped as a hand dropped onto my shoulder. I looked up to see Amos standing beside me. Powder was tied nearby, already dozing off. She had earned her keep today.

"Rebekkah, don't you dare blame yourself for this. You had no control over this situation. Even if you did attempt this trail, you recognized something was wrong. You stopped and acknowledged it. Dogs aren't perfect and dogs don't always have good days. You could not have altered what happened over there."

"Yes, I know that in my head, but the rest of me is feeling very guilty. Why did I try to work my dog when I knew he wasn't well?"

Amos chuckled and shook his head, which was rather unnerving. "Rebekkah, Ari is a solid dog. You trusted him because he has done his job well for years. He isn't perfect. Powder isn't perfect. But in your confidence, not your ego or pride, you believed your dog could work even if he wasn't feeling well. Now you know."

He gave my shoulder a squeeze as we both heard others approaching. Pushing back against the tree, I was able to get back to my feet without looking like the crippled old woman that I felt like.

Deputies nodded at us and I merely pointed. No words would need to be said. They looked and one went in to check, as Amos had done, for signs of life. I heard him quietly radio in and then switch to his cell phone to call in the details.

"Thank you guys. Not the ending we wanted, but at least there is an ending. They've stood the other teams down and we have a truck over on the road there to give you a lift back. Your guy at the trailer said you'll provide maps and reports?"

"Yes, we'll email them if that works for you. I'm really sorry, not a great way to end the day, eh?"

"This is the fourth time in a week he's wandered away. They found him the other times. It was inevitable I guess. I had suggested the family check out one of the programs in town. That's why he was at the clinic I guess. Life isn't all that we want it to be, is it?"

Arriving back at base, our law enforcement hosts offered to take us to dinner and we gratefully accepted. Ari, after a good meal and his first installment of antibiotics, was sleeping peacefully in my truck.

Sitting next to Al, I asked how things went while I was in Connecticut. It was the first opportunity I had to talk to anyone about the BWCAW search I had missed. I knew they had finally called it some days later when no clues were found and the dogs weren't getting anything anywhere. They were still doing over flights and other campers were asked to watch for him, but the subject was still missing.

"It was rather cool actually, flying up there. CAP flew us in. Amos said Powder left rather a slimy drool puddle in the back of the plane, but the pilot didn't seem to mind. Anyway, the real problem was getting her loaded onto the float plane. Oh my gosh, I never realized how big that dog is and how unagile she is – is that a word? Unagile?"

"How did the other dogs handle the flights?"

"Onyx and Chief slept I guess. They handled the float fine – they could climb up the steps and everything, no problem. I've never landed on a lake before, it was a rush actually. I almost hate to have enjoyed myself that much - the circumstances are so sad."

I nodded as I ate another bite of pizza. I think Law Enforcement personnel are pizza addicts or sub sandwich addicts. For some reason, they usually order one or the other when they provide meals to us.

"'Bekkah – I had those poor Forestry guys so nervous when they had to paddle Chief and me across the lake to portage to the next lake. Chief is rather excitable in a boat. He didn't seem to understand that you can't charge around in a canoe like you can on the Crestliner we have!" Karen's dog is well-known for being hyperactive on a boat.

We all laughed. Each person there knew that the search for a missing person is serious and not a laughing matter. However we also knew that if we didn't have an outlet, we would go crazy. The image of Kenny was still fresh in my own mind, joining the woman who died in the accident. Yet, I needed to let my own stress out in a positive way.

"Sheriff Tvrdik seemed like he really wanted to run this one right, but there were some odd things about the whole scene that didn't add up."

"What do you mean Amos?" Karen leaned across the table and snitched a piece of cheesy bread from Al's plate as he was turned toward Amos.

"I don't know exactly, but there are no witnesses to Hedstrom's arrival, no one saw him out on the trails, his car was left unlocked and while all his camping supplies were gone, it just seemed really strange that deputies found the receipts for their purchase neatly on the driver's seat, almost as though someone wanted them found. I don't know, it just felt weird."

"Alright, who took my bread?" Al looked at his nearly empty plate and Karen looked innocently around the table, as if trying to spy out the culprit for him. I just hid my smile and focused back on Amos.

"Did the dogs get any kind of trail? I know it was a time lapse of what, three days?"

"About ninety four hours actually, but no. Powder didn't get anything at all. Another dog – that good looking Shepherd from Park K9? – had the same experience. We even did trail checks around the area. Nothing."

"What does PARK9 stand for anyway?" Chris craftily removed the bread from Karen's plate back onto Al's.

"Park District K-9 I believe. The founding members were all park rangers if I remember right. They seem like a good unit. Haven't worked with them much yet. What did you think?"

"I liked them. Their dogs seemed to be well behaved, although of course we didn't get to watch them work. But the handlers were good and didn't come in and try to run things like, well you know…"

We all knew. It was Chris's old unit that was being referred to. While we tried as a group not to be political about search and rescue, sometimes it is hard.

"Anyway, none of the dogs had anything. Period. And last I heard, the reason they stood the search down was because there was some information coming in that put the whole area into question. Like maybe it was staged."

"Really? I hadn't heard that. I wondered why they stopped after only a few days. They are still doing over flights though?"

"Yes, but I think probably just for the family's peace of mind. Someone said he was out here with his dad who had business or something. I never saw or heard that he was on scene at anytime." Al, who had given up on his bread, suddenly noticed it was returned. A little colder and somewhat worse for wear, he ate it anyway.

"Wait a minute – what did you say his name was?" I froze, a strange chill swept over me as I tried to piece the information back together.

"Hedstrom. Thomas Hedstrom. Apparently his dad had some business here in Minnesota so they decided to make a vacation of it. The dad said his son wanted to check out the Boundary Waters, but he was too old to do that, so he was going to stay at the hotel, wherever that was. Son took the rental and went on a buying spree. Which, by the way, the father seemed rather surprised about, from what one deputy told me."

"Oh my gosh, listen, do you remember the dad's name? I know Hedstrom is a pretty common name, it's just well, McCaffrey House's new owner, or one of them, is a Jeremiah Hedstrom from Battle Creek in Colorado."

"Rebekkah, maybe you should call someone. I don't know for sure, but that does sound familiar."

Excusing myself from the table, I slipped away to the entrance and hit Bill's speed dial number.

"Rebekkah, where the heck are you? Did you forget I was coming up?"

"Bill, oh my gosh. Yes – I mean, no – what I mean is, I got called to a search and something kind of weird happened. Not today, I mean, just from the search that happened while I was in Connecticut. Did Jeremiah Hedstrom contact Terry yet?"

"Why? What do you know?" There was something in his voice that made the hair on the back of my neck stand on end.

"What do YOU know? You sound like you know something. Bill, the unit was called to a search for a Thomas Hedstrom who is from out of state and visiting here with his dad. He supposedly went camping and didn't return. Are they the same people?"

The silence on the other end confirmed what my stomach was already telling me.

"Ok, it is clear you are under some legal beagle code of silence, which only tells me it is the same people. When were you going to tell us?"

"Rebekkah, I'm only learning about it. There is something unorthodox about this situation. We – the lawyers and the advisory team – are meeting tomorrow and from that meeting will have more information to provide. I can confirm that Mr.

Hedstrom did communicate with Terry when they arrived. He said his son wanted to spend some time in the area, but it was planned for after they met with us. Mr. Hedstrom contacted us after his son went missing. As you can understand, he is very distressed and not sure what to do next. At this time, he's staying up in Ely until, well, we're not sure until when. Terry went up to meet with him and is coming back for the meeting tomorrow." There was a pause, and I could hear the strain in his voice as he finished, "Rebekkah, I honestly didn't know E.R. SAR was called on the search, that you would hear it there first. To be honest, they've tried to keep it fairly quiet from the media as well."

"All right. Bill, this all seems really odd to me. And I'm really sorry that I'm not there for dinner." I know as I returned to the table, my eyebrows were furrowed and everyone had to be aware that their missing person was now somehow related to McCaffrey House. They also had the good sense not to ask, which I was grateful for.

Bill had left by the time I got home, but at least I had one piece of good news. There was a small improvement with Ari. The medication appeared to take hold and his nose once again appeared damp and shiny. Other than that, the world seemed to be tumbling around like a whirlwind.

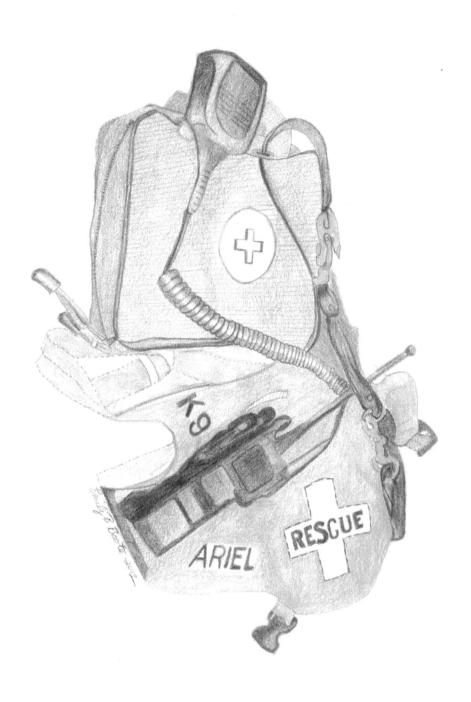

Chapter 6

Yet your heavenly Father feeds them.
Are you not much better than they?

It took two days before the new owners of McCaffrey House were officially notified about the situation of our co-owner. Terry called a meeting of everyone to go over the advisory board's recommendations as well as to discuss the situation with Mr. Jeremiah Hedstrom. I had said nothing to anyone else; not even to my mom. It was hard, as I really wanted advice that Bill couldn't really give me yet. I simply had to wait.

The meeting was set up in the McCaffrey House library, an official looking "Do Not Disturb" sign hung on the door to prevent uninvited guests. I sat down next to Margaret and Martha, with Bill to my left and Adam to his left. The advisory board sat across from us, thankfully all friends with the exception of Terrance, or Terry, O'Reilly. He looked as Irish as his name implied.

"Folks, this has been rather an odd few weeks for us. I know you're all curious about the fifth owner of McCaffrey House, but circumstances have prevented him from attending today. Mr. Jeremiah Hedstrom and his son Thomas arrived in Minnesota a few weeks ago. They intended to come here, however," Terry paused and I knew he was trying to find the words that would explain without saying too much, "as some of you may have heard, his son is missing."

There were only two audible gasps, from both Margaret and Martha. I glanced at Adam and saw in one look he had known; likely through his Law Enforcement connections. Although no longer our sheriff, he still remained on good terms with many of his old friends.

"Margaret, I told you that there would be trouble. Didn't I tell you?" Margaret looked steadily at her sister, her face curiously calm considering Martha's white hair was trembling at what was either outrage or fear. Looking back at the others, I could see their response was like mine. What on earth did the dear sisters know we didn't?

"Well, anyway," Terrance continued after a moment's pause, "The advisory board has gone over everything and wants to discuss with you their recommendations for McCaffrey House. Mr. Hedstrom has been apprised of the information and as of now sees no reason to object to them."

With a nod, Terry turned the meeting over to Dr. Sheffield. Gary was everyone's doctor in that room and he had even stitched up my dog on occasion. I trusted him with my life and I felt I could trust him with McCaffrey House as well.

"Let's get down to it. First, we found things have been running quite smoothly, so didn't see a need for very many changes. We do feel however there could be some improvements. Dave is handing out our recommendations. I'll read through them, but this is so you can keep a copy."

"First, reports were provided weekly as well as monthly in the past to Mr. McCaffrey, his lawyer, and Bill here as Rebekkah's representative. While we appreciate the effort, we believe quarterly reports will provide the same picture. They will be provided to ourselves and each of you. If you wish your lawyer or accountant to receive a copy, please let us know."

"Second, the insurance on the House and property has always been maintained by Mr. McCaffrey personally. That will now change to the business itself, as it should manage all of its own expenses now. It isn't cheap, as you can see by the attached."

"Finally - and this was the hardest decision or recommendation we had to make - we believe that the apartment rooms should be vacated by Rebekkah and her mom and turned over to Martha and Margaret."

I felt myself go cold. Prior to Pop's death I had started looking for another place to live, knowing his son Charles wanted me out. I just hadn't expected to be kicked out by my friends.

"Rebekkah, I understand this is coming as sort of a shock or blow, but I'd like you to hear the reasons."

I nodded, holding back the flood of tears that threatened to overwhelm me.

"First, the cost to drive the sisters back and forth every day adds up. Their presence is actually quite necessary to the running of the House. To be honest, yours isn't. You've been able to manage over the last year without being present full time. In addition, in the winter, if they can't make it, who will make the meals for your guests? So far you've been blessed, but the time might come when they can't be there. Plus there is the liability of having Harold driving them back and forth all the time. We truly felt this was the better option."

Several times I started to speak, but my brain seemed unable to formulate a word of defense. What they said made sense and was truly a good idea. I couldn't deny it. But without an adequate income, where would I find a home to live in?

"Rebekkah, we're not finished. We understand you aren't making any kind of actual salary for managing the business. That will change as of now. Your terms of employment are included in the attachment. In fact, everyone who is employed here is included as well. You're all owners; you need to know where the money is going. You will note there are two options listed for you

Rebekkah. You will need to decide which you'd prefer. You can either move into MiniMac or receive a housing stipend and move into your own place. As you can see, if you use MiniMac, your salary will be adjusted to reflect the loss of income it has brought in."

MiniMac. The beautiful little stable I had converted into a living space to add income to McCaffrey House. It wasn't currently set up for winter use, but I guessed that would be taken care of if I chose it. Did I want to though?

"Please give it some consideration. We know MiniMac isn't ready for use yet this spring, but if the owners are in agreement, we'd like to implement these recommendations by May 31st. Rebekkah, are you all right with this?" Gary's eyes were full of concern. I gave what I hoped was a smile and nodded. Less than two months to make a move of this kind was not long. Thankfully the pay they were offering would make a big difference for me, but it didn't stop the feeling of being lost and adrift. I also felt a bit as if I'd been stabbed in the back.

It only took a few minutes for us to vote to accept the recommendations. I agreed with them, knowing they were good for the business. After the meeting, Bill let everyone else leave before standing me up out of the chair and wrapping me in a bear hug. I held on tight, knowing right now he felt like the only thing solid in my life.

I began the task of house-hunting right away. Having three large dogs wasn't a benefit when looking for a rental, and yet I had no money to put down to buy. After striking out several times, I finally turned it over to my mom. I really needed to focus on getting some good training time for Ari as we approached his cadaver recertification.

My unit pitched in, setting up blind and double blind problems for us. I still had some concerns as I watched my dog each day. He'd locate the odor, but struggle to pinpoint it. Finding odor was good, but being able to get as close to the source as possible is a requirement of the test. If Ari struggled, I knew we might have a problem.

The night before the test, I noticed Ari's nose was dried out again, looking white against his black muzzle. He had just finished his prescription of antibiotics and seemed much better, but concern had me on the phone. Dr. Mikkelson cautioned me about going through with the test and asked me to bring him in instead.

"Doctor, I can't just cancel this late. It took two months just to get the thing scheduled! He seemed ok at training yesterday. I'll go and see what happens."

"I can't say I agree, but okay. Can you bring him in on the day after?"

"Monday? That would work for me. And Doctor, thanks."

Sunday, after church, I loaded both Ari and Gus. Driving the two hours to the testing area, I felt that familiar feeling I have before every test. Fear. Test Anxiety. Panic. Deep breathing helped, but I could still taste it in my mouth. As a kid in school, I hated testing mainly because I was terrified of failure. I wasn't competitive; I just didn't want to fail. Added to that, I was the leader of E.R. SAR. As the leader, failure just didn't seem to be an option. If I failed, what did that say about my credibility?

Parking my truck, I could see it was a small group which hopefully meant it wouldn't take hours to get through all the tests.

"Rebekkah James with K-9 Gus and K-9 Ari." I handed the evaluators my training logs and paperwork for requesting the test. With a nod, they told me Ari would be up next.

I waited while another dog tested and when they came back, I unloaded Ari. He immediately leaned into my leg and a small voice inside said "stop this now." I ignored that little voice and instead whispered in Ari's ear, "you can do this buddy, I know you can. Let's get caddy."

The start itself was good. He jogged out, his head held high. Ari had never been a speed demon, he worked methodically and that was fine. But thirty minutes into a two acre search without a find I knew I should have listened to that little voice. Ari continued to work until with relief I finally saw him give an alert. He slowed and worked in the wagon-wheel search pattern he had done for years. He went to center, went out, turned, and came back in from a different angle. By the time he completed the 'wheel', I knew where the source was. It was of course in the middle of the well-defined circle. But my dog still circled, looking tired and stressed.

"Ari, you're doing great buddy. You can do this." With an uncertain look toward me, he went to near the center and gave his final trained response of a down. Leaning in, I explained to the evaluators the source was likely about a foot to his left.

I didn't need to see the look that passed between the evaluator and their assistant to know that it was a bit unorthodox to point to an area a foot away from my dog. I knew the next find had better be solid.

With a nod, they told me to reward my dog and move on. As I gave Ari his treats, I felt my world crumble as the treats remained in my hands, uneaten and unwanted.

"Okay buddy, we have one more to go. You can do this big guy." I sent him out and watched as he stoically started the process all over again. Another thirty minutes and our time was running out when I finally saw another alert. What followed however broke my heart and, in reality, much of my spirit.

As my dog attempted to follow up on the odor, he jumped over a down tree. It was a small tree, totally devoid of branches. In agility, it would have been a jump for a toy breed, not a large breed like my German Shepherd. And yet he tripped. I watched his front feet catch on the log and my aging dog land head over tea kettle in the leaves.

Fear left me frozen for only a moment. I jogged over to him and watched as he shook and nearly fell again. Holding my hand against his groin, I felt the heat radiating from him.

"I'm calling the test. I never should have started it, I'm really really sorry. As you can see, my dog isn't well. I know this is asking a lot, but could I run my second dog Gus through his search area next instead of waiting? I want to get this dog to the vet, but I also drove two hours to test the dogs today." I waited, my arms around my dog, feeling his heart beat erratic and fast against my wrists.

"I'll ask the next person. Technically we should be going in order. Are you sure you want to try your second dog?"

"Definitely. He's healthy and ready to go. I'm really sorry. He was on antibiotics and he seemed better. I feel awful."

They only nodded and the assistant walked over to the person on deck for their test. I walked a visibly tired dog back to my truck. Sick at heart, I almost had agreed not to test Gus. It didn't seem worth the effort, still, he was all I had at this point.

Seeing the assistant wave to me, I pulled Gus out. His health was abundantly clear as he started bounding up and down beside me. I watched the evaluators size up my short partner and I could read what they were thinking. Too short to do the job, rather stocky too. What was this woman thinking? I'd heard it all before.

"Gus, we need to convince some folks you have the right stuff. Ready to work?" Gus responded with an exceptionally high pitched bark in my ear. "Alright, that is great, let's go."

Turning the dog loose in our new area, I watched Gus zoom off in his normal rocketing fashion. It never ceased to amaze me he actually found anything considering how fast he liked to go. Three minutes later we all watched him apply his air brakes, coming to a halt that would have screeched had he been on tarmac. Spinning back, he stuffed his nose into a small crevice and threw his body onto the ground, heaving out his bark at the same moment.

"I'm calling that. Source should be between his paws, likely inside the crevice there." Completely confident in my little dog, I waited patiently while the evaluators waited. I'd learned over the years that sometimes evaluators will sweat a handler who appears confident just to see if they really do trust their dog. I did.

"Reward your dog. Very nicely done. You have half the test done."

Gus spun off after a few treats and raced down a hillside and back up the other. He leaped over downed trees much larger than the one Ari had fallen over. He slipped under and through dead fall. As though he knew they questioned his physical ability, he did every agility move he could as he worked. I smiled as he disappeared over another hill, his energy giving me some of my own back. I walked along patiently, knowing he'd tell me if he found something.   The evaluators were good. They didn't hurry to watch the dog either. They were watching me.

Suddenly, in the distance I heard the bark.   That big whooshing bark of a dog that has thrown himself on the ground with everything he had.

"Good dog Gus, where the heck are you?"

A little golden head peeked over a hill top ahead of me, waited a moment, watching me. I waved and he disappeared and the bark came again. Closer this time. Cresting the hill, there was my dog parked under a large oak with sprawling branches. Only he wasn't looking at me, he was looking straight up.

"I'm calling that. While I'm guessing it is in the tree, I'd also check the ground around it in case the scent is chimneying up." I verbally praised my dog while the evaluators made their notes.

"It is in the tree, just above his head. Can you see it?" I gave a negative head shake and focused on my dog. The only working dog I had at the moment.

"You finished this test in 4 minutes. Excellent job. I'll be honest, I thought maybe you just couldn't train your dogs properly when I saw how out of shape your other dog was and how poorly he performed. He really is sick, isn't he?"

"Yes, and it is scaring the living daylights out of me. He's 8, almost 9 now. He's my first and favorite. I dread losing him. Thank you so much for understanding. Is there anything I need to do before I take off?"

After signing the two test forms, I headed home. Ari seemed no worse so I waited to call Dr. Mikkelson, but during the night he started to shake. A thermometer confirmed his temperature was nearly 105. After giving him baby aspirin, I carried my seventy five pound dog into the bathroom. Slowly I added cool wet towels around his body core. Gradually the shakes subsided and the thermometer confirmed that while he still had a temperature, it had dropped significantly from the initial reading.

I replaced the wet towels with dry and just sat with him. Holding his head in my lap, I felt wracked with guilt. First I asked him to work a search when it was clear he wasn't feeling well. Then I asked him to test which is actually more stressful. If he died, it would be my fault. Tears, unbidden and unwanted, slipped down my cheeks and into his fur. I couldn't stand the thought of losing this dog.

Bringing him into Dr. Mikkelson the next morning was hard. He had warned me and I hadn't listened.

He went over my dog head to toe. The fever had abated at 103, but was still high for the extended time he had been suffering with it. Taking another snap test, he came back with a shrug. Once again, it showed negative for any tick borne diseases. He drew more blood to send in for further tests for things like Rocky Mountain Spotted Fever, but also requested if he could take X-rays.

With a sick feeling, I helped lift my dog up to get the sedative and watched helpless as he fought to remain conscious. He gripped the table with his claws and his eyes started to bulge as he battled the meds flowing into him. Dr. Mikkelson, with a look of concern which concerned me, carefully added a bag valve mask type equipment to enhance the anesthesia. Slowly Ari had to let go and soon was asleep on the table.

Feeling more and more nauseous, I left the room as Nan and the doctor set about taking the X-rays. What had I done to my dog? The bottom was falling out of my world and I could do nothing to stop it.

"Dear God, I know I haven't been talking to you like I should. I'm doing exactly what my mom always used to teach me not to do. Using prayer as emergency rations instead of daily bread. I'm so sorry. Please God, please... I don't want to lose Ari. He's the world to me. I know you've given me Jael and I know I won't have Ari forever. But this isn't the way a great and noble dog should go. Please God....give me more time." I went into the bathroom and wept, feeling like the strength of my emotions would carry me away. Bev was right. Part of my heart was dying.

I'm not sure how long I hid away, but I finally made my way back to the lobby. I waited what felt like forever, but I'm sure it was only an hour at most when Dr. Mikkelson came to get me.

Ari's lungs looked like they were full of cotton balls and his heart was enlarged. Even I could see it and I'd never been taught to read X-rays of a dog's chest before.

"This could be Blasto; all that junk in his lungs. I need to do some more tests. He is a heckuva fighter Rebekkah. I've never seen a dog fight so hard from going under as he did."

I waited in the lobby again, taking time to call my mom and let her know. I hung up to find a very confused vet waiting for me.

"Nothing matches Blasto. It HAS to be a tick borne disease, but the tests are coming back negative. I'm going to put him on Doxycycline. Do you want to leave him here or take him home?"

"Take him home. How bad is it really?"

"I won't lie. He deteriorated rapidly over the last couple of days. If it is tick borne, he's likely had it for some time and it is just overwhelming his system. He might not make it."

Pushing back tears, I nodded and thanked him. He started to carry Ari, but my dog, dignified animal that he was, struggled loose. Once on the ground, he wobbled his own way back to my truck. Lifting him up myself, I promised to keep Dr. Mikkelson posted.

During the next weeks my focus was on Ari. I trained Gus and Jael, but Ari received the bulk of my attention. Often I had to help him get where he needed to go because he couldn't walk for more than five minutes. His heart rate would escalate and his breathing came in heaving, ragged breaths. A trip to the woods to go to the bathroom was too much for him and I found myself cleaning up after my dog just by the back of the garage.

At the end of the first week, I started to add boiled hamburger to his diet to encourage him to eat. The antibiotics were wreaking havoc to his digestive system and he was throwing up both food and meds. At least with the hamburger, he was able to keep things down.

It was the middle of the second week I finally saw the turnaround. While it was slow, it was definitely much surer than the last time. To my surprise, I realized the overfeeding and lack of exercise had caused my dog to put on weight. His next vet visit confirmed it when he weighed in at nearly 80 pounds, the heaviest he had ever been in his life.

"Rebekkah, I can't say if he'll ever recover completely. You do know he may never work again, right?" Dr. Mikkelson was gently petting Ari. I watched as the dog that had never worried about vet clinics was shaking just standing there.

"I know. I have Gus and Jael for that. But is it possible? He'll feel pretty rotten if he can't work."

"For now, let him recuperate. But if it helps his mental state to go to training, by all means, bring him along. Let him do simple easy problems. Don't strain him, ok? His heart and lungs are likely scarred from this." He watched me for a moment and finally asked, "What else is going on? I know this is bad news, but you know he'll live. Something else is bothering you."

Shocked it would show, I finally spoke my deepest fears to someone I hardly knew.

"I need to find a place to live. They've restructured McCaffrey House where I've lived the last, gosh I don't know how many years now. I'm not even sure where to begin. I need to find a place in less than two weeks now, and so far, while there are lot of places listed, no one wants to rent, or if they do, not to someone with three big dogs."

"Wow, not a lot of great news for you. Listen, I'll ask around. You never know, there might be something available that isn't listed. Have you thought about buying instead?"

"I wish I could, but I have no means of putting any money down. When I sold my last home, I used all the money to pay off the bills. I've worked at McCaffrey mainly for my room and board and essentials. I've put in some hours at a part time job I can do at home, but I've never earned enough to build a down payment. I'm sort of stuck."

"Well, you never know. Sometimes people are willing to work with you if they know the situation. In the meantime, you need to rest and recuperate yourself."

I went home to learn mom hadn't come up with anything except a place nearly two hours away. Giving her a hug for trying, I went in to help with dinner. My depression increased as I realized that both Martha and Margaret were unsure how to talk to me now.

"Ladies, don't worry about me. I'll be fine. This really will be the best for you and the House. I should have thought of it myself." Smiling what I felt was my bravest smile, I gave each a hug.

"Oh Rebekkah, we both are so worried about you. I'd offer you our little place to live, but really, with the three dogs, there wouldn't be room." I knew they were right. They lived above their old café, the café where I first met them. They now rented the store front to a young couple who planned to open a candy shop. I couldn't kick them out.

"It is okay, really. We're a family, always. Now give me a hug back and give me a task to do." After hugs, I went about doing the tasks I've always helped with, wondering if the new plan was for me to continue them or not.

That night as I sat contemplating yet another rental possibility, my cell phone rang.

"Rebekkah, I know you are pretty torn up about Ari and about the House. If I can help – in anyway – please tell me. In fact, I think you need an evening out and so I'm driving up tomorrow to take you out to dinner with Adam and Amy. And you can't say no. Your mom already agreed to watch Ari."

"Bill, I don't know..."

"You can't say no. Now, you can refuse, but I don't think you should. You need to take care of youself too. This is part of your therapy. I'll be there at 6:30 and pick you up. A good steak dinner will do you wonders."

"Seriously, it sounds wonderful, but Ari needs his meds at dinner time and..."

"Rebekkah, your mom is capable of feeding and medicating your dog. All of those that love you are starting to worry. This is our way of starting to pamper you a little."

"I won't be very good company Bill, are you sure?" I mentally tried to think of another excuse for not going. I hadn't been sleeping and I felt like I couldn't think straight lately.

"I don't care. If you don't want to talk, that's fine. You just need a change of scenery. Rebekkah, you must know how much I care about you, and I don't want to lose you to this. Okay?"

I realized suddenly that I hadn't spoken to Bill since the meeting. He had left messages, but I hadn't returned his calls. I was so wrapped up in my own misery I had forgotten those who truly did care.

Chapter 7

Which of you by being anxious can add to your height?

When they arrived, I was waiting, cleaned up and ready for a night out with friends. My mom smiled and poked me in the ribs with a whispered order to be thankful for those God puts in our lives.

Bill came to the door and greeted me with a hug and kiss on the cheek. I held onto the hug, wondering why I had argued against seeing him. He just held me, letting me lean against him.

"Thank you for being patient with me. I never knew life could be so hard."

Bill just squeezed me a little tighter and then whispered, "If we wait much longer, you'll hear my stomach growl. Really, I wouldn't sound very sympathetic about your situation with my stomach growling..."

I laughed, the first time in weeks. Bill went in with me to say goodnight to Ari, who flapped his tail against the floor and barely lifted his head in greeting.

"Ari old boy, you look like you need a vacation too. You rest up. I'll bring her back safe and sound later."

"Mom, his meds are by the food, and remember to give him the hamburger so he keeps it all down. He's gonna be a pig by the time we're done!"

I left with the full knowledge my mom was giving Bill "I told you so" looks behind my back. Joining Adam and Amy in Bill's modest sedan, I settled back and was truly thankful for the effort my friends had made.

Throughout the night Bill quietly held my hand under the table whenever he could, and part way through the meal, Amy finally whispered to me, "He's a good man, Rebekkah. Don't let your own fears make you lose sight of that." I gave her a gentle squeeze with my other hand and with some trepidation slid my hand into Bill's as it rested on the table. Lacing our fingers together, I felt at peace.

A few days later, my mom leaned into my office alcove and whispered, "Dr. Mikkelson is on the phone. Something about a place to rent?"

"Seriously? Oh dear Lord, please let it be good news," I picked up the phone and pushed the blinking button.

"Hi, Rebekkah! I was putting out some feelers through Nan and her husband. Not sure if it would work for you, but there is a place not far from Elk that isn't listed yet. The owner is from the Cities and is debating about selling it. It needs some work, but it is set up for year-round use. They might agree to a good price for rental if you do some fixing up to get it ready to sell."

"I'm not very handy, but my mom is, believe it or not. And I have a friend who is very handy. Where is it? Can I check it out today? I'm running out of time. OH – maybe I should ask what they want a month before I get too excited."

"I'll let you talk to them about that, but I suspect you can come to some sort of agreement. Good luck!"

An hour later, with directions in my hands and a phone number in case I got lost, my mom and I were on the road. Driving north out of Elk, I watched as we changed into the next county. It was always easy to see the change because the road signs were huge in comparison. The running joke was that they were either worried about tourists getting lost, or that the locals were all near-sighted. Checking my odometer, exactly at seventeen miles, Hummingbird Trail appeared. Turning to the east, I followed the wandering, scenic, and gravel road another two miles to the end where a small blue marker showed the numbers "14856" and we were there. Turning into the drive, I felt a little concerned as I realized it was going to be nestled far enough back to make the driveway an issue in the winter.

"Mom, we'd have to find someone to plow for us. I could never do it myself."

My mom just nodded as we made a gentle turn through the trees and found ourselves facing a home designed along the lines of Colonial Revival. Looking at it from the safety of my truck, I only knew that it looked much less Revival than Colonial in age.

"Rebekkah, we're here, we might as well look. They said it needed some work, you surely didn't expect a beautiful mansion? And it might not be as bad inside."

Stepping out of the truck, I studied the surrounding lawn. It definitely needed work. Flower pots left out over the winter were cracked and overgrown with weeds. Outside of my truck, I realized the house had not only an abandoned look. It looked worn out too.

Walking up the weedy path which I was surprised to find was brick, we arrived at the door. The pediment that crowned it looked hand-carved, but starting to dry rot. My mom, as if reading my thoughts, said softly, "Looks like someone loved this house once. Nicely done, but not craftsman of course." I only nodded and turned my attention to finding the lock box that held the key.

The lockbox located and the key removed, we entered through the front door and stopped to look around. I knew immediately Ari would have a problem. The floor was tiled and under a light layer of dust, appeared shiny.

"See that?" I turned to look where my mom was pointing and finally realized she was pointing out the window frames on either side of the door. "It is things like that they are likely talking about."

I had no idea what she was talking about. As just about everyone knew, I could barely swing a hammer without damaging something. If I did have to make repairs, I had to rely on my mom to walk me through them. I could accomplish certain tasks on my own, but not many. Windows were well beyond my abilities, especially as I didn't know what was wrong with them.

Mom led the tour, showing a quick grasp of the layout and noting that the ground floor held, beside the foyer, a sun room that faced east and would take in the morning sunrise. To the west was a living room that fed onto a dining room which led onto the kitchen. From the kitchen, it returned to the sunroom. Looking around corners, I finally located a ground-floor bathroom tucked under the staircase leading upstairs. While a fireplace appeared to be the focal point of the living room, it was also showing signs of age. Beautiful local stone had been used, but the grouting, or whatever it is they used, was chipping out from between them.

"One big downside Rebekkah is the lack of a bedroom on the main floor. I don't know if I can do those stairs every single day." We stood facing them, leading up to the second floor.

"I know. As it is just us, maybe we could make the sunroom your room?"

"Only if it is insulated and heated. I couldn't tell just walking through. We may not know until winter hits."

Climbing the stairs, we found typical bedrooms with a full bath over the sunroom. Over the living room was a rather large master bedroom with its own full bath. That surprised me, as nothing else about this house appeared to be modern.

We returned to the main floor and I descended to the basement solo. It was finished with a family room and laundry room. The laundry was under the kitchen area and included a full

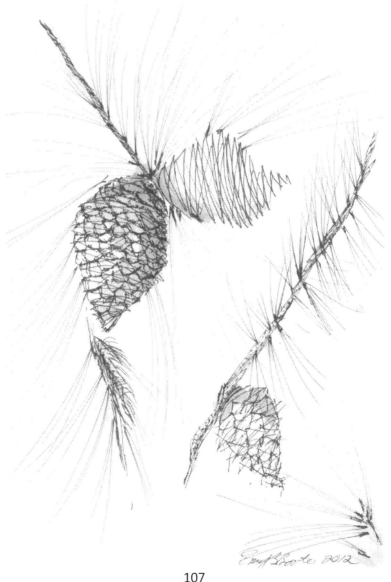

bathroom yet again. I started to wonder about the number of bathrooms, but decided not to question something that was good.

"Not much of a lawn, but then, we don't have to mow if there isn't much to take care of." Mom pointed out the kitchen door, a sliding glass thing I knew she would hate.

"Now THAT would be worth the extra money to rent the place!" We both laughed, as we had gotten very used to Harold handling all of the outdoor chores for us over the past few years.

Exiting the house, I found the garage tucked neatly to the back, but not attached to the house. It, too, was showing signs of age, but appeared solid and usable. As my mom had noted, the back yard was fenced, but small, and completely surrounded by the woods.

"What do you think?" I waited after posing the question, knowing her eyes would have picked up everything that needed repair. I only noticed the number of bathrooms.

"A lot of work, and not really a good fit for us. But do we have any other options?"

"Yes – Martha and Margaret's place if we want it. Which we don't. Or MiniMac, which I'm pretty sure we don't want either. I don't know what to do mom. Nothing seems to be going right lately."

My mom knew. When Pop died, it felt like everything finally fell into place. Then suddenly, it all fell apart again. While I got the puppy of my dreams, we struggled with her potty training. Ari got sick and lost his certification. I lost our home, and my SAR unit was somehow part of a case that linked McCaffrey House to a missing person. What else could go wrong?

"Never ask that question, pumpkin. You may find out." Once again, she had read my mind. She walked over and wrapped her arms around me. I don't know why, but I couldn't help it. I started to cry. My mom had never been a hugger, but every now and then, she knew I needed one.

After a short selfish, pity-party cry, I pulled myself back together and flipped my cell phone open.

"Bill, Ari's new vet found out about a place that I could possibly rent, but it needs work and that would be part of the deal. I'm wondering if you could maybe help?"

"Kinda depends on what needs to be done and when. I can do some things, but I can't do wiring and things like that. Did the owner tell you what they are expecting to be done?"

"I'm not sure what they expect or think needs to be done, so I can only go by what mom saw. Here, talk to her. I'm like Cary Grant in that old movie – you know the one, 'Mr. Blandings Builds His Dream House'. You could probably sell me a Zuzz-Zuzz water softener right about now."

Handing the phone over, I walked away to look over the lawn and property. My short conversation with the owner had only let me know that there was about 40 acres of land included, bordered on one side by Elk Creek. I tried to cheer myself with the reminder this wasn't a permanent place for us. It was just a stop over until I could find something better.

After giving Bill the low-down on the building, my mom handed the phone back to me.

"Well, what do you think?"

"Sounds doable from what she said. Is this really what you want to do though?" His voice softened as he continued, "You could move down here and work from home. You said Megan is doing most of the office tasks now. I know I could find you a good place."

"Thank you from the bottom of my heart Bill, but I don't want to live in the city."

"You don't have to live right in the city, you could live in the outskirts, like I do. Really Rebekkah, there are some really nice homes down here that we could get for a song."

"Yes, but I'd be so far from everything I love and enjoy Bill."

With something akin to fear, I realized what I had just said. The pause on the other end confirmed what my gut said. I had forgotten that Bill was supposed to be among the "everything I love and enjoy".

"I understand. Next time I come up, we'll go through it, see if I can help get it in order." There were those words again, 'I understand'. I was starting to hate them.

"Bill, do you understand? You know that I love the woods up here, the people who I see every day, my job, McCaffrey House," I waited a moment, hoping for a response. Getting none, I plowed on, feeling frustrated that I couldn't help Bill to see my side. "Really, don't you like being up here too? I thought you did. I thought perhaps that someday, you'd want to come and stay…"

"Rebekkah, I care deeply for you, but my life is here. I have a business, I have friends, I have a home. I think you could really be happy here too."

I saw my mom's face changing as the conversation went on. This was something I had never considered, that Bill wouldn't want to live where I wanted to live.

"Bill, maybe we could talk about this another time? For now, I think I need to stay up here close to McCaffrey House and my unit. You do understand?"

There was a deep sigh on the other end before he responded, "Yes, of course. I just look forward to when we can live a lot closer to each other than we do now. Listen, I'll see if I can come up this weekend and we can go out and talk. For now, you can put me down as slave labor to help fix the place up if you really do want it."

As I hung up, my mom's voice whispered from within my memory, "Never ask that question, pumpkin. You may find out." I only hoped that this wasn't really another thing going wrong in my life. I prayed Bill would be willing to consider living here as I knew I didn't want to move. I also knew I didn't want to deal with that kind of problem right now, especially not right now.

Locking the house and returning the key to the lockbox, I carefully dialed the number of the homeowner and with some trepidation, gave them Bill's office number to work out the legal details. Within a few days, the deed was done. Mom and I were moving. Bill, as promised, came up and, with the help of friends, moved us out of McCaffrey.

Our arrangement was set for a year at a monthly amount that would strain my budget. I asked to have first option to purchase it when it went officially up for sale. My request had Bill rolling his eyes. We in turn agreed to do the repairs requested by the homeowners which turned out to be less than my mom had anticipated.

Thankfully, we were too busy that weekend for Bill and me to have that talk he mentioned. I hated to admit it, but it seemed safer to avoid it for now. Perhaps I was a coward, but I already felt like a small boat on a storm-tossed sea. I had battened down

111

my hatches against further assault, something at which I'd learned to be quite adept.

Bill didn't pressure me about it. I loved him all the more for it, but deep down, I knew the time would come again when we would have to talk about it. I only prayed that given time, we'd work it out.

Life seemed to settle back down again. Ari's health finally improved, albeit with an enormous vet bill that should have been even more. I knew Dr Mikkelson had shaved it down for me, for which I was grateful. A month in our new home, we discovered Jael had a urinary tract infection. A prescription of antibiotics suddenly solved our potty training nightmares. The new home, while not perfect, would handle our needs for the time being. I still wasn't sleeping, and far too often was bursting into tears for no apparent reason. But life was normalizing and I believed all that would improve as well.

After moving Margaret and Martha into the apartment above the garage at McCaffrey House, I had to admit, the advisors were right. While I had said they were right before, now I actually meant it.

We learned that Mr. Hedstrom finally was going to make a visit to McCaffrey House shortly after I moved out. The staff had spent several days doing a thorough spit and polish cleaning in preparation for Jeremiah's visit. As I entered the library, I felt a sense of pride in everyone involved. Agnes, the housekeeper at McCaffrey House, had even gone so far as to have the library floor waxed.

Claiming the seat next to Amy, I could see she was finally starting to show improvement. Her cheeks bloomed with renewed health. She had decided to try a holistic approach to her cancer and it seemed to be working. We talked quietly, discussing the weather and Adam's plans to become a hunting guide. We both knew we were killing time until Mr. Hedstrom arrived, but it was pleasant nonetheless.

He arrived quietly, entering with little fanfare and no lawyer. Somehow I'd expected him to bring a lawyer. Glancing around, he smiled at Terry and, while they exchanged greetings, I studied him.

Jeremiah Hedstrom turned out to be a man somewhere in his eighties, although as he was a contemporary of Pop's, he could be older. Upright and lean, he carried himself as an old soldier would. As Pop would have had he not been in a wheelchair. Jeremiah however also seemed tired and gray, his energy at low ebb. A few whispers with Terry and with hand extended, he greeted me next.

"Ms. James?" Standing, I shook his hand and smiled back.

"Mr. Hedstrom, I'm so pleased to meet you. I'm also exceedingly sorry to hear about your son."

"Yes, thank you. I know this is all a mistake, I'm sure he is safe someplace, we're just not sure where or how. But it will all work out." Tears formed in his eyes, eyes that age had already blurred into a milky blue. With a single sniff, he smiled again and turned as Margaret and Martha entered, each holding the other's arm.

"The Miss Thwaites! Oh my goodness, I've been longing to see you both. It has been too many years. Jace wrote often of you both and your wonderful care of Ginie. It is such a pleasure!" He swept over to them and I think Margaret would have fled if Martha hadn't been holding onto her.

"Mr. Hedstrom, I'm sorry we hardly remember you, so you'll understand our being a little surprised at you being so forward."

Martha gave a prim smile and escorted a completely mute Margaret to the love seat by the window.

"Does anyone want coffee or tea? The pots are by the table there, as well as some of Margaret's amazing scotcheroo cookies. Please, help yourselves." I pointed out the goodie tray, hoping to smooth over what appeared to be complete rudeness to Mr. Hedstrom.

Bill poured himself a cup of coffee and chose a chair almost behind me. He gave my shoulder a gentle squeeze and I only wished he were sitting next to me.

Terrance stood up and I was glad to see a cookie in his hand as he began to speak.

"Folks, I know I've met most of you here, but in case we haven't been formally introduced, my name is Terrence O'Reilly, and you may call me Terry. I've been handling Jason Charles McCaffrey's Death Trust. Today we have all of the owners of McCaffrey House in one place, although under incredibly sad circumstances." Terry paused, glanced around and then continued, "First, Mr. Hedstrom has indicated he endorses the plans already laid out to everyone, and we understand that the Miss Thwaites are already installed into the apartment?"

He merely glanced at the two ladies in question before turning to look toward me. I nodded, confirming it.

"Good. The advisory board said they received the reports you made up Ms. James," Terry didn't notice me flinch at the word "Ms."; I had always hated it. Call me Miss, Rebekkah or even hey you, but I felt "Ms." compromised who I really was – a single woman able to stand on her own.

"The reports all look good and the board agrees they will work. Are there any questions?"

I was surprised to see Martha's hand lift, and after being acknowledged by Terry, saw her glance at Margaret before speaking. I wondered if she was making sure her sister would stay put as she spoke.

"Mr. O'Reilly, I know everyone has been so kind to explain to us about the Living Trust and the Death Trust and what-have-you, but who actually owns this building and the land?"

"Well, Ms. Thwaite, you do. Along with your sister, Ms. James, Mr. Drahota, and Mr. Hedstrom."

"So, if someone would want to sell the house, they have to get our permission first?"

"Yes, they would. Or if you wanted to sell, you'd have to get theirs. You have basically equal shares of ownership. Or of course, you could sell out to each other as well, if two parties would agree."

I glanced almost unwillingly at Bill behind me, but he remained just out of eyesight. What on earth was Martha thinking? I hoped we'd have some time later to talk alone.

"Any other questions?" Hearing none, Terry nodded twice and suggested that whoever wanted to join Mr. Hedstrom on a tour of the house was welcome. Bill stood up behind me and nudged me into a standing position. It was a clear order to be on the tour.

"Terry, I'd like to give the tour if that is ok?"

"You are probably the best one to give it, so thank you." Terry turned and touched Mr. Hedstrom's arm. We waited as the others left the room, leaving just the three of us. Even Bill had deserted me.

"Here is of course the library. It is my favorite room in the entire house. Mr. Hedstrom, have you ever been here before? I guess I should have asked?"

"Not since Jace made all these changes. I visited when we were both much younger and just out of the war you know."

"Ms. James," Terry spoke when I interrupted him, "Please, Terry, call me Rebekkah. I've never been a "MS" a day in my life."

"Sure, sorry. Rebekkah, the books, as I understand it, are all yours?"

"Yes, except some theology books Pop left for Pastor Michael. I'm still amazed – he knew how much I love books, but this was much more than I could have imagined as a gift."

Exiting the library, I took them on a guided tour, explaining the different rooms, how the House was set up, and which rooms we couldn't access as we had guests in them. We entered the kitchen and I saw Martha turn her back. Struggling to understand why a woman who was normally very friendly could be so rude, I kept everyone moving.

"Here is the apartment. My mom and I were using it, but the board thought it better that the sisters use it."

"Rebekkah, how do you really feel about it? I know it was hard for you to find another place to live." Terry seemed honestly interested, so I gave him an honest answer.

"I was upset and scared, but in reality, this is a good change." We spent only a short time in the apartment, respecting the privacy of the spinster sisters.

We finished with a short walk down to Mini-Mac, a four room private cottage we rented out to families. Mr. Hedstrom's eyes widened as we entered. He obviously remembered it as it was years ago; a stable that housed horses, tack and feed.

"This is amazing. I can't believe it. It is beautiful. Did Jace do this?"

"No, actually I did, with his permission of course. We were offered Mini-Mac as a place to live, but I decided to leave the income with the House and find a place of my own."

The tour ended back in the library and I waited for any questions, which there didn't appear to be any. With a handshake and thanks, Jeremiah Hedstrom turned to leave, but paused at the door.

"My son will love this place when he gets here. He loves the outdoors and this whole area is amazing."

I glanced at Terry, who shrugged.

"May I ask, Mr. Hedstrom, do you know what happened when your son..." I paused, not sure if I should ask or how to ask about Thomas's disappearance.

"Tom – his name is Tom. He was going to go to the Boundary Waters after our visit here. I know he wanted to pick up some camping gear, but it is so odd, him buying so much when he has all that stuff at home."

"Yes, I can see why it would seem odd. Did he know anyone out here?"

"No. We flew into Minneapolis, you know, and got a hotel room as he wanted to visit some of the big camping stores there before we drove up." He paused and I waited, wondering if I should actually be discussing it with him.

"Anyway, he went on his own as I was meeting with Terry and he just didn't come back. I waited for a day, you know, thinking maybe he just got lost or something. Then I reported him missing. I was surprised that they took it so seriously, but I guess I'm glad too. Did you know they found out through his credit cards where he'd been? Then they found the rental car up in a parking area in the Boundary Waters. It all seems so strange that he would go without telling me. But I'm sure he'll be located soon, probably feel a bit embarrassed – you know how young men can be."

I wondered briefly how young the son of a man in his 80's or 90's could be, but I guess for someone that age, everyone is young.

"Did you know Ms. - I mean, Rebekkah - is part of a search and rescue group here in Elk Ridge, Mr. Hedstrom?" Terry nodded towards me and went on, "She has dogs trained to find missing people."

"Really? They used dogs but apparently they couldn't find anything. I don't know much about it, but they are wondering if perhaps Tom didn't camp in that area after all. Maybe he got a ride someplace else?"

"I guess it is possible. Well – do you have any other questions about McCaffrey House?"

"No, not right now. Thank you for your time! I believe Mr. O'Reilly will be spending some time with the advisors, is it alright if I sit in here for a bit?"

Giving him an affirmative, I slipped out and bee-lined myself directly to the kitchen. Finding neither sister there, I tapped on the apartment door.

"Who is it?" Martha's voice, strong and serious, came clearly through the heavy wood.

"Rebekkah – can I come in and talk?"

"Of course dear, the door is open."

I entered and found both sitting at the familiar table, drinking tea and having some cookies. Martha tapped the chair next to her.

"Tea, dear?"

"No thank you. Unless it will help loosen your tongue. What is going on with you and Mr. Hedstrom?"

"Nothing dear," Martha patted Margaret's hand with a gentleness I'd never seen before.

"Would you care to expound on that statement, or am I to start the third degree?"

"Rebekkah, really, it is ancient history. Look at us; we're both ancient and so is he. He came once many years ago, right out of the war, and we met him then. Then he went away and we haven't seen him since."

"Then why are you being so rude to him?" I finally poured myself a cup of tea, hoping perhaps that it would make the ladies feel more like it was a hen party.

"Is Mr. Hedstrom staying with us?" Margaret's voice startled me. She rarely spoke to me directly, and in looking at her, I realized she wasn't.

"Not that I'm aware of Margie – don't you worry."

"Oh, I'm not worried now that meeting him again is over with. He's still very handsome, isn't he?"

A glimmer of light began to shine through my dense fog.

"Margaret, did you care for Mr. Hedstrom?"

"Yes. He was so very handsome in his uniform, and he would take us out to tea and cake, remember Martha?" Margaret smiled and I knew she was remembering a different time, a time when all things were possible and life was still ahead of her, instead of behind.

"Yes Margie, I remember. I also remember he left without a word and you wouldn't speak for days. I don't like him coming back and pretending friendship when he has no concept of it."

"Martha, did he, well, make overtures to Margaret he shouldn't have?"

"I don't know what you mean child. He was polite to us, he took us for tea and cakes and the movies, as Margaret said. He was here about two months I think. Then he just left. I don't know why."

"I do." Margaret dreamily stirred her cup of tea, and for a moment, I saw her as she must have been then, back in the late forties, young, beautiful and looking for romance and excitement.

"What? What did you say?" Martha's voice escalated and actually made Margaret and I both jump.

Margaret cowered down, and then seemed to develop a spine. Martha had always been the boss, and suddenly Margaret knew something her sister didn't. I could see her shoulders square back up and she responded, "I know why. He fell in love with me. I know he did, but he shouldn't have you know. He told me in the letter."

"Margaret, are you daft? What letter are you talking about?"

"No dear, I'm not daft. I remember – I still have the letter. He was already married – didn't you know? He wrote me a letter and Ginie gave it to me after he left." She smiled a secretive smile.

Margaret had completely silenced Martha and myself. The rumors for years about a romance with the single gentleman who had lived with them were nothing compared to a romance with a married man.

"Did you love him, Margaret?" I asked tentatively.

"Yes, he was a wonderful young man. When I heard he was coming back, I guess I got very nervous. I wondered if he even remembered me. But when he walked into the room…" Her voice trailed off and I wasn't sure she'd finish, but she did, "He looked right into my eyes and I knew. Is he still married?"

"I don't know Margaret." I glanced at Martha, who still sat in silence, her lips slightly parted, eyes blinking. She was as silenced as I'd ever seen her. "Do you think he still carries a torch for you Margaret?"

"I don't know dearie, but wouldn't it be nice if he did?"

"Only if he's no longer married, sister. I thought he was a cad all these years, flirting as he did and then just leaving without a word." Martha had finally found her voice, but it was subdued and possibly hurt.

"Of course you are right sister. I was afraid to tell you. I thought, well, I thought YOU were in love with him. When I read his letter, I was so afraid you would be hurt because he loved me instead. Do you forgive me?" Margaret studied her sister and I knew I was seeing the sisters as who they really were. Margaret, a romantic who loved a man she couldn't have and as a consequence, locked her love away and lived in her own dream world. And Martha, who loved a man who didn't love her back and to keep others away from her wounded heart became abrasive and bitter.

I wondered, but didn't ask, what Margaret would have done had Jeremiah not been married. Would she have risked losing her sister to gain the man she loved?

What price love? I thought about my situation with Bill, if I was willing to give up the life I loved and wanted in order to marry him. Or if I'd give up on possibly my only chance at love in order to keep doing what I loved to do.

Chapter 8

And why are you anxious for clothes?
Consider the lilies of the field, how they grow

I left the sisters, knowing the conversation was suddenly far more private than I had expected. In the past, I would have gone to my little alcove office, but even that was no longer mine. Megan was in the chair, on the phone, receiving a reservation. Smiling at her, I continued on to the kitchen and poured myself a cup of coffee and took a cookie from the jar.

"So, what did you learn?" Bill's voice came from nowhere. I never heard him come in, but he was suddenly there.

"Coffee?" I asked economically. At his nod, I poured another cup and handed it to him, pointing at the creamer on the butcher block table.

"Things that weren't any of my business, but shed light on the sisters. And how much they must love each other."

"Meaning?"

"That it isn't my information to share, but to put your mind at rest, it has nothing to do with McCaffrey House, the Trust, or anything else. It is personal and private. Something that happened many many years ago. Ancient history, as Martha put it."

Bill's hand settled over mine, which was tapping nervously on the table. He waited a moment for my hand to go still before asking, "What else?"

"I don't know Bill. I guess maybe I'm tired. I don't know what is going on anymore. Mr. Hedstrom showing up, finding out the unit is involved with the search for his son, then this with the sisters. Just getting through with Ari, I really am just tired."

Bill placed his other hand over my other hand and leaned in. I knew he was going to kiss me, but a bolt of fear shot through me and I pulled away.

"Why do you do that? I wish you would talk to me Rebekkah. There is something, and it isn't about your dog, the sisters or Mr. Hedstrom's issues."

"I don't know, please don't ask."

"But I am asking. I think I need to know. Why are you so afraid of getting close?"

I turned away and likely would have left if he wasn't still holding my hands. I felt tears in my eyes and wished I could run. I didn't want to cry in front of Bill. I also didn't know how to explain what I didn't yet understand myself.

"Tell me, Rebekkah. We have to get through this, or there isn't any point to talking about the rest of it. Your friend Connie mentioned you'd been hurt…"

"Connie doesn't know anything; it was before I met her."

"So she told me."

"I can't believe you asked her about me or my past."

"I didn't actually, she offered. Last time she was here, she said she knew you'd been hurt by someone and to be patient. Tell me."

"It is nothing. It was nothing. A guy I went to church with, he and I started to do a lot of flirting I guess. I don't know, I'm not sure if I encouraged it or not. He was divorced, his wife had left him high and dry. He was sweet and nice to me. We never dated, but…I thought we would. He had a, I guess you'd call it a pet name for me, and I had one for him. Sort of secret, no one else knew."

I paused and then stopped. Why was I even telling him all this? It didn't matter anymore. As Martha had said, it was ancient history.

"Go on Rebekkah. Please, we need to get it out of the way."

"Fine. One day I heard from a friend that his ex-wife had come home and he was dating her, hoping to rebuild his marriage. He wanted to do the right thing, the Biblical thing. He didn't tell me, he still talked to me as if...well anyway, I confronted him, asking what he meant by it all. His response..." I swallowed and looked away, my eyes glazing in tears. I don't know why that response, given to me so many years ago still hurt, but it did.

"He said he thought he was only risking his own feelings and not mine." I could feel the tears rolling down my cheeks. It all seemed so silly. An affair that wasn't.

"I'm sorry. He wasn't a man if he didn't realize his actions could affect you. I wouldn't do that Rebekkah."

I knew that, or at least my brain believed it. I also knew that little romance wasn't the first tear my heart had experienced. Over the years, I had several men do similar things to me. Treat me like I was special, that maybe I was "the one", only to leave my side for someone else. And every one of them had said words so similar, I wondered if there was some book written for men like them.

I had bad judgment in picking men and had learned to always be on my guard. I knew there would be that moment when they would find someone better. They'd say how glad they were I understood and that we would be friends as always.

Would Bill do that to me? I didn't think he would, but I also knew that my reactions to him belied my thoughts. I was afraid of yet another desertion.

"Rebekkah, how often has it happened like that? Can I ask?"

"Several times I guess. I'm everyone's fallback position when they can't get the one they want. Or maybe I'm the safe one, the one they think they can't hurt. I don't honestly know. I do know I've learned to not let it happen anymore."

Bill let my hands go, but I felt too drained to move. We sat quietly, and I was glad he asked no more questions. Looking at my life from the perspective of time, I sensibly knew that what had happened to me had been pretty minor. Many women had far worse things happen to them. I often wondered why I felt so scarred by it all. I had no answer, and yet the fears remained.

"When Jane died, I felt deserted. She had gone and I was left alone. I suppose I went into denial at first, believing that somehow it wasn't true. I only remember feeling abandoned. Then I got angry - I blamed her, I blamed myself; and for a while, I blamed God. I never wanted to risk myself again to something I couldn't control. I didn't, either, for years. Then I met you."

The tears I had managed to get under control started to flow again.

"Rebekkah, I tried very hard to ignore the feelings I felt stirring up when I talked to you. I pushed them away and at one point, tried to walk away. But God kept putting you in my path. At least, I believe it was God. I watched you run this place, keeping it going with a natural skill no one believed you had. Not even you. I've watched you love and care for those around you. You give of yourself and touch lives with your volunteer work. I see the dreams you sacrificed in order to do what you do for

126

others. And I also know that you feel the need to be loved and accepted. I suspect that every time a man left you for another, you felt as if you didn't measure up. I want you to know Rebekkah that it is those men that didn't measure up – they weren't good enough for you."

I felt myself take a deep shuddering breath, hoping to take control of my emotions. I had kept them under such a tight rein for so long, I didn't know how painful it was to let go. No words could make it past the tight ball in my throat, but I reached over and touched his hands.

"I have to head back to town, but before I go, Rebekkah, you do believe I wouldn't take advantage of you like those others did?"

I nodded, and, still holding his hands in mine, I leaned across and kissed him. He accepted the simple kiss, never demanding more. We sat for a long moment, our foreheads touching as we sat with our hands intertwined. The moment was broken by the sisters, who had come in to start prepping the kitchen for the next meal.

"Sister, look!" Margaret's voice sounded so young, I imagined again her as a young woman.

"Yes Margaret, leave them alone now." Martha, I noticed, had returned to calling her sister by her full name.

I stood up and swept both women into a hug, feeling the need to somehow convey the depth of what I had learned today from them. They didn't understand, or at least Martha didn't as she brushed me away. Margaret however wrapped me in her thin arms and held on tight. As we stood there, she whispered in my ear, "You mind you don't let love get away, dear. And find out if he's married, will you?"

127

With a sideways, darting glance at Martha, she moved away from me and disappeared into the large walk-in cooler. It took me a moment to realize she meant to find out if Mr. Hedstrom was single and not Bill. Smiling, I turned and walked with Bill, hand in hand, out to the front room. In front of God and everybody, as my dad used to say.

A few weeks later, Bill had gone home and things were more or less settling into a routine again. I learned driving to and from McCaffrey House afforded me the only time alone I had in a long time. I treasured it, and thanked the Advisors each time I got into my truck. I spent time praying and even singing. It was during one of these drives that my cell phone went off and I found myself talking with Sheriff Matthew Tvrdik.

"Is this Elk Ridge Search and Rescue?"

"Yes, this is Rebekkah James speaking, how can we help you?"

"This is Sheriff Tvrdik, that's T.v.r.d.i.k. I know it is pronounced like the V is a W, but it isn't."

"Yes sir, I understand. How can we help you?"

"We have a case that some of your dogs helped us on, for a Thomas Hedstrom?" The question mark was evident in his voice, wanting to confirm I knew something before having to tell me the entire story.

"Yes, of course. Three of our teams went up to the Boundary Waters. Do you need dogs again?" While I hoped he'd say yes, I also knew the trip would put my budget into the red.

"Well, sort of. I'm not sure. I've not worked with dogs very often, and I was impressed with them, I can tell you. We've come to think that Mr. Hedstrom was never there. Just about every dog handler that came said their dogs didn't get anything. How do they do that?"

"Training and lots of it. Before we proceed any further however, I do need to let you know that Mr. Jeremiah Hedstrom and I are co-owners of a business. I don't know if that will affect your ability to use myself or my search and rescue unit. We didn't know it the last time you called..."

"I didn't know that, but let me ask you this. Have you talked with him about the case? How much do you know?"

"We haven't talked much actually. I expressed my condolences on his situation; he only mentioned things which were the same things the K-9 teams were told at the initial call-out. I can tell he's in denial, although by this time, I'm sure his son is dead. I did not tell him that of course."

"Alright, well, I've made a note of it and will talk to the BCA agent who is working with us, but at this time, as long as you don't know the details...I don't think it will be problem. What we have is a bit of a situation that I'm not sure if the dogs can help or not. Can they really smell for people who are dead?"

"Yes, they can. We call them cadaver dogs, or HRD – Human Remains Detection – dogs. They are trained to only search for the odor of human remains decomposition. We proof them off dead animals and other anomalies."

"That is what one of the handlers said when they were here, but I wasn't sure it was true. Park K9 said the same thing, but they also said they didn't have any cadaver dogs. They recommended we call you," he paused and ended with what sounded like an apology, "I only called them first as they are closer to us."

"I understand. I haven't had the pleasure of working with them much, but I understand they are well-qualified with good dogs. We do have a cadaver dog but I could possibly find some more if you have a large area to search?"

"Not yet. It isn't large I mean. We have a report which, while I don't think it's real, we have to check out. Someone said they believe Mr. Hedstrom was abducted at the store, killed and his body was dumped on the way up here from the cities."

"Sheriff, that is a rather LARGE area...."

"No, yes that is, but they have a fairly specific location based on the rental car's GPS. It had a stop off I-35 that doesn't make sense. There isn't anything there except a small wooded area. Do you think you could come and check it for us?"

"Yes, just let me know when and where. I'll bring the dog and do what we can with him. Is it alright if I bring someone with me to provide support in the field?"

"Of course, that will work well. Can you come tomorrow? I'd like to get this done. Nothing is making any sense anymore."

"Tomorrow will work for me. You may not be able to share this with me, but did you have the car checked for human remains or fluids?"

"The BCA went over it – you know, the Bureau of Criminal Apprehension – but they didn't find anything. Why, do you think the dogs could?"

"Well, if there was a body in the car for even a few hours, the gases could still be present which normal forensics wouldn't pick up. It might be worth checking."

"Can your dogs do that as well? The car is in our impound, although the rental company is raising Cain to get it back."

"Why don't we talk about it more tomorrow," I was pulling into the driveway of McCaffrey and was glad to be able to stop before writing the directions and time on a pad of paper I kept in the truck. Phoning the other members of my unit, I quickly realized no one was available to help me; that I'd be on my own.

Driving out the next day, I glanced in the back of my truck at Gus. Mom would watch Ari and Jael today, and I prayed my new little "wild child" would behave. Gus was my only certified cadaver dog now, and while I hoped Ari would come back, I wasn't sure. In the meantime, he stayed home.

Arriving at the location on my map, I realized we were in for a rougher time than "small area" had led me to believe. The area was a swampy bog. That it was a terrific place to dispose of a body, there is no doubt. The reason being that no one in their right mind wants to search a swamp or a bog. I glanced over the terrain and was at least thankful for a young strong dog like Gus.

Sheriff Tvrdik was older than I had imagined, looking somewhere in his sixties. He had sounded so much younger on the phone, it surprised me. He was waiting beside an unmarked squad, although he was in uniform. Deep in conversation with him was a younger man in a three piece suit. The suit looked out of place in the setting, but I correctly guessed he was with the BCA.

"Rebekkah James?" The sheriff broke off the conversation and walked toward me. Offering his hand, he economically said, "Sheriff Tvrdik and Special Agent Paul Mason of the Minnesota BCA."

"Gentlemen, nice to meet you both. This is the area? Do you have a map we can take a look at?"

"Over here in my car." We walked over and the Sheriff pulled a pad folio from the front seat and flipped it open.

"Here is the GPS track from the rental. As you can see," he paused as he traced the yellow line with his finger, "the track heads straight up 35 until it hits this intersection and stops here." He stopped and glanced around at the uninviting surroundings.

The BCA Special Agent interjected, "Ms. James, I haven't worked with dogs much, but when I have, I haven't had good experiences with them. They have proven to be rather unreliable and their handlers had every excuse in the book why. What makes your dog different?" Paul Mason had a low voice that sounded faintly antagonistic, but at least he was honest with me.

"Rather a tough question when I don't know what the history is on the dogs, their handlers, training or certifications that you worked with. I can tell you that Gus has been tested and certified by more than one nationally recognized organization over the past several years. We maintain training logs and I track his proficiency. Gus has an average of 85% accuracy on what we call 'blind' problems. I can provide copies of his certifications and, if you want to see his training logs, I can show you those as well."

"What about in the real world? That is what we have here – real world."

"Proficiency can't be measured by real world searches."

"Why in heaven's name can't it? If the dog doesn't find something, they don't find something." S.A. Mason's eyebrows had gone up and his body language changed to defiant.

"Sir, have you ever worked with narcotics dogs?" I waited until he nodded. Most Law Enforcement have worked at some point with a narc dog, and it seemed the easiest way to answer his question.

132

"Suppose we have 100 cars out here, and you ask that dog and handler to check every one of them for the presence of drugs. They find drugs in one of those cars. Is the dog a failure because he only has one percent success?"

"Was there anything in the other cars?"

"We don't know – which is why I ask the question. Most narcotics dogs are called to check one car because there is a high probability drugs will be found. There is probable cause established. In the real world of cadaver dogs, we are asked to search many areas where there is no probable cause, only reasonable suspicion. Such as today. Do you believe there is a body here? If the dog says no, is the dog wrong?"

I watched the faces of both men as I spoke, and hoped it would make sense to them. It was a hard concept to grasp. But in reality, search and rescue dogs are more often used to eliminate areas than find missing persons.

"Gus has been on over twenty searches since he first certified. Of those, he has assisted law enforcement in about four or five recoveries. In the majority of the others, my dog said there wasn't a body in the area we were asked to search. To this date, no bodies, in whole or in part, have been recovered in those areas. As a point of fact, in several of them, the body was located miles away later on. So the dog was proven correct. The problem we face as K-9 handlers is people want to know our success rate."

"Why is that a problem? I'd think you'd know, it is rather important, isn't it?" Sheriff Tvrdik's question didn't sound quarrelsome, merely curious.

"You need to define success first. In my opinion, success on a real world search is this: Did my dog do what my dog was trained to do?"

"And that is?" Once again, I was glad it was the Sheriff who asked, not the Special Agent.

"To sniff and tell me if there is the odor of human remains in the area assigned to us. If he sniffs and says no, and no remains are found, that is success. If he sniffs and says yes, and remains are found, that is success."

"What happens if he sniffs, as you call it, and says yes, but nothing is found?"

"Those are the hard searches because I truly trust my dog." I paused, waited a response before continuing. Getting none, I went on, "We have found the dogs can detect lingering odor if human remains were in the area, but moved. Lingering versus residual is something narcotic dogs experience as well. Residual odor can be proven with forensics. Lingering can't."

I waited, wondering if I'd be stood down and sent home. It was often hard for anyone who has had a bad experience to trust again. I knew that from personal experience. By his response, I could tell that the Sheriff was listening.

"I think I understand what you are saying. It is sort of like when someone wearing lots of perfume walks into a room – even after they leave, you can still smell them. However, they left nothing that can be detected except the odor?"

"Exactly. And it does happen, especially if the body is in an area with a lot of scavengers."

"Okay, let's give your dog a chance at this. I've told the Sheriff what I think of this area, he's told me what he thinks," he paused and I jumped in before he could finish.

"Please don't tell me anything other than how much of this wet mess you want the dog to sniff. I don't want to be influenced by either one of you."

"No, no plans to do that at all. I was just going to finish with, 'let's see what your dog thinks'. We need the entire bog checked over. It is about 30 acres. Is that too much?"

"No, although it is larger than I expected. You can walk along and watch. He won't care."

I geared up, pulling out my neoprene boots to stay as dry as I could. Unloading Gus, I slipped his royal blue search harness over his head and clipped the girth strap. He was quivering, as he normally did before a search.

"Okay Gus-gus – go get caddy!" I released his leash and we watched as he took off like a little golden rocket. Walking toward the bog, I glanced just once and saw both men walking behind me in waders.

Gus raced along, his nose carried midway between the ground and the height of his shoulder. I knew many people who didn't think he could work at that speed, but I knew that was the speed at which he was happiest. I walked along the outer perimeter of the bog, letting Gus tackle the deeper parts as we walked along. I hoped that anyone who was going to dump a body wouldn't want to plow into the wet sludge any more than I did. That they would stick to the outside edge.

I only half-listened to the conversation behind me, keeping my focus on my dog. I saw nothing in his behaviors to indicate any type of human remains, but we still had to cut through the heart of it. As we came around the north side, I suddenly was aware that the ground had changed. A moment later, my foot went through and within seconds, my boot filled with water.

"Floating bog! Holy cow, that stinks." I spoke without thinking, but didn't care if they did hear me. I should have asked ahead of time, but the fact they put on waders should have been a clue for me. I got my leg free and turned to check where my dog was. I could see him struggling, his body undulating with the motion of the floating vegetation he was trying to bound across.

"Gus, slow down!" It was a futile command. Gus knew only two speeds – fast or frozen. I just had to keep going and hope he didn't drop through. If he did, I'd only have moments to save him from drowning. The vegetation would close over him that quickly.

I could hear the men behind me also trying to navigate the strange mat that floated above a pond of mucky water. I knew when someone went through from the tone of voice, as their words were lost to me. Gus continued to run along, as best he could over the top. He looked sort of like a dolphin as he reared up, coming clear of the vegetation and landing again with his back end flipping up behind him.

It felt like forever but was really only about an hour of trudging until we came out on firm ground again. I called Gus over and ran my hands over him, hoping he wasn't going to be hurt in any way. As my hand ran down his back, he flinched and whined.

"Is your dog okay?" Sheriff Tvrdik had caught up with us and was panting as heavily as I was.

"His back seems a bit sore, but I think now that we're out of the bog, he'll be alright." I still watched him closely as we went along. I noticed his speed had gone down and instead of hopping over logs, he was going around them.

We worked another hour, with two more traverses through the middle of the area. There was no change of behavior from Gus that would tell me there was human remains present, however there was significant changes of behavior as I tried to load him in the truck.

Gus stood and stared up at the open back end, but didn't even try to jump in. Slipping my arms under his chest and loin, I carefully lifted him in. Toweling him off, I realized he was shivering. Finding another towel, I wrapped it around him and felt my first twinge of concern. I gave him a few treats and left him to debrief with the Sheriff and Special Agent Mason.

"Gentleman, I can tell you that my dog didn't give any changes of behavior that would tell me there are human remains in this area. It was a tough area to cover, but I think we did a pretty fair job of it. The ground isn't conducive to a burial, however that floating bog is a prime place to drop a body. But I trust the dog on this one."

Mason stood to one side, peeling off his waders and stepping back into his polished dress shoes. He never once gave any indication of being tired or regretting going out with us. In fact, he looked rather as if he had enjoyed it.

"How is your dog? I saw you lift him into the truck," Sheriff Tvrdik glanced with evident concern over toward Gus. I looked back myself, and my initial twinge blossomed into a full-blown fear. The happy little cadaver dog that normally sat in that crate wasn't there. In his place was a dog that looked old and decrepit, wrapped in his blue towel. His eyes were squinted and I knew he was in pain.

"I think he tweaked his back going through the bog, but I'll get him checked when I get home. He's a tough little dog." I responded with more bravery than I felt.

"Yeah, a lot tougher than we were, I was really puffing in there!"

"Ms. James, I am not convinced yet, but I will tell you this – neither the Sheriff nor I believed there was a body in this area."

"Can I ask why? It does seem rather an obviously good location."

"Too obvious I think. If someone went to the effort to dispose of the body, why leave it on the GPS? Why not drive around to make it look like you were everywhere and nowhere. It doesn't make sense."

"Well, I'm glad I don't have to worry about all that, although honestly I will mentally speculate anyway. It is a bad habit."

"You do know this is all confidential, correct?" S.A. Mason looked up sharply as he spoke.

"Yes, I'm sorry, the speculation is all mine. My unit knows I'm here, but not the details."

He nodded and then paused, a pause that made me pause. I was about to say my usual spiel about submitting my maps and reports, and then leave. Something in his manner made me stop.

"Listen, Matt and I," S.A. Mason flicked a thumb in the direction of the Sheriff, "we decided before you arrived if you checked this area and gave it a negative, we'd like you to check the car as you suggested."

I felt myself freeze. Was this a test? Was this area just a test? As if reading my mind, the Sheriff said, "This area did need to be checked, but we basically knew it was a negative. The GPS did have this exit showing as a stopping point, but we learned this morning there was a glitch and it is just as likely the car never stopped here. The mileage doesn't match the odometer on the car."

"If you're wondering if this was a test, I guess, in a way, it was. However, if we completely believed it was negative, we wouldn't have followed you out there." The Special Agent looked out over the even less inviting bog.

I nodded, accepting what he said. I wondered if the car would also be a test. I had heard of certain members of law enforcement doing this, hoping to prove the dogs wrong. I just had never experienced it before.

We drove north and an hour later, arrived at an impound lot. A number of cars were there, and more than a few showed signs of dramatic damage from impact. One even had half the frame torn away. Paul waited a moment while I looked them over before he spoke.

"You can consider this a test as well, if you want. We have five cars inside the garage there. One is the rental, which I understand you have never seen and do not know what make, model or color it is. I'd like you to check them with your dog. An external check."

Following them inside, true to his word there were five cars, neatly lined up. One, like its counterparts outside, was smashed up.

"Sheriff, can you please tell me if any of the cars in this line up have had a death or bodily injury?"

"Don't you trust your dog?" The Special Agent's tone was starting to get under my skin. He truly wanted to prove my dog wrong.

"If one of these cars, unrelated to the Hedstrom case, had a person who bled or died in it, the dog will tell me about that car. I just want you to be aware of it. This isn't an excuse or not believing in my dog."

I left the garage and opened my truck. Gus was dozing and when I lifted the harness, he pushed himself up and wiggled. Feeling better about his back, but still not sure what happened, I lifted him down and brought him into the garage on leash.

Approaching the first car, I performed the line-up as I had been taught by law enforcement officers who did it all the time. Starting with the front grill, I walked backwards to keep my body out of the dog's way while still being able to watch him. I directed his movements with my hand as we circled clockwise, and then did a second sweep counterclockwise. I watched Gus as he sniffed the body of the car and knew there was nothing there.

Surprisingly, Gus had no reaction to the smashed car. I had expected a response; someone had to have been injured in that wreck. With a deep breath, I trusted my dog and kept going. I reached the fourth car without any reaction and took a breather for the dog and myself. My back was starting to hurt and I flexed it out.

As we started checking the fourth car, Gus suddenly yanked away and dragged me toward the fifth car. I felt the words reverberate through my head, "trust your dog".

"The dog has had a distinct change of behavior, skipping the Wrangler there to bring me to this four door Chevy Malibu. I'd like to go ahead and go over this one; however I want to go back to the Wrangler before we finish up."

Starting at the grill, Gus pulled me down the side of the vehicle, sucking in air through his nose and expelling it out the sides. As we reached the rear wheel well, he stopped and stuffed his head up into it, snuffing and snorting. I waited only a moment and then encouraged him to keep moving. Reaching the trunk, Gus again sniffed against the joining of the body and the trunk lid. Coming to a stop on the passenger side of the trunk, he threw himself to the ground and let out his trademark bark.

"Gentlemen, my dog has just given his final trained response on this Malibu. I'll finish up with this vehicle and then go back to the Wrangler."

Gus, ever ready to keep working, accepted a pat on his side and kept going. He showed far less interest in the rest of the passenger side of the car, although he did sniff up into the rear wheel well on that side.

With my heart beating at twice its normal rate, I directed Gus to finish the counterclockwise sweep of the car. Gus again yanked my arm as he made the turn at the back of the passenger side. Reaching the rear corner of the driver's side, Gus gave his final trained response. He had neatly bracketed the trunk with his nose.

I glanced over at Sheriff Tvrdik and Special Agent Mason, and realized immediately that Gus had located the rental. There was no mistaking the widened eyes, the sudden tightening of the body and facial muscles. To clinch it, I saw Mason's hand went almost instinctively to his cell phone.

Patting Gus again, I pulled him back and went over the Jeep without a single reaction except he kept trying to drag me back to the Malibu.

"Ms. James, thank you. You'll of course send us reports for our records?" Sheriff Tvrdik had put on a poker face, which I matched with my own.

"Yes of course. If there is anything else, please let me know." I turned and started for the door, when a strong hand caught my arm.

"I'm sorry. I can't let you take off without asking more questions. What can your dog actually detect?" S.A. Mason was serious this time, no mockery.

"Can I put my dog up? I'd like to get him warmed up and some food in his stomach. Can I join you inside?" He nodded and I took Gus out, helping him into the truck as he again refused to jump on his own. He inhaled his dinner and drank half his water dish as I rubbed his back muscles, hoping to ease some of his pain. Leaving him with a dog jacket on, I headed back inside.

They were both on the phone when I tapped on an office door and went in. How to explain to a skeptic that what he had just seen wasn't black magic was the question of the hour.

"Would you like something to eat too? We're ordering some sub sandwiches."

"Sure, turkey is fine." The Sheriff waited, an eyebrow raised, so I finished with, "Lettuce, mayo, cheese and black olives?" He nodded and I could hear him finish the order.

"Alrighty then. Paul told you he has had bad experiences with dogs. I have had few experiences with dogs, but the Boundary search impressed me with the dogs that were there. We're not totally sure what to think today. Can you tell us more about what the dogs are trained to find?"

"Sheriff," I started when he interrupted.

"Please, call me Matt,"

"Sure. Matt, in short, the dogs are trained to find – or detect – the decomposition of human remains to the exclusion of other things, such as dead animals. When I first started some years ago, it was popular to train the dogs to find a single drop of blood to prove how great the dogs work. The problem with that training was, the dogs would find single drops of blood."

"Well, that makes sense – we need that information."

"Yes, but do you need to know that a person nicked themselves with a knife while chopping a tomato for their salad last year? That is what was starting to happen. The flip side to that coin was the dogs were leery of large sources because no one had access to large sources to train with. You understand what I mean by large sources?"

"Full bodies?"

"Yes. Or larger body parts. It is a gray area of our law here, although in some states it is less gray. People can possess some human remains for the purpose of research. We sort of fall under that umbrella. Sort of. We don't talk about it much."

I was interrupted by the arrival of our sandwiches, but Paul asked me to continue as we ate.

"Times are changing as are training methods. We now work dogs on larger sources when we can. We don't train for single drops of blood. The dogs are challenged with more things – like vehicle searches. Training an HRD dog takes time, hard work, patience and lots of repetition. "

"So, the dogs I worked with might have been trained to the older methods?"

"Perhaps, I don't know. Were they certified by anyone?"

"They said they were. We just assumed they were, but I guess we never asked for proof."

I ate some of my sandwich before responding, "I will tell you, and Sheriff – Matt – you can confirm this hopefully, but when my unit members respond to a search, they not only provide you with a full search report, but also a copy of their curriculum vitae and copies of their certifications."

"Yes, I received all that information. I'll be honest, until this moment, I questioned the need for so much paperwork, but now I realize how important it can be." Matt pulled a file from his ever-present pad folio and showed us a file folder more than two inches thick, "It is all in here."

144

We finished the sandwiches and I politely excused myself. I wanted to get Gus home and out of the constraint of his crate. The search only piqued my interest. Who would abduct a man, a tourist yet, kill him, take his body, and dump it someplace and make it look like he went on his camping trip anyway? And why?

Chapter 9

*They toil not, nor do they spin, and yet, I say to you that even
Solomon, in all his glory, was not arrayed like one of these.*

Gus bounced back in a few days, as I expected him too. He was stiff and sore, but a few baby aspirin and a gentle back massage each day appeared to get him through it.

Ari, as though realizing Gus had taken over his spot as the sickly child, rebounded. I was happy to see it, but still questioned his long-term ability to work search again. I could still hear the deep huffing of his breathing as I began extending our walks. Damaged lungs don't just regenerate.

The real pleasure in those next few weeks and months was working with Jael. She took to search and rescue like a duck to water. I carefully mapped our progress in training logs and knew that as quickly as she was learning, we could certify in live find area search by the time she was two, or possibly sooner. I also saw in this dog the potential for my first disaster dog.

Jael threw herself into training, doing runaways with puppy abandon. As people teased her, holding her ball just out of reach, and then dashed away, she'd fling herself against my restraining arms, wanting to follow them as they disappeared behind a bush or tree.

Jael picked her reward with the same focus she put into her training. She discovered tennis balls. Really, she discovered that anything round had the potential to roll, be thrown, and caught. And in those actions, life opened up many new possibilities.

Her intelligence, while not quite as highly developed as Ari's, still was a vast improvement over Gus's. Jael would take her toys and test different places to put them. A box, a shelf, the coffee table. She even learned if she put it on the top of the stairs, it would, all on its own, roll down the full flight.

As she caught onto the game of hide, I had our hiders go further away, then closer but well hidden. Then further away again, but lying flat on the ground, or maybe curled in a ball. We challenged her with distance, position, and availability of the hider. As she touched them, they'd reward with a fast and furious game of fetch.

Knowing I didn't want my next large dog to jump on me as Ari always did, I chose a bringsel device for Jael's final trained response to finding her subject.

The bringsel can be just about anything that a dog can grab as a sign they have found what they are trained to find. While some people attached the bringsel to the dog's collar so the dog could grab it and carry it back to their handler, because of our wilderness work, we preferred the bringsel to hang from our belts.

The goal of course, was to have Jael grab, pull the bringsel, and run back to her missing person. Jael, however, had a mind of her own and had no intention of grabbing anything she didn't like. With a lot of trial and error, we finally found a fleece tug toy was acceptable to both of us. With a small carabineer, I hooked it to my belt loop.

Each day time was spent teaching her to grab the bringsel and get a reward. She'd grab, I'd click our little training clicker, and a treat was tossed her way. Soon, whenever she saw the bringsel, she'd run over and pull it. I laughingly called myself her Pez dispenser.

Just as she learned that finding people gave her tennis ball and a big playtime, she also learned pulling the bringsel gave her treats. Life, for all intents and purposes, was one happy playground for my newest K-9 partner.

Then came the big day when we changed the game and started to chain her behaviors. I wondered how she'd react as we placed my mom in a lawn chair while I stood next to her, my dog watching us closely. Reaching down, I tapped the bringsel dangling from my right hip. Jael happily grabbed it and yanked it.

I just as quickly touched my mom's shoulder and she threw Jael's tennis ball. I love my mom dearly, but tennis ball throwing isn't in her realm of expertise. The ball dropped a foot away, but Jael didn't care. This was a new game and one she clearly was going to enjoy.

Within days, we had progressed to having a person standing, sitting, lying down, bent over and in several other odd positions as they waited for my touch on their shoulder. Each time Jael grabbed that bringsel, she knew the person, not me, would throw her ball. She began to yank and swing around in a single motion.

As we began moving away from our helpers, Jael stuck with it. Distances between us and our helper were at first were only a few feet, then twenty feet, fifty, and more were added. Without hesitation, she'd tug the bringsel and race full tilt back to our helper. I'd run back with her and as soon as I touched our helper's shoulder, the game would begin again.

Three months into our training, I knew it was time to chain our bringsel work with our search work. Up until that day, we had kept the trainings separated, but Jael was now pulling the bringsel under almost any situation.

As my unit gathered around, we brainstormed the best way to incorporate the two activities.

"Rebekkah, I think it is important we put it back to baby steps as we're asking her to do something entirely new." Karen commented as Amos stood by, waiting to go hide for Jael. I started to nod when Chris jumped in with her question.

"Should we let her see her hider run this time? I know she hasn't been, but this is sort of new."

"What about letting her watch for the first 10 feet and then turning her?" Amos glanced over at me as yet another question was tossed in my direction.

"Good ideas, everyone. I tell you what I'll do – I'll let her watch for a few feet, then turn her."

I took Jael, a spindly, coyote-looking puppy who had a tendency to leap straight up at unexpected moments, out of the truck. Slipping on a borrowed vest, we walked to the area and Amos teased my puppy, calling her name and then suddenly running away. Before he went out of sight, I turned Jael and hung the bringsel on my pocket.

My puppy frantically yanked at the end of the leash and barked to be released. Unclipping the leash, I watched her zoom away, following where Amos had gone. I jogged along behind, but not fast enough to keep up. The point of the exercise was to see if she'd connect in her own brain that when Amos didn't reward her, she would come back to me. It would be the first time her hider didn't throw her ball when she arrived.

A few moments later, we heard her excited bark and then nothing. I was literally twitching when we heard our radio transmit, "she left me and is returning back toward you."

Seconds later my little sable search and rescue dog came racing toward me. She was going so fast, she missed the bringsel entirely, her teeth snapping thin air. Wheeling around, she plowed into my thigh with both front feet, grabbed the bringsel and pulled it so hard it ripped the belt loop on my pants. Without ever looking directly at me, she spun around and ran back toward where we knew Amos was hiding.

I ran behind her, tears in my eyes, as I knew she had linked her chain together on her own. I also knew this first time could be a fluke, that we'd have our fair share of errors going forward. But today, this first one was perfect. We reached Amos at about the same time and I touched Amos's shoulder. He immediately tossed her ball to her and she ran in a circle before returning to him and dropping the ball at his feet to throw again.

"Rebekkah, you need to get one of those ball thrower things. She's going to be a ball freak, might as well make it easier for everyone!" Amos tossed the ball again, this time further away.

Laughing, I agreed to do that soon. After running the other dogs on their training problems, we settled on the grass to chat and relax. Inevitably, the conversation turned to the Hedstrom search. Everyone knew I had been called and were wondering what, if anything, I could tell them.

"I seriously wish I could tell you everything, but all I can really say is, they had another area to check and Gus came up empty. As you knew, he also strained his back working that thing. I hate floating bogs – they are hard on everyone."

"I think the whole thing is bogus. Do you suppose he just took off?" Karen plucked at the grass and finally finding the right blade, pinned it between her thumbs and blew a piercing whistle before the blade split in two.

"Thanks Karen, now that I can't hear anymore..." Al poked her in the shoulder before turning back to me, "Rebekkah, you weren't up there in the Boundary Waters, but I have to agree with Karen. I think it is a bogus search at this point."

"I think I can tell all of you that they agree with the K-9 teams who went up there that Thomas was never there."

"So how did the rental get there? Someone steal it?"

"Sorry, no clue. Anyway, speculation doesn't really help. I've got to head back to McCaffrey House – anyone up for a mid-week run for my puppy?"

Karen and Chris both volunteered to come down to Elk Ridge and help me do some extra runs with Jael. Since moving out of McCaffrey, I'd discovered my training time had been reduced. I now had a long drive to and from work, instead of just walking out the door.

Arriving at McCaffrey an hour later, I did a quick walk through of the House, and then stopped in at the office. It was quiet, Megan apparently off doing other things. I sat behind the desk and went through the books as quickly as I could. While it was still my desk, Megan used it more often as she handled the reservations.

As I sat there, there was a tap on the door and I looked up to see Adam in the doorway. Smiling a welcome, I teasingly asked him if he was there to check on his new investment.

"Actually, I'm here to finally pick up that trunk of Pop's memorabilia. I wanted to make room for it in the spare room before I brought it over. If I remember right, it is a pretty large steamer trunk."

"Okay if I join you? At some point I need to go through all the other boxes, bags and trunks up there. I only know what is in one of them."

"Virginia's dresses?" Adam of course was referring to the one trunk I had been in. For a very formal event, Pop had given me permission to wear a dress from it. I never dreamed it would one day belong to me.

I followed him up to the attic, thankful for the spring-loaded stairs that dropped out of the ceiling. Standing at the top, I had almost a fatalistic feeling about the piles and stacks around me. There were just too many. Adam however went straight to the trunk he knew.

"I thought you said it was really big?" I touched the top of it, feeling the fine old grained leather and brass fittings.

"I was a lot younger and smaller then I guess. I remember it being gargantuan." Adam used the key I had given him earlier to open the lock and after opening it, he gave both lock and key back to me. "I won't need these anymore. Thank you for keeping it secure for me."

As he opened the trunk, I propped open a nearby box. A box that belonged to me and for all I knew contained a treasure. Instead, it contained packing peanuts. Pushing my hands deep into them, I realized that the box was merely a storage place for the peanuts. I wondered briefly if it was my mom's box. She was notorious for keeping everything, including every single packing peanut she ever received.

Closing the box back up, I opened another one next to it with the same result. More peanuts. The third box was different. It contained empty boxes of assorted sizes. Giving up, I returned to Adam's side and his far more fascinating trunk.

"I wanted to get here sooner, see if there was anything about Jeremiah Hedstrom that perhaps I just didn't remember. Life just gets in the way sometimes."

153

He carefully sorted out a stack of composition books and set them aside. With something akin to reverence, he carefully touched several boxes; boxes I recognized as holding military service medals.

Smiling, he picked up one and flipped it open, showing a purple heart. "He earned this one in France. He sort of laughed this one off because he felt it wasn't earned. A shell hit by the mess tent and he was injured while eating his dinner." I watched as he fingered the medal, and then finished, "He says the medal was actually for being brave enough to eat the food, not for the injury."

I smiled at the story, and could just about hear Pop saying those very words.

"So, all these boxes and stuff are yours. What have you found so far?"

"Packing peanuts. I almost would blame my mom, but she'd never get her boxes up here." I took another box from nearby and opened it. This one at least didn't hold packing materials. Instead, it was quilting squares.

"Rebekkah, are you feeling alright?"

"Sure, why do you ask?" I warily looked at Adam, wondering why he would ask.

"You seem really tired and distracted lately. Amy was worried about you I guess. She said to ask if I saw you today. I think she thinks maybe you and Bill had a fight."

"No, not at all. I guess I haven't been sleeping all that great, weird dreams, must be the new house or something." I opened another box and found more quilting squares. "Adam, did Virginia quilt?"

"She did. There was quite a little quilting club in town for many years. You know, now that you say that, I wonder what happened to all of those quilts. I guess they must be up here someplace."

"Well, one of these days I'll have to go through all of this. Do you think Amy would be willing to help me? It is quite a lot of boxes and trunks."

"I know she would," He paused and finished with, "Rebekkah, you've had a lot of stress lately. I wonder if maybe you should talk to Pastor Dave. Benjamin told me about the accident and he said you were really shook by it. Then that man you and Amos found. It could be, well, that you are having some issues with PTSD."

"Post traumatic stress? No, really, I'm fine." I nudged another box aside, and found myself refusing to look at Adam. He just closed up the trunk and together we carried it out to his pickup.

Two days later Amy and I sat in the attic and began sorting boxes. Well, actually I sorted and shifted them; Amy recorded what was in each and labeled it accordingly.

By the time we were done, we had sorted and stacked over twenty boxes. Most contained what I would term "junk" and I wondered how I'd get rid of it all. The trunks held the nicest things, including winter coats, boots and hats, dresses, candlesticks, and other household items that appeared to be antique. The final trunk held Virginia's quilts, which I planned to air and use at McCaffrey House.

"Rebekkah, what do you say to a garage sale? I'm sure you could sell most of the quilt squares and those books easily. Who knows, maybe you'll get rid of all this stuff that way!"

"Good idea. I could use it as a fundraiser for E.R. SAR, maybe bring in more people that way. I'm sure my mom has some stuff she'd like to get rid of too."

After Amy left, I toted the boxes to the garage, wondering if I could keep them there until the garage sale. Who knows, maybe people would even need some packing peanuts!

A week after our "Attic Attack", as Amy called it, we held the sale in the three bays of the McCaffrey House garage. I agreed to pay the House twenty five dollars for rental, and donate the proceeds to Elk Ridge Search and Rescue.

To say the sale went better than I expected was an understatement. By the time we were done, almost all of the things I thought of as junk were gone and E.R. SAR received nearly eight hundred dollars. I was left with only the things I had chosen to keep, which were really just the trunks.

As the summer wore on, Jael became the talk of my unit and McCaffrey House, but not because of her amazing accomplishments in her search training. No, she was becoming infamous for what I began to call my "guess what your dog did today" phone calls from my mom.

"Rebekkah, guess what your dog just ate? She ate…" and I could put just about anything in the blank. First was a bar of soap, which came out twenty four hours later like gray pudding. Then it was an ampoule of perfume. Mom wondered why she smelled like a brothel and discovered the broken bits of the vial in the bathroom. My only excuse was that Jael had a hot date and needed to be clean and smell pretty for it. My mom wasn't amused.

The worst however was when mom called in a panic because Jael had eaten a box of powdered enzymes designed to be put into the septic system to keep it clean and healthy. After numerous calls to Poison Control Center, the manufacturer, and Dr. Mikkelson, we learned it would only help keep Jael's digestive tract clean and healthy too. Meaning she had to go to the bathroom a lot over the next several days.

While Gus had merely disemboweled pillows, Jael actually ingested what she found interesting. God had given me a pup with a cast iron digestive tract and not much fazed her. I still had a horrible fear that one day she'd finally die from eating the wrong thing.

My mom, on the other hand, wasn't built quite so strongly as my pup. It wasn't long after the garage sale I noticed my mom seemed to forget things. We were mostly on our own for meals now, and often I'd go into the kitchen and find the stove or a burner still on. Sometimes in mid-sentence she'd forget what she was saying. I wasn't sure if I should worry or accept she was aging, like Ari was. I had to admit, on top of my sleepless nights, this new worry began to eat at me.

I wondered what I would do without her if something did happen. She was the rock that was always there for me. I relied on her far more than I had ever realized. She sacrificed every day for me to be able to do search and rescue. She gave up things so I could put gas in the truck or pay the vet bills. I knew that I was placed to take care of her, and I needed to do a better job than I had been doing.

In the midst of this new crisis in our lives, I found myself with another challenge. I had forgotten that Ari's air scent certification expired in August. Making the decision to re-certify Ari was difficult. Although technically he had remained certified while he was sick, I couldn't have deployed him. I knew that it would take one more year to get Jael ready, which meant a year without a live-find dog.

I had continued to train with him, and realized over the summer, he had actually gained much of his endurance back, although he still got tired faster than he used to. The question was could he complete a hundred and sixty acre test.

It was Ari that made the decision for me. Looking into his eyes, I knew he still wanted to work. I had to give him the chance. Picking up the phone, I called E.R. SAR's training officer. She was the one who could give us the nod to test outside of the unit or not.

"Marge, I'd like to set up a certification test for Ari. He really only needs to go one more year, then Jael can take over. I think he can do it, his nose still works, and he still loves his job." I held the phone while rubbing Ari's head with my other hand.

"Talk about timing - I was talking to Paul just this morning and he mentioned they were doing some certs down by Duluth and asked if we needed anyone done."

Flipping through my desk-top calendar, I didn't see anything on my calendar, but after the last few mix-ups with Bill, I figured I'd better be safe than sorry. "Marge, let me make a call and I'll let you know. I might have something on Saturday, I can't remember."

Dialing Bill's office a moment later, I wondered how I should ask him if we had anything scheduled for the weekend. I was actually relieved when Tracy answered instead of Bill.

"Tracy, I'm working on my calendar and I think I'm getting old, but I can't remember if we have anything scheduled. Can you check his schedule?"

"I don't need to look; he is traveling to Boston for a trial, leaving tomorrow. Do you want me to leave him a note?" Tracy sounded so competent, I felt almost like an idiot.

"Well, just ask him to give me a call. I can assume he's not coming here then for the weekend. I'm trying to schedule a test for Ari and didn't want to mess up like I've been doing lately."

"No problem, he's in court now, back probably by 3:00 or so. Take care and good luck on your test!"

Hanging up, I called Marge back and within an hour, Ari's retest was scheduled. While apprehensive, I knew that if we accomplished the test, I'd likely let his trailing certification expire. With Gus fully certified for water and land cadaver, and after Jael certified area search next year, I could consider retiring Ari.

Bill called back promptly at 3:15 and I was happy to wish him a good trip, find out he would be back by Wednesday, and arrange a date for the following weekend.

Saturday dawned bright and clear. Evelyn asked to come with me, and I was glad for the moral support. She had made the decision to join a few weeks before and I knew this would be a good eye-opener for her on search work.

A gentle five to ten mile an hour wind was predicted for the day, although the heat had me a little worried. As I drove to Duluth, I focused on a cheery conversation with Evelyn, not on the test. I still had my normal anxiety, however.

Arriving at the state park, with great confidence I received my briefing, explained my search plan and was given the nod to get my dog out.

Ari was on; I could feel it in the leash as soon as he got out of the vehicle. The park had given permission to the teams to use it for the test, and, based on the parking area, I suspected there were lots of Saturday visitors we'd have to work around.

Going over the map, I could see in the very center of our assigned area was a large swamp. There seemed to be dry land all the way around it, but as the acreage was a full one hundred and sixty, I knew the swamp was included in our search.

Scenting Ari on the article left for us, I gave him his search command "FIND" and watched as he trotted away, head toward the ground. He was looking for a ground trail first, as usual. Finding none in the immediate area, his head came up and began working the air around him.

My search plan was to split the area in three, the two dry sides and the swamp in the middle. I didn't want to work that swamp, but would if necessary. As we made our way around to the first area to the east, Ari worked steadily, but with no interest. Until we reached the causeway between the two sections of dry land, then my dog lifted his head and gave a solid change of behaviors. He had caught the odor of his subject here at the southern edge of our search area.

The wind was coming in from the north, and even as we stood there, it switched. It was now coming from the northeast, and straight from the area we were heading towards. Feeling pretty confident this would at least not be a long search, we moved on, covering the lower part of the swamp. As we reached the first area, I realized what wasn't on my micro-sized park map. The swamp was in a hollow, and the dry areas around it were all much higher in elevation. I was searching what we commonly called a bowl. Bowls are often the hardest to search because any wind that comes in simply circles around and around, with no real escape route.

The end result was that, the odor Ari had picked up on the wind coming from the swamp could have come from anywhere in our search area. It was likely just pooling and blowing around.

Ari worked the deep inclines on the east side and gave no further changes of behavior, and I knew an hour of our four hour allotment was gone. Returning to the causeway, I watched my dog throw his head up and sniff intently toward the north and the swamp again. Would they really hide someone in a swamp for a test? Or was it just scent blowing around?

Sending Ari toward the west, we worked along the edge of the swamp in the hopes of using our northeasterly wind to help figure out if our subject was in the swamp. Almost as soon as we started to the north, the wind switched again, blowing from the northwest and away from us.

Sighing, I pushed Ari into the woods on the west side of the swamp and watched another hour tick off of our clock. He acknowledged several hikers in the area but didn't deviate from his own search plans. I knew they weren't our subject.

Taking a risk, I decided to enter the swamp from the north side, testing how deep and wet it really was. Within minutes, water was over my boot cuffs and my lead evaluator said "I don't plan to get wet for this." Pulling back out, I was now stumped. I had searched the east and west sides; the only thing left was the swamp. But my evaluator just said, without really saying it, my subject wasn't in the swamp.

As I dithered for a moment, I felt Ari lean against my leg. Looking down, I realized his breathing wasn't normal. He was doing the slow, deep huffing he did when he was so sick earlier in the year. The scarred lungs were starting to take their toll. I reached down, putting my hand on his side. His heart rate was elevated and rapid. Glancing at my watch, I knew we were in trouble.

Chapter 10

"'d like to give my dog a break if we can. I think my Training Officer, Marge, let you know Ari was pretty sick earlier this year. I need to let him rest for a bit, see if his breathing normalizes."

"No problem. We can grab some more water and take a breather ourselves. The temps are a lot higher than we expected today, and with this humidity, I think your dog is doing pretty well."

"Thanks – I can tell you that we're getting most of our scent on the southern end of the swamp, but with the winds switching from the northwest to the north to the northeast and back again..." I paused, and looked at the map again, wondering suddenly if I had missed something on the eastern side.

"I can tell you that dog of yours has the heart of a lion. He won't give up, will he?"

"No, he won't, but I also don't want to kill him for this." Returning to our vehicles, I gave Ari a break with water and just some time sitting in front of a battery operated fan I always carried in the truck in summer.

Looking over my GPS and the map, I made a new search plan, went over it with my evaluators, and with only an hour left on my test clock, we returned to the area.

I rapidly rechecked the east side then returned to the west, using a road to get to the northwest edge faster. As we came around, I looked again at my dog, his breathing becoming even more ragged. I turned to my evaluators, ready to call the test off.

I had said I wouldn't kill my dog over this, and his breathing was really starting to scare me.

As I turned however, Ari suddenly threw his head up and jogged ahead of us. I heard a whispered "he is all heart, that dog," behind me. I couldn't quit when Ari was still trying so hard. Following him, I watched his behaviors change and strengthen. While not running, I knew that if he could, my dog would have been flying through the woods; straight east, straight toward the swamp.

Coming out of the woods, he paused, tested the air, turned left and pushed his way into the swamp grasses and thick reeds. I was dripping sweat, both from exertion and stress. This was it, there was no more time left for us. As he disappeared behind yet another clump of reeds about fifteen feet into the swamp, I saw it. Ari's tail gave a slow wag that he always did when he found his subject. I slowed my walk, knowing that finding wasn't everything. He also had to come tell me he had found his subject.

Looking into my dog's eyes as he looked up, I saw the hesitancy. He was exhausted, yet he knew his job wasn't over. With supreme effort, he came back to me, not running, not even jogging, but walking. Reaching me, he used one paw to swat my leg before turning around and walking back in. I went with him, praising him and encouraging him. Reaching our hider, I handed her Ari's reward, a whole bag of his favorite raw beef satin balls.

Standing next to the subject, I realized I felt absolutely no wind. Nothing. It was perfectly still where she had been hiding. Looking back to the direction we had come from, I could see the leaves were moving about twenty feet up, but under that canopy, no wind at all. How my dog had found odor was beyond my comprehension. I knew we had walked near this place at least two times before with no reaction.

"Rebekkah, that was an incredibly difficult test. We had no idea the winds would do what they did, but you worked it really well. You trusted the dog and the fact the odor was coming from around the swamp, it was a matter of placing your dog into a position to get it. And that dog, wow, I almost thought he wasn't going to come back to you for the recall and indication, but he did. Amazing animal."

"My guess is, there is no odor directly around our subject – it appears to be going straight up, getting caught in the wind and swirled to the south. By putting him at the higher elevation coming back through the woods, he was able to get some of the odor and then worked it out himself. I'm still not sure how."

"Yes, I was a bit concerned when we went by here two times with no reaction from your dog. I thought perhaps he wasn't working, but then he'd hit odor way down at the end there, so I knew he was. Good job – seriously, that dog is all heart!"

Ari had just passed his scent specific area search test one more time. I knew that this would be the last time. Ari had given me a gift, which was giving everything he had to find his subject. It was only a test, our subject was never in any danger, but he didn't know that. He only knew that he needed to find them. I only hoped I hadn't caused more damage to his lungs or heart.

Evelyn gave me a hug, whispering in my ear that she couldn't believe how stressful this could be.

While we waited for the evaluators to finish my paperwork, another K-9 handler there for testing approached us. She was running next and had a lovely German Wire-haired Pointer.

"Congratulations on passing. I'm Lillian Weber." She seemed very pleasant and appallingly relaxed for someone about to test.

"Rebekkah James and Evelyn Cavanaugh. Where are you hailing from?"

"My husband and I actually just moved up this way and are looking for a new unit to join. We're only about an hour or so away from Elk Ridge. Do you think we could join you for training sometime?"

"Sure, here is a card with our email and website – drop us an email and we'll get you our schedule." I never declined a potential new member, although something in the woman's manner had me slightly on guard. I couldn't place what it was though. "Does your husband work a dog as well?"

"Oh no! He likes the field work and is a whiz at navigation." She smiled and Evelyn responded with a smile in return.

"Did you belong to a unit before you moved? I'm new to Elk Ridge SAR myself." Evelyn asked what appeared to be a pretty basic question. Yet I saw Lillian hesitate before answering.

"We belonged to Park K9 before we moved."

"Really? We've worked with them on a search or two this year." My cell phone rang at that moment and I apologized as I took the call. Marge's voice came on, "Rebekkah – how did it go? I've been waiting and finally decided to call."

"Hey Marge, he did it. I don't know how, and he gave it his all. I'm going to stop and get him some ice cream for a reward, although he's fast asleep right now. We used every minute of our four hours."

"Congratulations! I'll let everyone know. I'm so happy for you; after all you guys have gone through. I was worried, I knew he still gets tired quickly now."

166

"Yes, but he worked like a lion – in fact, one of the evaluators said a couple of times he had the heart of a lion. And they didn't even know what his name means!"

"Well, he does. He loves what he does and he loves working with you. I'm so happy for you," Marge repeated again.

Hanging up, I was happy too. Although I made the decision to drop his trailing certification, maybe, just maybe, we'd try for cadaver again next year. But for now, Ari had earned a break from testing.

Over the next few days, I finally had a few nights of uninterrupted sleep. It was amazing how much difference it made. I felt a renewed vigor and looked forward to my date with Bill. It would be our first true date with no one else with us and to be honest, I was terrified.

Bill picked me up at my home and got the grand tour now that we were fully moved in. The majority of the repairs were done and Bill had helped with several of them. After the tour, we left for Lake Andersen and the restaurant we had planned to go to some months before.

At least, we tried to go to the restaurant. After many missed turns, I finally learned the directions Bill had gotten were from Elk Ridge and not from my new location. An hour into what should have been a fifteen minute drive, I could sense he was getting frustrated.

"Bill, it isn't a big deal. I think if we turn here, we'll be fine. No, I meant turn right…." I patiently waited as he turned the vehicle around and went back. Getting back to the main road, I pointed out the correct road and although late, we did arrive. To find the restaurant was closed. I hardly dared look at Bill as we read the for sale sign. It likely had been closed for some weeks, but neither of us had checked on it.

"Well, so much for a nice romantic date." Bill sat staring at the building, and I wondered if I should offer a different suggestion. I hated to admit I was very hungry and wanted some dinner. My stomach did it for me as a moment later it growled. And loudly, too.

"Do you have any suggestions?" Bill glanced at me and I could see he was trying hard to remain calm. Normally Bill was always calm, so this was a new experience for me.

"Well, there is the casino about twenty miles to our east, or there is a resort about fifteen miles south of here, they have a restaurant. I think they are known for their walleye, and, as it is Friday, they likely have a fish fry special."

"Known for their walleye? Have you ever eaten there?" Bill looked at me suspiciously.

"I don't eat fish, I thought you knew that. I mean, I do if I have to, but I prefer not to. So I have eaten there, mom says their walleye is very good, but I can't tell you one way or the other."

"Alright, let's go there. I don't like casino food to be honest. Usually overcooked and mushy." I forgot that Bill was a connoisseur, he was used to eating well and expensively. I only hoped Rupert's on the Lake would meet with his approval.

Thankfully they had a table open when we arrived, likely because we were past the normal time for most people to eat. And they had a walleye fry special as predicted.

Sitting down, Bill pushed the sconce to the side, the candle inside sputtering and barely making a go of it. The plastic table cloth bunched as he shoved, and along with it, the sconce flipped over, spilling wax onto the floor. Thankfully the candle went out in the wash of wax and no fire was imminent.

"Bill, what is wrong? You're very, well, nervous tonight. I don't think I've ever seen you nervous before."

A waitress had come over and the hot wax, now rapidly cooling, was scraped up, the sconce replaced and menus placed in front of us. Bill waited until she had walked away before answering me.

"I'm not nervous." As he spoke, he brushed against the salt shaker and sent it rolling towards me. I grabbed it before it rolled off onto the floor and set it upright.

"Okay, so I'm a little nervous. I haven't felt like this in years. I'll be honest, I'm terrified. I feel like I'm seventeen again, not, well, in my fifties."

"Are you in your fifties? I've never asked how old you are before."

"Fifty-two, actually," The normal question and answer seemed to help him, but I could still see his hands fidgeting. I tried to fathom this new insecure nervous man across from me. It was a very new sensation, being the one who was calm and not twitching.

"Well, you old goat you, what do you want to eat?" I looked over my menu, although I knew what I would order already. Most people who knew me only casually assumed I was adventurous because I was in search and rescue. They didn't know that I very much like things to be the same. I rarely order anything new, and hardly ever take a risk unless it is carefully calculated first. Which of course obviates the risk factor. I planned to order chicken fried steak, a tried and true meal at Rupert's.

"Walleye of course. I can't believe you don't like fish! You live in Minnesota! You have to like fish."

"Sorry, I don't. I don't eat crustaceans either. Bottom feeders, yuck. And remember, I'm not a native born Minnesotan," I said laughingly.

A moment later, Bill managed to send a fork off the table and onto the floor, followed shortly thereafter by tipping his water glass over. We both reached for the glass at the same time, hoping to prevent not only the flood but breakage.

As my hand caught the glass, Bill's wrapped around mine and for a moment, we remained frozen. I know for me, it wasn't about the glass, but the electric shock that ran up my arm. It wasn't real, and yet it was more real than the glass in my hand.

Bill must have experienced it as I did, because he immediately let go, which prompted me to release my grip. The glass finished its descent onto the table and water cascaded all over the table and floor.

Standing up, I started to laugh. I couldn't help it. It was likely the messiest date Rupert's had ever experienced. Bill, eyes wide with shock and horror, looked up at me, and then he, too, began to laugh. Wrapping his arms around me, we laughed together while trying to apologize to the wait staff at the same time.

Sitting down to a dry table without a plastic covering, we ordered and spent the rest of the evening talking and laughing as we'd always done before. Driving home, Bill held my hand and told me that was the most embarrassing time he'd ever had at a restaurant. He wondered if they'd ever let us back in. I knew the twenty dollar tip he tried to secretly leave covered a multitude of sins and they'd welcome us back again.

Standing in the foyer of the house, he glanced around for my mom. It took me a few moments to realize he wanted to kiss me goodnight, but the idea my mom might walk in on us rather inhibited him.

"She's in her room – come to the kitchen with me, have some coffee."

We sat and talked, three rather large dogs sprawled on the floor around us. I felt so safe and suddenly this strange house felt like home as it hadn't before. Bill made it that way. I wondered if he felt it too.

The night ended with a discreet kiss in the kitchen with six eyes watching, but none of them my mom's. Bill left for Adam's home and I went to bed and had the best sleep I'd had in months.

A few weeks after Ari's test, Lillian and her husband Frank joined E.R. SAR for training. Both were charming and friendly. They appeared to understand search and rescue well, and the fact they had been members of Park K9 spoke in their favor. Everyone seemed to like them and after watching her work her dog Cyrus, I could see she knew what she was doing as a K-9 handler. Through Frank, I learned she had passed her area search test the same day Ari did. In fact, he went into great detail about her test, which gave me some insight into him.

After training was over, Lillian asked if it was possible she and Frank could join our unit. Chris, as our operations officer, let them know she'd send the membership documents and a reminder they would need to get an FBI background check done.

After they left, Al asked what everyone thought of them, and I wondered briefly if he had a reason for asking.

"I liked her a lot. She is really smart and knows a lot about working dogs." Evelyn chimed in first, and I knew she had spent a good part of the day with Lillian in conversation.

"They appear to have a good grasp of things, and they sure present a nice, professional and charming appearance. What do you think, Rebekkah?"

"It is never easy to make a snap judgment on one day's training of course, but they seem very pleasant and knowledgeable."

The entire unit seemed pleased to accept their request for membership, although Al did ask to review their documents first. Knowing he was also a deputy, I wondered again if I should ask him what was going on or not. Making the decision that if it were important, he'd tell me, I let it go, and Lillian and Frank were welcomed into E.R. SAR.

Bill, now that our first official date was lived through, if barely, decided that I should come down, meet some of his friends and see his home. I had never been to Bill's home and was rather excited to see where and how he lived.

I met him at the office on Friday afternoon, enjoying a few hours to myself on the drive down, and glad my mom was willing to once again baby-sit my three four-legged furry kids for me.

Greeting Tracy, I waited while Bill finished up with a client and then took me to a modest hotel where I'd stay for the weekend. He explained he had made arrangements for a couple of his friends to meet us for dinner, but Saturday would be just the two of us, and on Sunday, I'd join him at his church before going home.

I was glad he had warned me ahead of time to come with a good dress for the evening. I had only a few of my own, but now that I owned the trunk of Virginia's dresses, I let the ladies of McCaffrey House decide what I should wear.

They had selected a tea-length dress that wasn't over the top dressy, but still gave the appearance of elegance. I had a pair of black heels to wear with it and my pearls for the finishing touch.

Bill seemed proud to have me on his arm as we entered the restaurant and I was incredibly happy that I had managed to wear the correct thing as the two couples we met were also dressed up.

"Rebekkah James, please meet Byron Mitchell and his wife Joanna, and this is Theo and his wife Stephanie. This is Rebekkah."

"How do you do? Bill has mentioned you often lately, we're so happy to finally meet you! I understand you manage a hotel?"

"Well, actually it is a bed and breakfast in Elk Ridge."

"Ah yes, we should stay there sometime By!" Joanna smiled warmly and tapped her husband Byron's arm as she spoke.

"Oh, of course darling, sounds wonderful. Maybe for the holidays," he responded laconically.

As we were escorted to our table, I realized I was out of my depth as the conversation was focused on local society events, names thrown about that I didn't know. I had learned many years ago to do two things in that situation. Smile and nod. I smiled and I nodded.

After the hors d'oeuvres and our salad course, Bill, By and Stephanie began talking shop, which is how I learned all three were attorneys. This left Joanna, Theo, and I to talk. My smile and nod method no longer worked.

"So tell me Rebekkah, what do you do when you're not managing your B&B?" Joanna appeared interested, but I also knew most people didn't want to hear about my odd community service.

"I serve as a K-9 handler for a search and rescue unit in Elk Ridge."

"Excuse me? Really?" Theo's eyes brightened and where he had not spoken much previously, he suddenly appeared interested.

"Whatever is that?" Joanna, her interest was obviously waning and she was only being polite.

"I train my dogs to help find missing people, then when law enforcement has a search for a person, they can call us." I smiled at the waiter as he came by with more water. I really wanted coffee, but that appeared not to be on the menu yet.

"Truly, that is amazing. I was just reading about it. Tell, me what type of dogs do you have?" Within minutes, I found myself deep in conversation about dogs and missing people with Theo.

"Um, Rebekkah, I know you don't want lobster so I ordered you steak. I hope that is alright?" Bill's eyes said more than the menu choices. I smiled and nodded once again, understanding I had gone outside the bounds of propriety in my conversation. I wasn't sure how, as I never actually talked about cadavers, body parts or things like that.

"Say, Bill, you never said what a fascinating person Rebekkah is. That is just so interesting. I can't imagine the stories you could tell."

"Well, Rebekkah has many things about her that are fascinating actually. Theo, how is your thesis coming along?"

Bill smoothly changed the subject and I wondered if he was embarrassed by my involvement in search and rescue.

The dinner finally ended and I realized my leg had actually gone numb from sitting so long. Standing tentatively as Bill held my chair, I took his offered arm and was grateful for it as the tingling went clear down and back up.

"Is something wrong?" A whispered question, meaning the answer needs to be 'no' unless there was something wrong.

"Only that my leg fell asleep. It is tingling madly and I would have fallen over had you not bravely saved me by offering your arm." I whispered back. I was rewarded with a laugh and was relieved. I wondered if the stilted dinner was normal or simply because we both were worried I'd make a mistake.

I called my mom when I got back to the hotel, unsure if I was happy or not about the dinner. Theo was the only person there who seemed to have a spark of fun, and it got quashed.

"Rebekkah, what on earth are you doing, calling this late? Is something wrong?"

"I don't know mom. We had dinner with two of Bill's lawyer friends and their spouses. It was weird and not very comfortable. Bill wasn't like he is up here."

"Well, it was likely sort of on trial, you know. He was probably nervous, and you were too I'm sure."

"Maybe, but one of the men asked me about my SAR work and Bill, well, he stopped it. As if he was embarrassed about it."

"I can't imagine that being true. Maybe he was more worried about you getting rolling and talking about something unsavory like you do sometimes."

"WHAT? I am very careful who I talk to about cadaver stuff. I don't go around telling people we find dead bodies mom. Bill should know that by now."

"Well, ask him tomorrow, don't stew about it and go to bed."

I did as I was told, however my sleep was once again fitful and disturbed by dreams of Kenny lying tangled in the rocks and the young woman covered by snow. I woke tired and distressed, wishing I could make the dreams stop.

The knock on the door at 9:00 I knew was Bill coming to take me for breakfast. After which, we'd go on to his home. I had to ask about the conversation the night before, but I wasn't even sure how to begin.

A simple breakfast and we were off, driving out of town and into the suburbs. Built into the hillsides, the homes seemed to get bigger as we drove, the yards longer and more distant from the road. Bill reached over and took my hand as we drove.

"Want to talk about it?" He squeezed my hand and lifted it to his lips for a kiss.

"Not really, but I guess I need to. Are you embarrassed by my SAR work?" I'm not sure how I managed to just spit it out like I did, but I really needed to know.

"Not at all, I just don't think of that as being your whole life. There is so much more to you than that."

His response silenced me. I wasn't sure if I was pleased or upset by it. What else was there? I managed McCaffrey House and I trained dogs to find missing people. Of the two, McCaffrey House paled in comparison on topics of interest. At least for me. While I loved McCaffrey, SAR was really more about who I was.

"Bill, you do realize how important SAR is to me, don't you?"

"Yes, I think so. Why do you ask?" He clearly was stumped. He really didn't know.

"Last night when, what was his name – Theo? Yes, Theo asked about my SAR work, you cut it off. I finally had someone who was asking me things I could answer or talk intelligently about, and you stopped us. Why?"

"Honestly? I guess I was worried you were leaving Joanna out of your conversation."

I know I blinked several times as I thought about what he had just said. I thought back over and realized he was right, Joanna had lost interest and we left her out of the conversation. A polite hostess wouldn't have done that.

"I shouldn't have gotten into talking about that case over dinner. It did leave you rather stranded." He squeezed my hand again, and then let go to point up the hill, "There is my place. Well, Jane and I lived there of course. We never had any kids, but we had hoped to. Jane loved to give parties, have people over."

The home was huge. I wondered how anyone could live there all by themselves and not go crazy. I learned quickly that Bill didn't live alone however. A house keeper of epic proportions opened the door and with a strong German accent, welcomed me to the home.

"Greta, this is Rebekkah. Greta lives in the maid's quarters off of the kitchen area, and Roberts lives over the garage."

"Roberts?" I had the feeling I'd walked into some episode of Dynasty.

"My chauffer, butler, valet and whatever else I need him for. Often he gets to listen to me practicing my summing up for court."

"Ah, alright. I didn't realize you lived..." I wasn't even sure how to finish my sentence, so I let it trail off.

"So wealthily?"

"I guess. I expected a modest little suburban home. I don't know why. Maybe because you are so down to earth and drive that safe old sedan. You live differently here, don't you?"

"I have a Mercedes in the garage, which I do use when I entertain clients. It was really Jane's car. After I lost her, I hated living completely alone. The house is an investment, so I didn't want to sell it. And I figured maybe someday, if I remarried, we'd have parties again. So, I hired Greta and Roberts and stayed on."

"You need a dog Bill. A loping big Great Dane or St. Bernard..."

"No, I don't think so!" He shook his head and showed me into the main room.

"Well, how about a couple of German Shepherds and a Basset cross?" I laughed, but part of me wanted to know the answer.

He laughed as he said, "No, I'm thinking more along the lines of a tiny little white dog – what are they called?"

"Westie? Llasa Apso?"

"Yes, something like that!" Putting his arm around my shoulder, he took me on his grand tour. It really was grand too, although I knew immediately when we got into where Bill really lived. The tone of the rooms changed from museum to library.

Soft leather chairs, books scattered around, and warm woods. Just like his office, it felt lived in.

"I like this room." I slid into one of the large chairs and curled my legs up under me, "I could sit in here and read for hours."

"And what would you read?" I looked around at the book cases and idly pointed out one that looked interesting.

Bill pulled it from the shelf and handed it to me. It was a leather-bound law book.

"Okay, maybe not that specific book. But still, a good place to wile away the time."

"I think so too. Now, come on, there is more to see."

By lunchtime we'd finally finished the tour, from the basement to the garrets, from the swimming pool to the tennis court. Sitting across from him over luncheon made by Greta, I wondered what happened to that homey feeling I had just a week before, sitting in my kitchen with three dogs and Bill.

The weekend went fairly well, but I know Bill sensed something wasn't quite right. I didn't have the heart to tell him I was uncomfortable in his mausoleum of a house.

On the other hand, church was wonderful and I met people who seemed more real than the couples we had dinner with on Friday. Bill talked about the next Habitat for Humanity project they would be working on. There, over a wonderful pot-luck dinner, I found many people to talk to about many subjects.

It was on the way home, with time to think, I realized Bill led two lives. He maintained one life for work, another for everything else. That was why I didn't feel at home in his house; it was a place to rest his head, not to live. Did Bill think by marrying me and bringing me there, his house would become the home he craved? Like the homey feeling when he came to Elk Ridge? The question weighed heavily on me.

Chapter 11

Which today is, and tomorrow cast into the oven,

Winter was coming, and we prepared McCaffrey House as part of our normal routine. Chimneys were swept, windows sealed, wood hauled in and a myriad number of other tasks done each year.

In E.R. SAR, our K-9 training became far more limited as we had to work around the hunting and trapping. When I first started in search and rescue, I didn't know anything about trapping, and I could never keep track of the hunting seasons. Firearm, muzzle loader, bow, deer, elk, and moose. Then there were the small game. Furbearing, raccoon, fox and even squirrel. Or the birds; turkey, goose, and duck.

Now, however, as we arranged for training areas, we had to not only make sure there was no hunting but also no trapping in the area. Thankfully we still had access to McCaffrey House land as well as Marge's land. I was happy, because Jael's training had stalled.

Finding people was easy for her, but finding the right person was causing her problems.

Talking to Bev after training, I was somewhat despairing of her ever becoming certified. What was causing her to not use her nose and find the right person? When we had decoys out, she'd pick whoever she saw first, not bothering to even sniff them.

Ari had spoiled me, I knew that. He had trained scent specific from the beginning and never seemed to have a problem finding the right person. Often on searches I'd watch him lift his head, sniff, and walk away. Moments later, other searchers would come out. I always knew when someone was there, and I always knew if they were his subject.

Our newest member, Lillian, had several ideas on correcting Jael's problem, but I knew her ideas wouldn't work. Nor would I ever use them as she and her husband leaned toward compulsion training. If the dog isn't doing it correctly, force them to, then reward when they finally get it right.

It was Chris who actually figured it out for me. Jael didn't care who she found, because eventually, someone would reward her. So in her mind, she would check every single person, just in case.

"However did you come up with that?" I was stumped. I couldn't see how she could know that.

"Rebekkah, watch her next time. When she finds the decoy first, she doesn't come tell you. She's still got it locked in her brain someplace that if she finds someone, they'll play with her. But when she finds the right person, she runs back to you. I saw her three times today doing that!"

Rubbing my pup's head, I felt a bit stupid. Jael was bright enough to figure out that finding people meant finding a ball, but not bright enough to realize not everyone would carry a ball. Great. How do I train that out of her?

A few days later, we tried again, and this time, we had her hider hold her ball, not me. We didn't put out a decoy. She did a beautiful find, recall, indication and refind, as normal, but this time, Al played ball with her as soon as she went back in. I hoped it would work, but I had a feeling it wouldn't.

The fall was unusually hot, and, taking a break after running the dogs, we let them splash in the lake. Ari of course had no intention of getting wet, but waded in until his chest hairs were brushing the surface.

Kicking off my boots and socks, I waded out with Gus, letting him swim around me. He clearly enjoyed himself, the PFD helping him float even when he stopped paddling. Gus, likeable goofball that he was, sometimes forgot to paddle when he was swimming. When he stopped, he rolled over like a log. He never had figured out that to stay upright, he had to keep paddling. With the life vest, he could spend as much time as he wanted in the water and never worry about rolling over.

Despite wishing the warm weather would last longer, two days later winter struck. Waking up to a freezing house, we realized immediately the furnace should have been on our list of repairs. A few calls and some hours later, the furnace repair man found us huddled around the fireplace.

Thankfully, as soon as the furnace kicked in, we found out the sunroom was insulated. It was a happy moment as neither mom nor I wanted to move her upstairs; or downstairs for that matter. She was happily settled in the sunroom and glad to stay there.

It was actually larger than the bedroom she had at McCaffrey, and so we were able to put in a small office space for her. Mom was not only my chief cook and bottle washer at home, she was also my accountant and secretary.

With the cold came another search. A couple of friends had gone out camping and one came out without the other. Benjamin called us, knowing that while he hoped the missing man was alive and well, it was also just as likely he was dead and gone. A quick search of their campsite revealed a weekend of drugs, booze and firearms.

Shrugging into my winter gear, I noticed dark stains on the ski pants and sleeves of my jacket. Trying to remember when I wore them last, I suddenly had a flashback. A woman, young and vibrant, dying in the snow in front of me. A pool of blood, dark as the night all around her, and me kneeling in it.

"Mom, didn't we get my winter gear to the cleaners this year?" I don't know why, but I didn't want to wear them.

"Sweetheart, we didn't have the money. I didn't realize how dirty they were. Where were you? I'll send them out as soon as you get home."

"Doesn't help me now." Even as I stood there, Gus came up, sniffing deeply at the knees of the pants and with great joy, lay down at my feet and gave a little woof.

"Good dog Gus, yes you are right, it is. Mom, give him a treat, will you? No buddy, you can't come tonight. Only Ari gets to go buddy, they hope he is alive."

Driving into the night, I went over the information in my head. It was already over twenty-four hours after he went missing. His friend had claimed he didn't know he could call in sooner. Maybe he was telling the truth, many people still believed

184

you had to wait twenty four hours before reporting an adult as missing. Laws were, however, changing.

Arriving at the entrance to the park, I realized it was the park I stayed at my first night in Elk Ridge. Long before I had moved here, and it held good memories for me.

After the briefing, I pulled Ari out of the truck and strapped his blaze orange vest on, hooked a glow light on him and uncovered his bear bell. I wanted all my senses on the dog tonight. I prayed for no accidental shots, strange traps or snares to catch and harm my dog in the dark.

Scenting him on a cigarette pack, apparently the only thing left for us to use, I told Ari to go find. He ranged out and picking a small trail, started jogging down it. With the light on his shoulders, I could see his head set and knew he was actually trailing. He had found where our missing man had walked at some point. I just didn't know when.

Ari moved slowly, not quite a jog, not quite a walk. I knew this would be his speed from now on, and actually rather liked it. I could keep up without gasping for air. We hadn't gone far when Ari lifted his head and sniffed the air. I felt it too. It was water. I don't know why, but the air is different by a lake, even a partially frozen lake.

Al radioed back to base our change of direction and requested someone bring life vests to the beach area of the lake as well as a PFD for the dog out of my truck. I knew he was thinking what I was thinking. If our man walked to the lake, he was likely in it. Ari would try to follow him out there, and none of us wanted to get wet.

As we came out of the woods, ATV's rolled up to the beach. The ground was frozen and I couldn't see any tracks, but Ari kept moving toward the water. Calling him back, I put his vest on and my own. For extra security, I also attached a long line to his harness.

"Rebekkah, we need to be careful. The lake isn't solid yet." Al was with me, but we carefully placed ourselves a fair distance apart from each other to even out the weight.

Ari moved out across the ice, the slippery surface not bothering him in the least. Feeling the ice moving under my feet, I started to get down on my knees when I felt the ground give out from under me. With a deep reverberating crack, I was in the water. Not just in, but under as my weight carried me down.

Feeling the water close over my head, I had a brief moment of fear. But the life vest I had put on, zipped up and buckled brought me back to the surface. Sputtering and feeling intensely cold very fast, I had a moment when I couldn't breathe at all. Somewhere in the back of my memory banks, I remembered the words "mammalian dive reflex". I knew my body was trying to protect itself from the cold water and immediately was shutting down systems not required for life in order to protect the core.

As I came out, I tried to look around for my dog. I had lost hold of the long line and was terror stricken for a moment I had dragged him in with me. I couldn't lose Ari, not like this.

Water had washed my contact lenses out of my eyes, and in reality, the whole world looked blurry and wet. Like a water color caught in the rain. I finally saw him, indistinct, but definitely dog shaped. I didn't dare call for fear he'd leave safety to come to me.

He came anyway, creeping along the ice toward me. I heard Al telling him "NO – ARI – go back" and yet onward my dog came. His long line swished by my arm and I made a grab for it.

I missed, but back he came again, edging closer. All the while I heard everyone yelling at him to go back.

"Ari, my love. BACK – go to Al. You can't come over here." He hesitated. I could sense his concern, his fear that something bad had happened to me. I had seen it only once before. The first and only time we trained for disaster work together. I had broken through a rotted board, nearly disappearing under the pile. As I got up, I saw the same look I saw now. Ari was more worried about me than himself. That is, if a dog actually worries. There are some that believe they don't. Looking at my dog's face, I knew he did.

Al managed to crawl up and unhook Ari's long line. He was safe where he was, if he would stay there.

"Ari – stay buddy. Don't move. Rebekkah, tell him to stay." Al sounded scared, but I didn't know why. I had a life vest on, and plenty of rescuers there.

"Ari – STAY. Al, I'm getting tired. I'm going to try to crawl out, ok?"

"NO, Rebekkah – I'm going to toss the end of Ari's long line to you. See if you can grab it. The ice is really thin and will just bow and slide you back under."

"Okay, but I'm tired Al." Feeling slow and stupid, I turned toward him, but the world was shadowy. I didn't know if I'd be able to grab something I couldn't even see.

I didn't have to; the line hit me. More accurately, the alligator clip that normally attaches to the dog hit me. The metal cut into my cold skin, but I didn't really feel the cut, only the impact.

Looking at it lying on the ice in front of me, I was glad the line was black and the ice white. Or it looked white anyway. With something akin to flapping, I tried to make my hands work. Finally I felt it. The clasp was in my glove, but curling my fingers around was impossible.

"Rebekkah, can you squeeze it open? If you can, maybe you can clip it to your life vest strap. Try." Al was calmer, but perhaps it was because I was so numb, I didn't hear the fear anymore.

An alligator clip is one that instead of pulling back a little ratchet to open, all you do is push the opposing ends together and the jaw on the other side opens. It sounds so simple, and is. I had more than once accidentally let my dog loose by opening this same clip.

However, it wasn't so easy with frozen hands that wouldn't work. I got it open, but the strap was too wide and I couldn't seem to squish it. Giving up, I slowly wrapped the line around my arm. Once, twice, three times. Then with inspiration, I clipped the line to itself. It fit.

I'm sure it went faster than I thought it did, but I was nearly asleep by the time I was pulled free. Ari was, I was told later, ecstatic that I had been rescued. He wouldn't leave my side, and they finally let him lie down in the warming blanket with me.

I was being warmed in the ambulance when Benjamin showed up. He reminded me of my father as he entered the ambulance. Concern, care and anger all rolled up into one. I had loved my dad, but he could be at times moody and angry too.

"Are you alright? You could have died out there. What were you two thinking? Going onto thin ice, knowing you were going onto thin ice…Why didn't you wait until the rescue squad could get here in the morning to help?"

"I didn't think. I'm sorry." Al looked very contrite, which seemed odd on the normally cheerful, cowboy kind of man he is.

"It was pretty apparent you didn't think. Rebekkah, you could have died out there. Do you realize that?"

"Not really Benjamin. I had my life vest on, there were people there. I was okay, honestly."

"No you weren't. No one could get to you because of the ice. If Al hadn't been out there already, you would have frozen to death before we could get people out to you."

"Well, Al, I guess we're even. I saved you when you had the heart attack; you saved me from freezing to death. I think we deserve some hot chocolate – with marshmallows." I was still shaking, but I had retained my sense of humor. At least Al thought so as he laughed shakily, but one look at Benjamin's stormy countenance and he stopped and quietly left me alone with his boss. The coward.

Ari suddenly popped his head up from beside me and with a smile that could melt the hardest heart, he looked at Benjamin.

"Ari, you should have had more sense too." The anger was gone, the voice back to normal. Stepping over to us, he rubbed Ari's head. "Old man, you could have lost her out there. Next time, stop and let the ones trained to deal with ice find the victim, okay?" Ari leaned into his hand and I watched as the two communicated without saying a word.

"He sure likes you. So does Gus and Jael for that matter. You have a way with dogs. I don't understand why you don't get one for yourself."

"Probably because you have the best ones, and, unless they can move in with me, I'd be getting second best."

Laughing, I gave Ari an awkward pat on the head. He was right of course, I had great dogs. As I stroked Ari, Benjamin suddenly put his hand on mine, stilling it as it rested on Ari's soft fur.

"Rebekkah, you really scared me tonight. Please don't ever do that again. I love what you do for SAR and people, and I respect it, but there are times when you need to let others do their jobs." He left the ambulance and I opened my mouth to talk to Ari when a voice came out of nowhere.

"Your boyfriend?" I nearly jumped out of the warming blanket as I realized we had not been alone, but a paramedic was sitting just out of my sight.

"No, he's just a good friend."

"Ah. A very good friend then. You should have heard him before he got in here. I guess he dressed down every person out there. How are you doing? Do you want us to transport you?"

"No. I'm fine, just cold. Thank you for the use of the hall." I don't know why, but I felt giddy. "I don't suppose anyone brought me a change of clothes?

"Not that I'm aware of, but I'll check."

After he left, I whispered in Ari's ear, "You like him don't you? You always have. I think he was afraid of you at one time, thinking you were a bite dog, but you aren't." I paused, listened for intruders before finishing, "I like him too. I just wish he was a good Christian man like Bill."

I immediately wished I hadn't thought it, let alone said it. Benjamin was not only a good looking man, but also had a lot more dashing and daring-do about him than Bill ever would have. The difference between them was night and day. Bill wasn't nearly as handsome as Benjamin, but he was a good man.

Sighing, I had to remind myself I was in my late forties, graying and just a bit pudgy. Benjamin could have any woman he wanted, why would he want someone like me? He wouldn't. No, I was sure he wouldn't. I was just a good friend.

The paramedic returned with a huge pair of boots, snowmobile pants that were oversized and a jacket to match. But they were warm. I had to have help getting up and out of the ambulance as I was still wobbly. During the long slow walk toward my truck, I realized I had forgotten Jael. She had been sitting in a cold truck for hours!

And then I saw Benjamin come around the side of my Yukon with her on leash. Jael had taken to barking at anyone strange coming up to my truck, yet there was our sheriff, walking her around like she belonged to him.

"She needed a break. Can you drive in that get up?" He looked me over, from oversized, falling off boots to the coat that was at minimum three sizes too big.

"No, but I can kick the boots off and drive in my stocking feet."

"Yeah, not happening. Your hands are still swollen too, aren't they? Al – you take the squad, I'll drive her and the dogs home. Meet me there."

"Are you really as mad at him as you sounded?" I let him help me into the passenger side, and watched as he expertly loaded both of my dogs.

"Yes and no. He reminded me we haven't ever done an ice rescue class up here. I intend to change that. We all need it, even your unit members. He took a huge risk that nearly killed a great dog and a good woman."

"Golly, glad the dog came first!"

"Actually, she is a great woman too, but I can't tell her that, it might go to her head." Benjamin in one smooth motion put the truck in drive and dropped his hand on the top of the steering wheel. "I admire you a great deal Rebekkah. Not many would do what you do, and then when you nearly drowned, laugh it off."

"You have to laugh it off or it will hang with you forever. Now it's just a goofy thing that happened, not a scary thing." His face went glacier cold and focused on the road. I don't know why, but I wondered what it would be like to live in Benjamin's world. All fire and physical passion? Stormy arguments? Would there be any calm peace like I had with Bill?

Dragging my thoughts away from that subject, I returned to the reason we were out there, "Benjamin, what will happen with the search? I know Ari was on a trail when I went through. Do you think he's in the lake?"

"It's very likely. Probably went to take a…" he glanced at me, measured the words a moment and then rephrased it, "To take a bathroom break. A lot of us guys tend to go to water to do that. Don't ask;, I don't know why."

"Barbara Jennings, my search management instructor, once said a high majority of drowning victims are male, and of those, most are found with their zippers down."

"Yes, well, you see what I mean then."

"We women don't have that problem. We develop strong bladders, if you excuse the word, so we can hold it until we reach land." I smiled up at him, hoping to ease his rock-like countenance. It worked.

"All right, you win. We'll have the divers check the open area just ahead of where Ari left off. They like an ice dive once in a while, the crazy loons."

"Good. I'd hate to go back out there just to finish it and risk your wrath." As I spoke Ari stood up and stretched his head into the front seat area between our shoulders. I reached up to pet him and instead came in contact with Benjamin's warm hand. He was also reaching out to pet my dog.

He didn't pull away, but gently felt the hand, "The swelling will go down, but it will hurt for a while. Frostbite is nasty stuff, get it checked." Feeling a bit like the air was kicked out of me a second time, I only nodded. Once again, I had been thinking thoughts that would only cause pain later.

"Rebekkah, I know what SAR means to you. I know each search is important to you. So if we don't find him in the lake, you'll be back because I'll call you myself to come. It is what you do and I... well, admire and respect you for it." In the moment of silence, I soaked up the words he had spoken instead.

Benjamin stopped the truck and didn't give me a chance to answer, even if I could have. He got out and I heard him tell Al to help me into the house and he'd bring the dogs. Benjamin left shortly afterwards without another word.

I didn't see him for several days, which was a good thing. Bill came to visit, coming in the middle of the week unexpectedly. We spent several nights playing games with my mom, Adam and Amy. Bill or mom usually won, but we still had fun. We held hands, walked in the woods and kissed goodnight as good couples do. We had a wonderful, peaceful and calm time. So when the phone rang the last night of his visit and I heard Benjamin's voice on the other end, I don't know why my heart skipped a beat.

"Rebekkah, just wanted you to know that they found him. Just as you said, found with, well, evidence he needed to use the facilities. Definitely accidental, but preventable. How are you doing?"

"Great, hands are ok, but Doc agreed I'll likely always have problems with cold from now on. Benjamin, Bill's here, we've been playing games and just spending some quiet time together." I reached over and took Bill's hand, a reminder of who I was really dating.

"Oh. I'm glad to hear that. Tell him I said hello." And he was gone.

"Benjamin says hello. Just a follow up to that search where I went through the ice, and he kept me warm."

"How did he keep you warm?" Bill looked at me curiously and, I wasn't sure, but possibly a little jealousy flickered there.

"What?" Why I suddenly felt guilty, I didn't know. Or I did, and didn't want to admit it.

"After you went in – I thought you said Al pulled you out and put you in some blanket to warm you up, but you just said Benjamin kept you warm?"

"No, Ari kept me warm. They let him share the blanket with me. Really, he wouldn't leave my side."

"Well, you shouldn't have been out there. I don't care if someone was in the lake. It isn't safe for you to be doing this stuff."

"Bill, you know this is my service – for God, for my community. I can't just not go if the going gets tough, or wet or cold. I love what I do."

"I don't know, Rebekkah. There are so many ways to serve God, and to live your life to helping others. Look at what you do at McCaffrey! I know it may not be quite as exciting, but you help people. I can tell you have the gift of hospitality and it is used well there."

While Bill was right, I did love to serve people and help them, I knew that McCaffrey was being run mostly by my staff now. I managed, but I no longer was helping in the day to day operations. In search and rescue, I was there, working and serving. I didn't often see the families or the people I've helped, but that was okay. That wasn't the point.

Deciding to drop the subject, I also avoided telling him E.R. SAR would be participating in the ice rescue training Benjamin was putting together. I knew he'd not like that anymore than my responding to searches lately. I, on the other hand, was looking forward to it.

Chapter 12

Shall he not even more clothe you, o ye of little faith?

The morning of the training dawned bright and cloudless. A sure sign the temperatures would be great for ice, but horrible for humans standing on it. Though a typical January in Minnesota, I still winced as I looked at our outdoor thermometer. Twenty below zero would definitely ensure solid ice, but I suddenly questioned what I was thinking, wanting to put on some weird orange suit and actually get into the water.

Driving to the lake, I talked to the dogs to avoid thinking about the cold. Benjamin had asked that we do a demonstration of how dogs can find humans under the ice. Glancing back at Gus, I told him all about the demo he'd be doing. I knew he loved people, the action, and it would be lots of fun for him. Ari and Jael could also run the problem after we were all done for training.

Arriving, Benjamin told me to pull out onto the ice and park near what appeared to be giant ice cubes. I had never, in all my years of living in the great and cold state of Minnesota, driven on ice.

As much as Bill thought I was too adventurous, I really wasn't. With extreme caution and windows open just in case, I drove down the boat ramp and onto the ice. I could hear the ice under the truck give deep creaking sounds but kept moving. Parking where directed, I got an up close look at the ice cubes. Each was about three feet by five feet in size. They were the blocks cut out of the lake to create a hole for our training. The ice was a solid three feet thick. My truck was perfectly safe, although the entire day, I wore my personal floatation device under my coat.

Talking to the rescue divers, I asked if one would be interested in diving to see if my dog could locate him under the ice. I didn't tell him I'd be using my cadaver dog.

"Rebekkah, can Gus really locate a live person? He's never done live before, has he?" Karen had been in the field with me more than any other person in E.R. SAR and knew my dogs well.

"I know, but I know he can detect the anomaly. We need to show the law enforcement and firemen here that the dogs can locate a person under the ice, even if decomposition hasn't really started yet due to the cold. He'll be fine."

First however, I had to get through rescue training myself. I was handed my orange suit and, watching the others, I figured out I had to remove my boots and outer winter wear to put it on. Standing behind my truck, I tentatively slid out of my first boot and even with my merino wool socks, felt the cold bite into me. It definitely made me finish changing out of my boots and into the Stearns suit much faster.

Standing there with my hands unable to do much of anything, I turned to the first person I could see, a tall strapping young fireman who was assisting others.

"Can you zip me up? I'm starting to get cold and these stupid gloves don't work for someone with small hands." I flapped the giant things at him, my fingers not coming close to the tips of the gloves.

He laughed and easily slid the industrial strength zipper up to mid-chest, where it got stuck. With some concentration, he unzipped it partway and tried again. It stuck at the same location. The third time he tried, he bent his head down to look at the zipper close up.

With a suddenness that nearly knocked me over if he hadn't been holding onto me, he swung his blond head up and I watched the red blush rush up his cheeks.

"I'm not being fresh, really." His blue eyes were wide, but he continued to hold the suit and zipper at my chest.

Trying not to laugh, as the poor boy was serious, I responded, "I look like a giant Oompa Loompa, not a sexy starlet, I'm not worried. And I feel like a block of ice. It's okay, just get that zipper up."

With some more effort, the zipper finally slid to the top and sealed me in. Jeremy, my blonde helper, explained how to expel the air out of the suit; otherwise known as burping it. Crouching down, I pulled the little tab by my jaw and squeezed my body into as tight of a ball as I could. I felt the hot air rush past my cheek and as I stood up, I felt instantly like a piece of shrink-wrapped frozen meat.

The suit was sucked tight against me. I felt more conscious of my body than when Jeremy was trying to zip me in. Even the gloves seemed to fit better. I looked around, feeling a bit embarrassed, until I saw everyone looked very much the same. I was hard pressed to tell who was male and who was female. That is until Karen nudged me and informed me I was the only woman going in first.

Waddling over to the huge square cut into the ice, I watched as the Border Patrol Dive Rescue walked out onto a clear sheet of ice in the square. While the hole had been cut the night before, with the sub-zero temperatures during the night, another two inches of ice had formed over the hole. With some effort, they broke through and I watched as they clambered in and out of the water like some sort of seals.

"Bekkah – aren't you cold?" Chris had arrived and I had to completely turn to look at her. The suits didn't allow for much articulation of my neck.

"Actually, no. This thing really blocks out the wind and retains my body heat. My feet on the other hand, just standing here, are getting cold." We all looked down at my feet, which looked like they were in clown shoes.

"First rescuers – we need tenders to hold the lines and we need people to get in the water!"

Shuffling over, I learned how to tend the lines for rescuers going in, although I still struggled with the over-sized gloves. Then I rotated out and was told to get into the lake.

The moment had come. I had watched others struggle to maintain their balance in the water. Instructions were to point your toes and paddle just a bit, but still people would suddenly flip. Their legs would pop up and they would look like upside turtles. Orange, but turtles nonetheless.

Sliding into the water, I could hear my unit members yelling encouragement to me. I also heard young Jeremy tell me to burp the suit again. As my body went in, all the nice hot air remaining in the suit rose to the top and I looked like a football player with full pads on. Only it was all air. Curling my body up into a ball in the water was easy as it wanted to turn turtle anyway. Feeling more hot air rush out as I pulled the tab, I realized why everyone before me struggled. Once on your back, it was very difficult to force your legs back down.

I was exhausted within minutes, but I did manage to get my legs down, my toes pointed, and miracle of miracles, I was in position to start helping rescue our "victims". I learned to slip a retrieval sling over a buoyant victim, help float an unconscious victim to the edge of the ice, and even, while a bit embarrassing, help push a victim out of the water from behind. Placing my hands as instructed, I shoved up and thankfully never had to look the poor man in the face. It was a lot of fun until the instructor told me to try and get out on my own.

Paddling over to the thin sheet of ice left from the Border Patrol guys, I tried to slide up onto it. Nothing happened. Paddling harder, I tried to grasp something – anything – to help pull myself up. Everything was too slippery. With supreme effort, I finally was able to paddle myself up onto the thin ice shelf, only to feel it bow under my weight and I slid back into the water. I started to choke as I ingested and inhaled icy water. Holding on tight to the edge of the thin ice, I was suddenly thankful for the oversized gloves I was wearing.

"Rebekkah James! How does it feel?" The instructor yelled out to me.

My lungs were burning, I was still sputtering out water, but I managed to yell back, "Way too familiar!"

"Okay, I'm going to throw you some ice picks. They float, don't worry. They're also retractable so they won't poke any holes where you don't want holes. Please use them only on the ice, not the suit!"

The picks landed near my right hand and I grabbed them. Taking a moment to orient them and myself, I started the self-rescue process one more time. I paddled hard, put my right arm up onto the ice shelf and with the pick pointed down, slammed it into the thin ice. It stuck. Holding tight, I paddled harder and got my left arm up, close under my chest. Feeling the thin ice shelf start to bow, I slammed the pick into the ice. It held and I pulled myself up a few more inches. Pick by pick, I pulled myself out of the water.

I finally got close enough so I could put my knee up onto the shelf. With some effort, I rolled myself onto the thick solid ice. I sat gasping; trying to drag in air but the air was icy cold and burned as I sucked it in.

Chris helped me to stand up. I'm not sure I could have otherwise. Making my way over to the instructor, I handed him the picks. "I'm buying a pair of those today. I went in a month ago and I never knew what those things could mean to a person."

He nodded and smiled through a very bushy mustache. "Benjamin told me about your incident. I have to say, I didn't expect you to go into the water after that. Good job. And these things only cost around ten dollars. Well worth the money. Now go over to the other hole over there. They'll teach you to do rescues with the banana boat."

Making my way to another hole in the ice, I watched in amazement as they used the blow-up yellow boat designed for water and ice rescues. Its formal name of course is the Rapid Deployment Craft, or RDC, but it truly looked like a giant banana. Over the next thirty minutes I spent learning how to use the boat.

My favorite part was learning to use the leverage of my own body weight to pull a victim into the boat. I watched in amazement as others did it and finally it was my turn. Kneeling down, I slipped the sling around the victim and, pushing myself upright, I pulled hard on the webbing. My weight carried me back as planned and I fell onto the floor of the craft. What I didn't actually expect was to have the fireman land on me. I wondered what Bill would think as I lay on my back with a man on top of me.

Thankfully Bill wasn't there, and thankfully we were both wearing the orange ice suits. I couldn't tell if the man was young or old, fat or skinny, handsome or not. All I knew was, I had managed to pull him out of the water and I could do it again if I had to.

Patting my head as instructed to notify the line tenders I was ready, I yelled as loudly as I could "PULL" and suddenly the boat rapidly came out of the water and brought us safely back onto solid ice.

"Thanks for saving me, Rebekkah. How do I get up without squashing you?" I started to laugh as I realized I had just yanked Amos out of the water. It wasn't a fireman; it was my own unit member.

We untangled and I surrendered my spot on the boat to the next person so he could learn to use it. I took the place of Amos in the water, swam out to wait for my rescue.

While having a man land on me in the boat was rather disconcerting, falling face-first into the lap of the young man who rescued me was infinitely more so. As I landed, I knew very well what Bill would have thought had he seen me then.

Going back to where my street clothes were, I happily realized I had finished all the training and was now certified. Just as quickly, I realized I had to hurry up and get Gus out for his ice demo.

Rounding up Marge and Benjamin, I let them know how I wanted the six holes drilled into the deep ice. Then I walked away to get out of the suit while they set up the cadaver problem. I was going to do something we don't often do. Work a demonstration blind.

"Rebekkah, we need the suit. How fast can you peel out of it?" Jeremy waited where I had left him, although I could tell by the ice on his suit he had been in the lake already.

"Don't know, can you help me? I can't get a hold of this stupid zipper." Jeremy pulled and sure enough, the zipper got stuck in the same spot.

"Go into that trailer and lean over the space heater. It will help thaw the zipper out. Bring your boots and stuff in there and you can dress in the warmth."

A few minutes later, I slid out of the suit and handed it out the door before dressing myself and returning to the world of cold. I couldn't believe how warm I had felt in the water.

"Jeremy, if I could have, I'd have stayed in the water longer."

"The water is about thirty-three degrees, our ambient air temperature today is hovering around seventeen below zero. The water is definitely warmer!"

In a short time, I had Gus out of the truck in his little blue search harness. A volunteer diver had gone down under the water in one of our training holes and Gus's job was to figure out where our live diver was hanging out under the ice.

I put a long line on my dog, worried he'd take a flying leap into the water. Unaware of my fears, Gus performed a beautiful search pattern around the giant hole in the ice, returning repeatedly to one corner. With a rather confused look on his normally jovial face, he put his chest down in a play bow, but didn't completely lay down as he did for cadaver.

With two hard tugs by his tender, the diver rose to the surface and Gus was rewarded for picking the correct location. He didn't even seem to care that the diver looked more like a sea monster than a human. He gave him food and that was all that Gus cared about.

Moving over to our drilled holes, I had Marge explain to the gathering crowd what Gus was looking for this time. Human remains were placed in a cage and dropped down through one of the holes in the ice. Secured to the surface by a thin line, all of the holes had a similar line attached so the dog wouldn't cue off of it.

Gus gave his excited, high-pitched bark and, with the crowd approaching well over one hundred, he zoomed off. I had unhooked the long line, knowing I wouldn't be able to keep up with him.

I loved watching my little Gus-Gus as he threw himself into his job. He happily checked the giant ice cubes and even more happily discovered a half-eaten apple on the ice. Scooping it up as he ran, he came to a stop as I told him to drop it. Spitting it out, he waited until I turned to explain to the crowd what they couldn't see – a distraction. Gus took advantage of me being distracted to scoop it up again.

"GUS – bring it here buddy." Gus ran to my side and put the apple in my hand. Placing it on a nearby giant ice cube, I flipped my hand, a non-verbal command to get back to work.

Gus dashed off again, leaving the food behind and in minutes, was throwing himself against the ice while letting out his trademark bark. It was the correct hole; I could see Marge give me a quick nod.

"YEAH GUS!! Good job!" I praised him as Marge explained what Gus had found. Walking over, she reached down to pull the suet cage with the bones in it out of the lake, only to find that the hole was completely iced over.

Cracking it, she lifted out the cage and showed those who were interested what we had used. I heard several people commenting on how surprised they were that the dog could find the correct hole even when it had iced over.

"Ice is actually porous, and the water freezing on the surface would already have absorbed the odor." Marge did a good job of explaining while several people came over to meet the star of the show. Gus took it as his due and was a complete ham.

"Excuse me, but is it true they can smell bodies under the water? I know I just saw your dog do something, but what exactly did he do?"

Turning, I found someone I knew standing beside me. "Sheriff Tvrdik! I didn't know you were going to be here today. Gus just sniffed the ice and water to locate which hole was closest to the source of the odor he is trained to detect."

"Yes, but under water? How?"

"When a person dies, decomposition, or decomp, begins immediately. I'm not an expert in the science; there are plenty of people who can explain it better. The best way I learned to understand it is this. Decomp produces gases. Like pop in a glass, the bubbles rise to the surface and burst. We can see it in our glass. But under water, a body is also producing gases that rise to the surface and burst. We can't see or smell it. But the dogs are trained to find that odor. They search for the strongest point where it comes out of the water."

"How long will a body continue to produce those gases?"

"As long as there are remains in the water, they continually produce odor. The problem is, the deeper they are, the colder the water, the more decomp is slowed. Thermoclines can affect scent movement as well. You understand thermoclines?"

"Sure, where there are like two layers of water in the lake with dramatically different temperatures. My dad used to say it was like an invisible blanket."

"Good description, because like a blanket, it can block odor from coming up – or deflect it. The blanket, as your dad called it, rarely covers the entire lake, so odor can travel under the thermocline and pop up in weird areas."

"The other problem is if a body is disarticulated – a clean tidy way of saying destroyed or taken apart. Snapping turtles can wreak havoc on a body, I hate to say. In those cases, the dog will get odor all over, because there are parts all over."

"Thank you. More information, more things to learn about. Your sheriff invited me, I'm glad he did!"

As I watched him walk away, I loved up Gus. He was an awesome little demo dog and I was thankful to have him. He sold more law enforcement officers on the use of dogs than I ever could.

Chapter 13

Therefore, be not anxious saying,
"what shall we eat or drink?"

The rest of the winter went by quickly it seemed. While we continued to train, I was noticing our unit cohesion was fraying. Not really understanding why, I put it down to cabin fever.

I'd seen it often enough before. When there weren't any searches, or other units were getting searches but yours weren't, people get edgy. They start harping at each other. Or looking for things to fix, whether they are broken or not. I got that way myself. Nothing to worry about, the next search would solve the problem.

The problem was; it didn't. The next search was for a snowmobiler through the ice, and Gus was called to assist. I learned as I made the calls, that our newest member, Lillian, believed we should deploy all the dogs that were certified. I disagreed. I knew that ice searches are different than land searches. Dogs often don't understand the three dimensional nature of the search. And handlers who hadn't trained for it didn't know what to watch for in their dogs.

I didn't make a friend that day, but Al, Marge and Amos stood by my decision. Chris and Evelyn however questioned it. The search itself went smoothly. Gus gave a beautiful solid trained response on the southern edge of the hole pattern drilled for us. Ice divers went in and located the snowmobile and the driver, both thirty feet down and still relatively close together.

Returning toward the shelter put up for Incident Command, I found Lillian in front of the entry. She walked me away from the shelter and while I stood holding my dog on the ice, gave me a lecture on everything we had done wrong.

Not having any clue what would prompt someone to do this at a search, I merely responded, "Thank you for your input, but this isn't the time for this discussion. I need to put my dog up and report in." I turned to walk away when she grabbed my arm. I was surprised when Gus growled at her.

"And a dog that is aggressive doesn't belong in search and rescue." Her words only added fuel to my stoking fire.

Clamping down on my anger, I stepped away again but she continued to follow me. I realized that one more step and she would have grabbed me again when suddenly Al appeared.

"Hello Al. Rebekkah and I were just talking about how we can deploy our K-9 teams better." I watched as Lillian turned on the charm and pleasantness I remember from the first time I met her. Maybe I was imagining things, but I was glad Al had shown up. I really wasn't sure what her motives were.

I found myself listening much closer to things Lillian and her husband were saying after that. I began to realize there was nothing in the words that caused concern. But often it was the tone or turn of phrase that made my hackles go up. I only hoped it really was just my imagination.

Putting it out of my mind, I focused instead on prepping Jael for her area search certification. I knew I needed to add some cadaver to her training skills. Often by the time we were called in, our subjects were already deceased. I wanted to make sure Jael could handle the odor of human remains even if I didn't plan to test her to become a cadaver dog.

Calling Marge, I asked her to set up a mannequin sign-off for Jael. Marge would put the unit's human remains training aids into the mannequin's body, dress it in clothes her husband Martin had worn and hide it in the woods. I would work Jael on her normal live find command, using Martin's hat as our scent article. The goal was to see what she would do upon finding her "subject" deceased.

The day of the sign-off training, Jael was, as normal, raring to go. I scented her on the hat left in a bag on the edge of the woods. I knew the area was about 40 acres of land, and the topographical map told me that some of it was ravine.

I loved the ravines, but only to look at. The colors are amazing with the red of the iron ore, the black of the slate and the changing vegetation. Trees grow and flourish out of breaks in the rocks, clinging to I knew not what in order to survive.

For an odor detection dog, deep rifts in the landscape create some interesting scent movement. In this area, rocky edifices are common. I was used to working my dogs through them, but it usually meant a longer search time. It also meant the likelihood my compass wouldn't work properly due to the amount of iron ore in the rock. In addition to that, twisting a foot into a crevice was a pretty common occurrence.

Jael didn't care about any of that; the beauty or the challenge. She only knew if she found her subject, she'd get to play with her beloved tennis ball. I worked her so she could catch the wind as it came over the area to her nose. Watching her, I saw her head pop up almost immediately, then the odor was lost and she kept moving.

Ten minutes later, my pup disappeared, her bell getting fainter as she raced away from us. I continued to walk, hoping she would remember to come get me, even if what she found wasn't normal to her. It was some five minutes later when my girl raced back to me and grabbed the bringsel. The grab was tentative, somewhat uncertain. Praising her, I told her to "show me".

Turning, she ran back and I could see where they had placed the mannequin. It was lying flat on its back at the bottom of the ravine. It, of course, was not moving. As Jael approached the mannequin, she sort of crept up to it before poking it with her nose.

Receiving no response, she ran back to me, pulled the bringsel again before running back to the mannequin and promptly sitting on its chest. She looked rather proud of herself. Marge chuckled next to me and when I looked at her, she said, "She looks like one of those Egyptian cat statues – look how tight and upright that sit is. Rebekkah, Jael sure loved this!"

Nodding, I threw Jael's ball to her and we celebrated with a great game of fetch. Periodically she'd bring the ball to the mannequin, sit the ball on its chest, and watch it roll off. Scooping it up, she'd race back to me to have me throw it again for her.

"Rebekkah, do you realize she's having a better time than I've ever seen her have finding live people?" Al had walked along with us and I had to admit he was right.

"Have you thought of training her for cadaver?"

"No, I need a live find dog guys!"

"But, if your dog really likes this better…" Marge was serious, I could see that. I just didn't understand why they thought after watching one cadaver training they'd think I would switch my dog over to a discipline I didn't need a dog for. Gus was a terrific cadaver dog. That is all he did.

Shaking my head, I rounded up my dog and praised her again. She immediately pulled away and ran over to the mannequin where it still lay on the ground, and popping onto its chest, she sat again. Another round of fetch, I finally managed to get a leash on her and with a shrug, told Marge and Al I'd think about it.

A few weeks later, a flyer showed up regarding a spring cadaver dog seminar being held a few hours away. Looking at the three dogs at my feet, I wondered if this was a good time to take Jael. I could at least see if it would be worth my time to train her for cadaver as well as area search. A dual-purpose dog wasn't wholly a bad idea in our area.

It was just a few days later at unit training that I also was told by the others that I should really consider retesting Ari for his water cadaver certification. It would be a good semi-retirement discipline for an aging dog, and we could always use another water dog.

Making the decision, I carefully budgeted out the $245.00 required to attend and signed Jael up for the seminar. I also eked out another $50.00 and requested a water certification for Ari. My unit was right; water is a much easier venue for an aging dog as they usually just rode in a boat.

The seminar was a turning point for Jael and for me as well. My young pup, with little actual cadaver training, started racking up finds without breaking a sweat. It was as if it were hard-wired into her system. Her only drawback was, as one evaluator put it, maturity. She was still young and in many ways exhibited the symptoms of attention deficit hyperactivity disorder, or ADHD. While her sit at a find was amazing, she had a hard time holding it, bouncing up and down and around.

"Rebekkah, we'd pass her right now except for that, so what I'd recommend is, give her a few months, come back and test her then." Marcia finished with, "She's a firecracker and when she hits maturity, she'll be rocking as a cadaver dog. If you want, we can schedule a test for, how about the first weekend in June?"

Sensing a shift in the tides, I agreed. I wasn't surprised when Ari passed his water certification that weekend, solid and steady as always. Arriving home, I let my unit members know that Jael was now in training as a cadaver dog.

While most of the unit praised the decision, a few seemed more upset than happy about it. Marge, sensing I was frustrated, told me to let it go. Things would settle down.

In late May, Sheriff Tvrdik contacted us again. The Hedstrom case was still open and he had what he hoped was new information to work with. There was an area near where the rental was located that someone found a possible clue. Could we come?

Al came with me and we were surprised to see Jeremiah Hedstrom in the briefing room. Al had never met him, but one nudge from me, and he figured it out.

"Mr. Hedstrom, how are you doing, sir?" I asked, hoping for some insight as to why they would bring him in.

"Please, call me Jack, everyone does. I'm doing alright. They called me last night to let me know about the jacket." I raised my eyebrows toward Sheriff Tvrdik. A jacket? This long afterwards?

"Well, it is good to see you again. May I ask if your wife is staying here in Minnesota or back in Colorado?" I felt rather proud of myself for remembering Margaret's request.

"I'm a widower. Tom is all I really have left you know." I nodded and patted his arm. He still hadn't accepted his son was likely dead which made things much harder.

Matt tapped on the table before saying, "Sit down everyone and we'll fill you in. Two days ago, a person of interest was picked up trying to hock some things at a local pawn shop. One of the items was on a watch list for Thomas Hedstrom's gear. It was a very expensive coat that was purchased the day he disappeared. Very distinctive in that he had it embroidered with his father's name. We assume it was to be a gift."

"So it wasn't found near where the rental car was located?" I had to ask the question, this wasn't making sense.

"The person of interest claims to have found the jacket, and, when asked to show us where, he brought us to a location about one mile from where the Hedstrom rental Jeep was found."

I nearly choked. For a moment, only one word made its way through my head. Jeep. Not Malibu, not Chevy, but JEEP. My hands started to shake and my gut started rolling. Why on earth was I even here? My dog had picked the wrong vehicle. Why would they ever call me back? What was going on?

Seeing my face, Matt gave me a "hold on" sign, and I held on. I had no other options at that point.

"Rebekkah, what is wrong? You are as white as a sheet right now." Al whispered into my ear.

"Gus got it wrong – why did they call us back? Gus said there was HRD in a Chevy Malibu, not a Jeep Wrangler. Oh, Al, we blew it. I don't understand." I wanted to cry and run, but of course I couldn't.

It only got worse as Special Agent Paul Mason walked into the room. Seeing me, he gave me a nod and settled himself in a chair a few feet away. Feeling queasy, I sat motionless. Al put a comforting hand on my shoulder, but it didn't help.

I missed much of the briefing, except the final word about safety. Matt and Paul asked Al and I to wait for a moment and when it was only the four of us, my internal shaking got worse.

215

"Rebekkah, glad you could come. We need to check the area we showed everyone on the map. Most of the people here are Department of Natural Resources and Forestry. They will provide our support today. It isn't a huge area as you could see," I didn't know, I had missed that part, but waited, "But I think Gus can handle it."

"Sir, I'm really confused. That day in the garage...Gus picked a Chevy Malibu. He was positive. I trust my dog... and the fact you called us back... I don't understand."

"Yes, well, Paul didn't trust dogs, remember? He asked that we have at least one vehicle with forensically proven human remains in the line-up. I wasn't sure I liked the idea, but he told me about the last two K-9's he'd worked with and we had to know."

Paul glanced up and continued, "Matt had a car where a man committed suicide and wasn't found until about a week later, lying in the back seat of his Chevy Malibu. That was the car your dog located. Your dog was correct."

"Then the rental was the Jeep and it was clean?" I don't even know why I asked, but I did.

With a very different smile than I had seen the last time I met Paul Mason, he responded, "Don't you trust your dog? Yes, the Jeep was clean forensically. Your dog showed us it was also not used to transport a body which would have left lingering odor. Oh, and in case you are wondering, the car that appeared to be in an accident wasn't. It was an old clunker the local fire department used to train on to recover accident victims."

I sat back, completely drained. I loved knowing for a fact my dog was right, but to be tested in such a manner wasn't the way I'd prefer to find out.

As if realizing my thoughts, Paul finished with, "I'm sorry, but I've had handlers tell me their dogs are never wrong, and watch them walk right past a known blood spill. Then I've had that same handler give me every excuse in the book why their dog missed what we all could see."

"My dog isn't always right, but he's usually pretty accurate. Alrighty then, I hate to say it, but you'll need to go over the briefing one more time for me. I sort of faded out when you said Jeep earlier."

"I saw that. No worries. The area is about fifty acres, but all high ground and jack pines. Not much for floor vegetation. The wind today is pretty decent, not too hot either. Here is a map, the guys who already left with Mr. Hedstrom are simply to make sure hikers aren't disturbed or if they are, to explain why you have a loose dog; without explaining in detail of course."

"Can I ask if Mr. Hedstrom is going to be out there?"

"Yes, he wanted to be. We are trying to keep him involved – in fact Al here suggested it that first night. Not to lose touch or communication with the family. I'd prefer him to not be so closely involved, but we are a small county with few resources to assign directly to him. So he is more involved than... well, anyway. Let's get started."

A few hours later, we finished searching and found nothing. Gus once more had a squint-eyed, pained look on his face and wouldn't get in the truck on his own. Al gently lifted him up for me and Gus nipped him, something he'd never done before. Thankfully he only connected Al's shirt sleeve with his teeth.

"Bekkah, he's hurting badly. I've never seen your dog ever do that. Something has to be wrong."

I suddenly wondered if Gus's growl at Lillian was more because of pain than defending me, "I'll bring him in to Dr. Mikkelson. I guess maybe he hurt his back worse than I originally thought. I'm really sorry."

"No worries for me, he didn't get skin, but that's not normal behavior for Gus. We're buddies." Al rubbed Gus's face and Gus leaned into his hand, giving it a gentle lick as if in apology. As we stood by Gus, Matt walked up to us.

"Rebekkah, thanks again for coming. If we get anything new, we'll call."

With final goodbyes, which included an additional thank you from Special Agent Mason, Al and I left. We talked on the way home about the case. Al was still convinced Tom was never at that parking area of the Powwow Trail. I wasn't as convinced as when I thought there had been a dead body in the rental.

The following day, Dr. Mikkelson made room for me in his schedule. What that really meant was it was his normal day off. Gus was still in pain and I had to lift him out of the truck and help him up the two steps into the clinic. Even walking seemed to hurt him.

An hour later, x-rays revealed the problem. My little Basset cross's heritage had caught up to him. The last three lumbar vertebras were calcified and bone spurs had developed to such an extent they were actually encroaching on the nerves that exit out of them.

"Surgery?" I asked with an edge of concern.

"It is possible, but expensive. I can't do it here. You'd have to take him to the University of Minnesota or another clinic that specializes. I'll send the X-rays to the U, see what they think. Don't worry yet, but I'd put him on light duty for a while until we get this figured out. We'll put him on an anti-inflammatory as well."

Going home, I told Gus all would be fine. The pain meds would kick in, and with some time off, his back would improve. I only hoped surgery wasn't the answer as there was no way I could afford it.

After church on Sunday, I was handed an envelope by Pastor Dave, who only said it was from a friend. Inside was a certified check for $500.00 with a note at the bottom that it was for Gus's vet care. Blinking back tears, I felt strange not having someone to thank.

Two days later, another envelope was dropped off at McCaffrey House with more money, and then another. By the end of the week, people had donated nearly $2,000.00 for Gus.

Putting Gus on medical leave was hard on everyone. He still had energy; he just couldn't expel it like he wanted to. I could take him for walks, but no running, no jumping, no playing. I iced his back each day, and prayed the U of M would come through with something soon.

The word came the day after I returned from Duluth with Jael. She passed the cadaver certification test with flying colors. Her focus and maturity had definitely improved. In fact, although I hated to admit it, she actually did a better job on her first test than Gus did on his. Feeling on the top of the world, I confirmed a time with Doc Mikkelson to stop in and go over the U of M's recommendations.

The next day however I felt as if I had been hit by a sledgehammer. The U of M did not recommend surgery. Based on the X-rays, the damage was too extensive and surgery would likely cause more harm than good. Their notes only said they were surprised the dog hadn't exhibited more evidence of pain long before and recommended non-steroidal anti-inflammatory medication and rest.

Sitting down, I wrapped my arms around Gus's thick and furry-soft neck. Without realizing it, I was crying. Tears were streaming down my face and I just let them fall. I was going to lose Gus. They didn't have to finish that sentence for me to know what they really meant. Medication and rest until the dog was in too much pain; then put him down. Life just didn't seem fair.

"How long?"

"We don't know Rebekkah. With rest, meds, he might be fine for quite a while. But he can't work again. You do understand that?"

Doc sat down next to us and gently rubbed Gus's head and my shoulder. I hardly noticed. I had nearly lost Ari, now Gus? Where was God in all this? Where was He? "What about surgery? I have enough money for surgery, couldn't we at least try?"

"Rebekkah, I did ask about surgery, but they said the odds were high that the nerves, and possibly the spinal column, would be damaged. He'd lose the use of his back legs, or worse. It isn't worth it. Let him live out the time he has left with basically full function."

"It isn't fair Doc. He's only six years old. It isn't FAIR."

"I know. I wish there was more I can do. We'll just try to keep him comfortable as long as we can."

That night my dreams returned, Kenny and that poor woman I watched die while trying to save her. Feeling like I was being crushed with their deaths, I started to cry. I wanted it all to stop. I wanted the world to just stop for a moment and let me catch up; to figure out what I was supposed to do next. Part of me wanted to stop too, to quit search and rescue, to quit McCaffrey House, to just quit. The chasm before me seemed too great to cross over.

I felt a wet nose press against my hand and gathered Jael into my arms. Her fur, still as soft as a bunny rabbit's, was soothing and I cried myself to sleep with her warm body snuggled into mine.

The next morning, I pulled myself together and went to work as normal. Entering the kitchen at McCaffrey House, Margaret came over immediately and gave me a hug. Martha patted my hand and said how sorry she was. I nodded and just went to work. I went through the motions of the day, speaking little, not looking anyone in the eyes. When Adam stopped by I actually avoided him. Going to bed that night however, I couldn't avoid my dreams.

I began to get quite good at steering clear of everyone, cloistering myself into my own world. I still trained my dogs, although telling Gus he couldn't was like cutting off my arm and his leg. I still went to work; I just didn't interact with anyone. I found it safer that way. I ignored phone calls and messages, knowing they'd just rake up the pain again.

I'm not sure how long I would have gone on like that. The lack of sleep was taking its toll and I knew people were worried about me. I suppose what they say is true, a person has to hit bottom before they can look up.

Chapter 14
Or, "What shall we be clothed?"

It was Pastor Dave who finally broke through my shell of protection. At the end of church service some weeks after I had the news on Gus, he simply took my arm and led me to his small office. Sitting me down, he closed the door and said only four words.

"We need to talk."

"Really, Dave there isn't anything to talk about. I don't want to hear how sorry everyone is about Gus. I just need time."

"No, you really don't need time right now. You need to listen first, and then hopefully you will talk to me. How long have you been having nightmares?"

"What? What are you talking about?" I dodged verbally, not knowing how he could know about my dreams.

"Rebekkah, you are a walking zombie. I can tell you I know this started after that bad accident in that spring snow storm. Then shortly afterwards, you and Amos found that poor man. After that, it has been one thing after another for you. I don't know how you've been keeping going. I do actually; you are one stubborn, strong willed and egotistical woman."

"Excuse me? Is this supposed to somehow help me? I agree, I can be somewhat stubborn," At his snort, I rephrased myself, "Okay, very stubborn, I inherited it from my mother. I guess I might be strong willed, but egotistical? I am not."

"What word would you use to describe someone in desperate need of help who thinks she can get through it on her own?"

"I'm not in desperate need of help Dave. I'm fine, I can get through it. I just need time."

"Ah – there you go again. You're fine. Do you realize in the past two weeks you haven't said one word to your mother? She says you walk in, take the dogs out, come in, eat dinner, and go to your room. She doesn't even see you in the morning because you are going to work so early now. And Bill has left you message after message. He drove up here to see you, did you know that? No, of course you don't, because you ignored the emails and phone calls. He stayed with Adam and they both came to see me. Your staff at McCaffrey is scared to death of you right now. Did you know that?"

"Afraid of me? Why? I hardly talk to them lately."

"Bingo, sister. You are not acting normally. You look like death warmed over. You hardly eat, you've dropped weight, and yet you tell us you are fine. You're not. You need help Bekkah."

"No, I mean, I know I've lost some weight, but that's good, I needed to. I didn't know people were afraid of me. Afraid? I'm sorry…." I paused, wondering what I had been doing, what I had been saying. I didn't even know.

"Are you sure you don't want to talk about it?" Dave leaned forward, his elbows resting on his knees as he spoke. "Rebekkah, I'd like to pray with you if nothing else."

I was raised a good Christian. One never refuses to have their pastor pray with or for you. I wanted to refuse because I felt so angry that people were talking about me. I was angry that he should force me into talking about it. But I could never refuse an offer from someone to pray for me. It would be, well, heathen for lack of a better word. Especially if he is your pastor.

Reaching over, he took my clenched hands in his and began to pray. I don't even know what he said at first. I only hoped I could hold out from crying longer than he could pray. And then the words began to soak into my hearing, even if I didn't want them to.

"Father, you are the creator of all, you are the sustainer. You have the life of my sister here in the palm of your hand. She has suffered some things this year that have strained her, have tested her, and have pushed her beyond what she thinks she is capable of handling. I know that you would never do that. I know that she will come shining through with you there, holding her up. I pray the dreams will stop, that she will find peace in sleep, not fear. I pray the desire to live will return and thrive within her. I also pray for the gifts, both spiritual and physical you have given her; that she will recognize them for what they are and use them for your glory. Go with my sister Rebekkah, fulfill your wonderful grace in her. Amen."

The tears, kept in secret for so long, poured down my cheeks. I sat, humbled by the prayer, wishing for that peace I used to have and had lost. Dave sat quietly, just holding my hands. We were there a long time when I finally took in a shuddering breath and could stop the crying.

"I've had dreams. I've tried to block them out. I don't understand why they keep coming back to haunt me. I feel like the world has thrown everything it can at me, and with the news about Gus, I finally thought the world had won. I was defeated, but Dave, I couldn't let anyone know."

"I know. I'm a pastor and I've had times like that, especially about not letting anyone know. As your pastor, I'm supposed to tell you the Jesus has already conquered the world. I also know some days; it is hard to see the truth for all the lies that are put in our way. Rebekkah, I'd like you to get counseling. I think you know you need it. I can recommend someone, or if you want, I can be your listening ear. By talking these things out, you realize how much you've kept bottled up."

"Yes, I guess so. I didn't realize how much it was affecting my life though. I don't know if I can pull it all back together again."

"You can if you stop being so proud."

With a sniff, I laughed, "I think you said egotistical before."

"Yes, well, that was just to get your attention. Pride and ego can be our worst enemy sometimes."

I nodded and reached out for a hug. Dave obliged and gave me a box of tissues to clean my wet face and running nose. Blowing noisily a few times and several tissues later, I knew I still looked awful.

"We all love you Rebekkah. Everyone has been worried. Please, don't fall back into a bad pattern of ignoring your friends and family."

"Okay. I'd better go now or mom will wonder."

"I doubt that. This was a community effort." He walked me to the door and I found everyone I knew waiting outside for me. My mom was first to hug me, whispering in my ear, "You're not mad at me are you?"

"No, I love you mom, I'm just sort of messed up right now. I'll be okay."

I met with Pastor Dave once a week to talk things out. I found myself able to sleep through the night again, although I'd still periodically start crying for no reason. I accepted what was happening with Gus and learned to give him small fun finds to keep him mentally active.

On returning to the land of the living I also remembered to tell Margaret that Mr. Hedstrom was a widower and therefore single, and tell Adam to check for the name of Jack in Pop's diaries.

Passing the messages along brought almost immediate results from Adam. There were many references to a Jack in the diaries, though never with a last name listed. From what he gleaned, they really were best friends up to and through the war. It was only after the war their paths seemed to split. Confirming what I learned from the Thwaite sisters, the separation came after an extended visit by Jack to Elk Ridge. They still maintained some type of friendship, but not like before.

With the coming of fall, I retired Gus completely. There was no improvement, and in reality, he was declining as he experienced more and more pain. He still looked good, his coat glowing with health. But one look into his eyes and you knew. Eyes that once twinkled with life and joy now were dulled with pain.

It was during this time that Sheriff Hedstrom called again. There was a lake they wanted checked. He remembered Gus's ice demo and wondered if perhaps, even this long afterwards, a dog could smell a body under the water.

It seemed another witness had come forward, saying they were sure they had seen someone of Tom's description near one of the old mine pit lakes. It was going on two years now since his disappearance, but anything was possible.

Mine pit lakes are literally lakes that developed naturally from the old man-made mining pits. During mining operations, the ground water and normal precipitation is continually pumped out. After a mine closes, however, the pumping stops. The water gradually fills the open pit, often becoming even larger as the land around it erodes and collapses.

Minnesota law now requires mines to resolve environmental issues and basically reclaim the land they've used after they are finished with it. But many mines closed long before the law was enacted. Some are quite large and deep. Stocked by the DNR with native species, they have become destinations for fishermen. The one we were going to be searching had a depth of some two hundred feet in places and was around two miles or more in length.

It was cold but calm as we left the anchorage. A beautiful day, actually. Jael and Gus had remained at home, and I was exceedingly glad I had recertified Ari when I did.

At the Sheriff's request, I had requested additional dogs from other units to help do some shoreline searches. I also knew that on another boat, a different K-9 team from southern Minnesota would be working. Karen rode beside me in the Boston Whaler and we covered the area fairly quickly. The only response I had, I felt was an anomaly, not a human body or human remains. Ari had sniffed intently over the side of the boat, but then disregarded it on a second pass.

The driver still tossed a buoy and divers checked the location, finding only a sunken boat. As I had thought, it was an anomaly. When we got back to shore, we learned the other K-9 team had a similar reaction in that same area. It never ceased to amaze me that the dogs could detect a sunken boat, acknowledge its presence with a few extra sniffs, and then dismiss it.

The shoreline dogs located nothing of interest either and we went home, knowing that we had only eliminated one more small area from what we commonly called "ROW" or Rest of the World. We can't search the rest of the world, but we can chip away at it.

As I returned with Ari to my truck, I was surprised to find Jack Hedstrom waiting for us.

"Miss James, I'm sorry, Rebekkah, I wanted to talk to you if I could. Sheriff Tvrdik said it was alright."

"Of course! Let me get Ari settled and maybe we could get a cup of coffee in the café there? We're supposed to meet Matt there anyway."

Moments later, I sat across from my fellow owner of McCaffrey House and the father of the man we were looking for. I wondered which I would be talking to when he hit me with a curve ball.

"I know you don't know much about me, but I used to know Jace – Jason – his wife Ginie, and Martha and Margaret Thwaite very well. I stayed with them after the war; W.W.II, of course. I was married, a nice girl from back home in Colorado. Married her before I left for the Army and well, as with most war marriages, it was in a hurry and I was gone. Little Tricia was a sweet thing. She stayed with her parents until I got home, and well, I went to visit Jace and his wife about six months after I got home. To be honest, I was scared. I wasn't sure how to be a husband. I knew Jace would set me straight. He loved his wife like no tomorrow. Anyway," Jack paused to take a sip of coffee and then continued on, "I met the Thwaite sisters. They were both so pretty and friendly and amusing. We had lots of fun going to movies and getting sodas and things. Jace wasn't happy with me, he knew I was married; so did Ginie. I didn't think much about it, I was just having fun. I was young and all that. I didn't expect to fall in love. I really didn't. But Margie was, well as I used to say, the cat's meow, although I doubt anyone would say that now."

"I did hear that Margaret and Martha did spend time with you and that, well, Margaret especially…" I waited, hoping he'd fill in the rest. He did.

"Yes, well, Jace reminded me I was married and I was leading the girls on. He got downright angry you know? Told me I should go home to my wife and live a good life with her. I couldn't bear to tell Margie, so I wrote a letter instead. Maybe I was a coward, but I couldn't face her and tell her. I often wondered over the years what she thought of me. Ginie agreed to give her the letter, but only after she read it and made sure I was clear. I tried to be. It was hard."

He stopped again and looked out at other K-9 teams coming in and flagged the waitress for more coffee. I was patient, although shortly I'd have to leave him and report to the Sheriff, who I could see coming towards the café.

"I didn't hear from her again, didn't hear from Jace for a while either. I went home, I made a good go of my marriage with Tricia and we had Tom. Tom is the light of my life. He got married himself, although that didn't go so well. Too much like his old man; he didn't have a friend like Jason McCaffrey. Rebekkah, I'll tell you truly, I know my son is dead. I just can't speak of him in the past tense. Not yet."

I touched his hand and watched the tears form. I knew I was getting into dangerous waters. But Jack simply sniffed and returned to his first topic, Margaret.

"I walked into that room the other day and there she was. I know she's changed, she lost weight, she's got white hair, but she was still the same beautiful fun-loving Margie I remembered. Our

230

eyes met and I knew; she never forgot me. I assume she never married, did she? I hope it wasn't my fault. She deserved a good life. I'd like to marry her, Rebekkah. That is what I wanted to talk to you about. I don't want to let love slip away from me a second time."

I could have fallen off the chair. I only hoped I didn't look like a fish with my mouth gaping open. Purposefully squaring my shoulders, I took a deep breath in through my nose and held it a moment before answering.

"I think she still cares for you sir, but I will be honest. She loves her sister dearly. I don't know if she'd have the strength to break away and be on her own. Especially if it meant moving so far from all she has known her entire life."

"She wouldn't have to move though. Don't you see? I can move. I have no one left. I'm retired. I can go where I please. I'm healthy, and for someone as old as I am, I'm pretty active yet. So is she. We could still have a few years together. I know this might sound so strange, as we sit in a place trying to find my only son, but it just underlines that life is shorter than we realize. I don't want to lose her again."

Smiling through some tears I hadn't realized sprang up, I squeezed his hand and kissed his cheek, whispering, "Go and ask her. Don't wait, Mr. Hedstrom, go now."

I walked away, joining the other K-9 handlers and law enforcement to provide a debriefing. While our search was unfruitful, I was very glad I was here today. I hoped Jack would go and ask the love of his life to marry him and that she would say yes. I also hoped Martha would understand and let her sister go.

I didn't have to wait long to find out. I got home and found five messages waiting for me. My mom held them up, saying before she handed them to me, "Not sure what happened today, but Martha, Margaret, Pastor Dave, Martha and then Margaret all called. Margaret – I don't think I've ever talked to her on the phone before. Hardly even in person! She sounded… like she was sixteen. It was strange, all giddy."

"How did Martha sound?" I dreaded to ask, and wondered in what order I'd call them back.

"Not sure. She wasn't normal either, very subdued."

"Ah. I'll start with Pastor Dave."

"Wimp," I laughed and walked away to call him. I figured he was the safest person to call first.

"Rebekkah, want to let me know what you've been up to today?" He sounded friendly, but the question seemed odd.

"At a search…why, what have you been up to today?"

"Helping Margaret Thwaite make a decision. And at the same time hoping Martha doesn't collapse completely. It appears that Jeremiah Hedstrom asked Margaret to marry him. And she agreed."

"I'm so happy for them! Can you imagine waiting that many years to finally marry the love of your life?"

"It sounds good in theory, Rebekkah. Jack did mention he talked to you first. The problem is that Martha is devastated. She has no idea what to do if Margaret leaves her. I need some help."

"They both called me twice. Who do you recommend I call first?"

"As they both live in the same place, it likely doesn't matter who you want to talk to first, the other one will answer."

Hanging up from Dave, I made the decision to drive into McCaffrey to speak to both sisters at once and not look like I was trying to pick sides. As I drove, another thought suddenly went through my head. If Margaret got married, I'd likely lose Martha as well. And then what would McCaffrey House do for cooks?

Opening the kitchen door, I could see they weren't there, however Agnes, Megan, Bella and even Pauline, our on-call nurse, were all in the kitchen; looking terrified.

"What happened?"

"The sisters – they haven't started dinner and we have a full house. Agnes thought we could maybe make something ourselves? But we have no idea where to start."

Sighing, I could have kicked myself for ever suggesting that Jack propose to one of my chefs.

"Agnes, see what meats we have available. Usually the sisters have things well prepped for meals. It is likely already laid out and ready to just cook. See what you can figure out while I go talk to them."

Knocking on the apartment door, there was only silence. I knocked again and hearing nothing, I opened the door anyway. Sure enough, both sisters were sitting at the table, staring away from each other. Not speaking.

"Grow up, both of you. You have jobs to do and sitting here like spoiled children will not resolve anything."

I suspected a parent-like attack would work best, and I wasn't disappointed. Martha gave me a startled look, stood up and grabbed her apron which was draped over her chair. Margaret didn't look at me, but responded in a similar fashion. Moments later I heard Martha telling everyone to get out of their kitchen.

Dinner was only delayed by about fifteen minutes, but was still superb. Gathering the rest of the staff, I explained the sisters where having a bit of a personal issue. Sensing my frustration, they volunteered to clean up after dinner. I would talk to the sisters and see what I could do.

I went into the apartment and waited for them. As they entered, I pointed at the two chairs and poured tea.

"Now, please tell me what is going on."

They both started talking at once, and then stopped at the same time. Martha ranged from angry to depressed; Margaret from cowering to proud.

"Margaret, did you accept Mr. Hedstrom's offer of marriage?"

"How did you know? What do you know?" Martha snapped back at me.

"I know. That's enough for now. I suspect everyone knows by now. Margaret?"

"Yes, I did accept him. Now Martha hates me. I don't know what to do."

"Do you hate her Martha?" I knew she didn't. She might be angry, jealous and hurt, but not hateful.

"I don't understand why she would desert me to marry a man who left her for over fifty years because he was already married. He was a cad!"

"Would you?" I looked at Martha.

"Would I what? Marry a man who left me like that? Of course not."

"No, Martha. Would you marry a man who loves you and you love in return?" Martha didn't respond. I could see the pain in her eyes, but, so much like me, I knew she wouldn't cry. She'd hold it in.

"Can I tell you both a little story?" Getting no response, I continued, "Good. I know of a girl who was terrified of falling in love. She was hurt and so hid away to avoid being hurt again. She lived with a dear friend who relied on her, and she learned to rely on. They were both used to taking care of each other for many years. Then one day, a man came along. A good man and he fell in love with my friend. He wants to marry her, but she isn't sure what to do. She has a good life, she's not unhappy. She has friends, a good job, hobbies she enjoys, a lovely home. Should she accept this man who wants to marry her? It might mean leaving all she loves behind. Or it might just mean keeping it all and him as well. But she won't know until she says yes."

I waited, watching their faces as they listened, finishing with, "What should she do?"

"Rebekkah, is it you and Bill?" Margaret's eyes teared over. Martha looked up at me, her eyes widening.

"It could be Bill and me, Margaret. I love him, but I'm very afraid that if I say yes, he'll want me to leave here and go live with him in a house I don't like, in a city I don't like, and yet, I'll be with the man I love. What should I do?"

"I'm sorry Margie. I'm sorry. I want you to be happy, I'm just so afraid. Like Rebekkah says. I'm afraid I'll lose my best friend, you'll move away, and what will I do?"

"Oh Martha, Jack says he'll move here, that I can remain in Elk with you and still work here. I wanted to ask if after we're married, if Jack could live here. He and I could have one room, you the other. Then you won't be alone."

"No. If you get married, you live with your husband. That is how it should be. I don't know what I'll do, but will you still help me here?"

"Yes, if you want me to. I want to. I love being here. But Martha, I have loved Jack for a very long time."

Martha waited, hoping, I suspect, that I would jump in but I remained quiet. Finally, she nodded, then reached over and took her sister's hand in hers. I knew it wasn't completely over. There would be issues that would come up. But for now, McCaffrey House still had its chefs, the sisters had each other, and Jack and Margaret would marry.

Calling Dave on the way home, I informed him all was well for the moment. Getting home, I let my mom know what had transpired, wondering what she would think.

"Martha must be really scared. To be left all alone, at her age? I can't imagine what that would be like."

I blinked back a few tears, suddenly realizing my story to the sisters was more accurate than I expected. Biting my lip, I went upstairs to change clothes. Was I, like Margaret, locked into my life because of the person I lived with?

Chapter 15

For after all these things do the Nations seek.

That night, Gus attacked Ari. I heard Ari trot down the stairs with Jael as they did each night before bedtime. My mom would let them into the backyard and let them back in. As I was brushing my teeth, I heard a snarl and a yelp. Dashing downstairs, I saw Gus snapping at Ari's muzzle, leaving a bleeding cut.

As fast it had happened, it was over. Gus suddenly seemed normal again, and even tried to approach Ari to clean his face as part of their normal nightly routine. Ari, terrified of another attack, ducked and scuttled to my side.

My mom stood to one side, her face drained of all color and her hand to her chest. Worried she was having a heart attack, I went to her first.

"I'm fine, I'm fine. Is Ari okay?" I then checked my gentle old Shepherd and found two bite marks on his face. He had not retaliated; he had not bitten Gus back. Washing his face, I told him I was sorry.

"Rebekkah, this isn't the first time Gus has done that. He's just never drawn blood before."

"Why didn't you tell me?" I glanced almost unwillingly at my dog, who still didn't seem to understand there was something wrong.

"Nothing happened before, he'd just snap at Jael or Ari and they'd move. But this was different. It was like he totally lost his mind. And now he's back. I don't understand."

"I don't either. I'll call and ask Dr. Mikkelson. I'm so sorry buddy." Repeating the apology to Ari, I leaned over and rubbed Gus. He immediately and gently licked my hand.

The next morning there were no problems. Gus was his normal self, although much more subdued. After a call to the vet Gus was prescribed another medication, one to help with the pain. Two days later, I almost wished I hadn't agreed to put him on it. Gus had become a zombie, his personality and mind shut down from the medication. Calling Dr. Mikkelson once more, he suggested a half dose, just to keep him calmer and in less pain.

It did seem to work, and so we went on for a while without any more attacks. I now realized it was just a matter of time before we put Gus down.

Bill called me early in the week, wanting to know if I could visit him again. While I wanted to see Bill, I truly didn't want to go. I had Gus to worry about, but instinctively, I also knew he wouldn't understand that reason. Agreeing to come down the following weekend, I let my mom know first. She wasn't entirely thrilled to be once again left alone with the dogs, but she agreed as there hadn't been any more attacks since Gus went on the medication.

It was Sheriff Matt who got me off the hook of the unwanted trip. He called two days before I was to leave for Bill's. He needed more water dogs because he wanted to search the entire lake this time. I didn't ask a lot of questions, just agreed to find what dogs I could. My next call was to Bill.

"It's me. I hate to do this, but I have a search this weekend. I need to cancel."

"Rebekkah, I made plans for us. Can't you get out of it? Let someone else go instead."

"Bill, I really can't. This is the search for Mr. Hedstrom's son. I feel sort of obligated to keep trying for him. You understand, don't you?" I suddenly realized what I had said. I often had thought how much I hated when Bill said 'I understand' and now I was asking him to say it.

"No, actually I don't. You are not the only dog handler in this state. There are others who could go in your place. You are not indispensable."

I had no words to respond to him. He was, of course, right. I wasn't indispensable. There were other K-9 handlers who could go instead of me. The problem was I wanted to go. And I wanted Bill to understand that. Search and rescue was important to me, to my life.

"I can't explain it Bill. I wish you did understand. I want to be out there on that boat with my dog. I want to help Sheriff Tvrdik with his case. I want to help solve this mystery. It's like it is a part of my DNA."

"More like an addiction Rebekkah. You simply can't give it up, can you?"

"No, I don't think I can. Can you live with that? Accept it?" I prayed he'd say yes. That he would finally realize my life, and his I hoped, would be here.

"I don't know. I need to pray about it. Just be safe this weekend. Don't do anything stupid and come back in one piece, alright?"

With Bill's safety message in mind, I packed up the truck for a water search. I didn't realize I was humming until my mom poked her head into the garage and murmured something about how inappropriate "what do you do with a drunken sailor" was for a good Christian girl to be humming.

"Sorry, didn't realize it. What do you need?"

"Are you taking Jael? I know Gus can't go, but can you take the nutball?"

"Admit it mom, you like her."

"No, I really don't. She doesn't listen, she climbs on the furniture, she steals food off the counter, she steals the other dog's toys and she thinks she has to go potty every hour on the hour. Not because she does, but because she gets bored."

"Mom, if I take her, she'll be sitting in the truck for hours. That isn't fair. You know that. And it is November - she will get cold. Besides, I thought if she stayed home, Gus wouldn't feel quite so left out?"

"Rebekkah, I'm still so afraid of what Gus might do. If he has another attack and really hurts Jael, what would I do?"

"Call Dr. Mikkelson, he'll come. I'm sorry mom, I really need to leave Jael home, and I really need to go to this search. But thank you. I'll take you out to dinner when I get back."

"Sure you will, at eleven at night? You rarely get home earlier than that from training or a search. I know this is what you train for, so just be safe." There was reservation in her voice, but I knew she meant it.

"Thanks Mom, I love you." I gave her a hug, whether she wanted one or not. She usually didn't.

Saturday morning dawned bright, the sun making its grand appearance over the trees and the world felt a little warmer. I had packed the gear the night before. Ari, now almost ten years old, loaded happily into the truck. He loved being one on one with me, not sharing my attention with the other dogs.

Driving to the search area, I noticed as I drove the weather began to change. The sun disappeared behind lead gray clouds and the wind increased. I was struggling to hold the truck on the road with the driving wind. I kept expecting a call to cancel, but no call came.

Sheriff Tvrdik explained why during our briefing. We all huddled behind our trucks to keep out of the wind. I noticed some of the handlers from further away hadn't arrived yet, but everyone from E.R. SAR was present. I glanced up and found Lillian watching me. Her husband stood next to her and for a moment, I felt uncomfortable. I dismissed it and focused on Matt.

"I know you are all wondering why I didn't call this off today. The reason is, I've arranged for a lot of underwater equipment to come in tomorrow. It is being supplied by other agencies, from all across the state actually. And it is only available tomorrow. Our goal today is to narrow the search area to a more reasonable size than almost the entire lake."

I personally didn't think the goal was achievable, at least not today. The dogs were a solid tool in helping find drowning victims, but not with these weather conditions. It was only my opinion, of course, but I wasn't convinced we should even attempt it.

"Rebekkah, I'd like you and Ari on the Whaler there. It is the only boat we'll be deploying today as it is stable no matter what the weather. We'd like to use the balance of the dogs to work the shoreline on the eastern side of the lake. We have information that our subject, Thomas Hedstrom, might have been in that area."

The briefing over, I tapped Karen and asked her to go with me as my field support. I needed someone I could trust and who knew my dog. I glanced out over the lake, dismal and gray, the waves constant and white-crested. So intent was I on the conditions, I was startled when someone grabbed my elbow.

"Rebekkah, I'd highly recommend you not spend too much time out there on the lake. You should plan to come back in an hour or so and let another dog go out."

Lillian didn't let go of my elbow as she spoke. Having someone who had never trained or certified for water recovery telling me how to deploy my dog seemed rather brazen, but I told myself to at least listen to her reasons.

"I believe your dog won't be able to handle this cold for that long. He is old you know." Somehow she made old sound decrepit, ancient, and dying.

"Thank you Lillian, I'll keep that in mind. Who are you going out with?"

"Frank is going out with the handler over there, from Michigan I think? I'm going out with a handler from south of here."

"Well, be safe."

Gearing up to go on the boat, I layered carefully, finishing with my life vest. Strapping Ari's onto him as well, I knew it would also help keep his core warmer. Stepping over the gunwale, I greeted the undersheriff and realized the sheriff was also on the boat.

As we left the protected anchorage of the dock, Ariel raced to the front of the boat, wanting to get to work as soon as he could. Within minutes, I found myself hanging on for dear life as I watched as my dog was literally lifted up off the deck and slammed back down as the boat crashed into the first roller. He landed, four legs splayed out, and his jaw snapped shut as he hit.

Not to be stopped by a mere bump, he tried once again to approach the bow of the boat. He hit the white plastic deck again as another watery wall hammered the boat. I settled myself as best I could and held tighter onto my dog. My other hand was latched firmly on the rail. It was going to be a rough ride and I thanked God for good personal flotation devices.

Within minutes, I knew I needed to move. As the boat hung suspended between the waves for a brief moment, I scrambled for the safety of the captain's console. Ari and I skittered behind it as I felt the boat lift for the next roller. Another crash, another dousing of icy cold water washed over us.

I looked at my dog, hugging the back of the console, and didn't see how we could work this search. Ari apparently had no intentions of doing anything more than stand there. I didn't blame him, I didn't want to let go of the metal pole that held the law enforcement light bar over my head. Karen glanced at me and yelled something about grandkids over the sound of the crashing icy waves. Matt laughed, but my own laugh was shaky by comparison.

We went on, heading north and directly into the teeth of the cold wind. My hand remained clenched on Ari's leash. I used to love leather leashes, but was sincerely glad this one wasn't leather. It was a newer material that didn't get slippery when it was wet. The last thing I needed today was a slippery leash. Karen held on with one hand and I could see she kept one hand free to grab the dog if he went sailing.

Unlike most boat rides, this one afforded no beautiful scenery, just the gray skies that blended uneasily with the gray waves. I could barely see a small peninsula of an island come up on our left. As we cleared the tip, the sheriff yelled that we were now in the middle of the lake and at its deepest point. Nodding, I realized a moment too late he was warning me.

Released from the protection of the island, the wind became more of a gale. The boat turned its port side to the wind in order to get around the rocky outcropping and instinctively I knew this was the most dangerous part of our boat ride. When the boat turned, I could hear the props spinning freely out of the water.

As I looked across the vast lake, I noticed for the first time we were alone out there. If something should happen, who would rescue us? The relief of everyone on board was almost tangible as the propellers finally caught and pushed the boat forward again.

The undersheriff broke my spiral of worry when he tapped my shoulder and pointed at some distant point to the north. Waving an imaginary loop in the air with his hand, I assumed he meant that is where we would turn around to begin the actual search. I nodded and patted the dog who still seemed unfazed by the whole thing.

Shortly after we passed the island however, my dog suddenly moved. Ari stretched out and away from the console, pushing his way to Karen's side of the boat, and leaning over the railing. I could see him take a deep breath and prayed fervently that Karen would grab him if we hit another roller while he stood so unprotected. The leash in my hand just didn't seem strong enough. Just as quickly, he returned to the back of the console and I gave Karen a "mark the GPS" signal. What would cause a dog to risk his life? The scent he is trained and rewarded to find. A moment later, timed perfectly, he returned to the rail again, took a deep breath, and just as smoothly returned to the console. Yes, the dog was working.

We reached that invisible distant point and the boat came about, putting the wind at our back. The ride took a new and definitely queasier turn. The motion had changed, from hard crashing up and down, to a see-saw back and forth. Ari could more safely move to the side rails and set about scenting, but personally I felt seasick.

As Ari gave another check of the wind, I could see it was much lower in intensity. Although the ride smoothed for him, he no longer appeared to be getting anything; the scent was behind us. Shaking my head, I mentally questioned again why I had agreed to do this search today.

We slowly worked our way back toward the south, toward the island, and the dreaded center of the lake. Again the boat lost momentum when the propellers came out of the water during the turn. I was thankful, however, as we skirted the large rocky shoreline because it brought us around to the lea side of the island.

The wind suddenly stopped and we could actually hear ourselves. I slowly loosened one finger at a time from the pole and watched the ice falling off as I let go. Allowing my body to relax for the first time in two hours, I found myself actually admiring the view. And then I realized the boat was being directed to the island itself. Normally connected to the mainland by a small bar of land, during high water season it was covered in water, as it was today.

"We're hoping we can get you on the island, but there isn't a beach or anyplace to dock. We'll have to climb out of the boat and risk the rocks and water. Are you alright with that?" I studied the sheriff a moment. Although in his sixties, he was a solidly built man not much taller than I was. I looked over at Karen, who shrugged – whatever I decided, she'd be fine with.

"I'm assuming you want to make sure he didn't make it to shore," at his nod, I continued, "I agree it is a good idea, but how do we get off the boat?"

"Ken will stay with the boat and so he can help us out and back in again. We can lift the dog out pretty easily. The island isn't very big, but as no one is ever out here, I think we'd be remiss if we didn't at least check it over."

"As long as we can get back on the boat, let's go for it. As Karen said, it is an adventure to talk about someday," I paused and added under my breath, "If we live to tell about it."

The boat approached the lowest point they could see and Ken grabbed onto some branches of an overhanging tree to pull the boat closer to shore. It didn't seem close enough really. I looked down over the bow and was reminded how incredibly high the front of a Boston Whaler really is.

The sheriff climbed out first and asked me to hand the dog down, which I did. He carefully set Ari down, and the dog promptly dashed off toward the north and wiped out on the moss covered icy rocks.

I wish I could say I didn't wait for help because I was hurrying to my dog's aid, but it really was pride that overrode caution and I climbed off the bow without waiting for help. I found myself face first in the cold water, my bad left leg twisted and caught on the rocks.

I felt the knee give way, a very old injury that surgical repairs had never made quite normal. Realizing I was being watched by a very concerned sheriff, a very concerned field support, and even a concerned undersheriff, I stood up, flexed the knee and pronounced myself fine. I watched as Karen smartly allowed the sheriff to help her out of the boat and had no mishaps at all. As they say, pride goes before a fall.

Soaked to the skin, I waded ashore and told the dog to get to work. He obviously didn't get injured when he hit like I did, because he tore off across the swampy, wooded and heavily vegetated island. I was stunned as I saw my dog give a strong, hard alert, a natural change of body behavior indicating he had encountered the scent that he was looking for; the scent of a deceased person. He took an almost direct route across the small island and we soon found ourselves overlooking the lake on the other side, facing north and into the hostile wind.

Ari stood on a natural dirt berm above the rock strewn beach, his head high and nostrils flaring. I studied the beach and noticed the debris of broken boards, torn off canopies from boat lifts, wood from what appeared to be boats, and the typical washed up garbage. But my dog was ignoring these things, his muzzle working hard to find the source of the scent which was wafting to him on the 15 to 20 mile per hour breeze. I found myself wishing my camera was working, but the cold had drained the battery. The sight of my dog so beautifully framed against the wild and crashing water almost made my heart ache.

The sheriff made his way over to us and I pointed out the dog, explaining whatever he was getting was coming in from a distance and over the water from the north. That it was consistent with the alert he had on the boat. I asked Karen to mark the point on the GPS.

"How far away do you think?" He had asked a lot of questions about how the dogs work, and I knew this was the question he really needed answered before he could put ROV's, remote operated vehicles, cameras, and whatever other equipment he had coming into the lake.

I shook my head and tried to explain that I didn't know for sure. While Ari's head was very high, he wasn't checking the actual water, so my guess was that it was a fair distance. With the strong winds, it could be upwards of a mile or more. Or closer than that; there were no guarantees. He nodded; we both knew that the search dogs working the shoreline along the main body of land would hopefully bring in additional information.

We searched the remainder of the island, finding nothing of interest, and walked back to the boat where the undersheriff waited patiently. As we walked, the sheriff explained that this island was considered sacred ground by the Indians. Each year they came here when the land bar was dry and spent days performing cleansing rituals. It explained why there was no dock or place to put a boat in; this island wasn't meant to be utilized by anyone.

As we approached the Whaler, I felt trepidation, wondering how we could ever get back in. Karen went first with the undersheriff leaning down to help lift her up while the sheriff boosted from below. I started to lift Ari with the handle of his life vest when the sheriff brushed my hand out of the way and quite easily hefted my 75 pound dog up to the undersheriff who lifted him the last two feet over the bow. I'm not sure how, but a moment later I found myself on the boat, rather like being tossed onto the back of a horse. I was still straightening up when I realized the sheriff was already in the boat with us. How on earth he managed to jump in like that was something I thought about for quite a while and never figured out.

Leaving the island, Ari enjoyed a respite from the wind and waves as we stayed on the south side, protected from the weather. Not that it did anything to help the search effort. Ari continued to search, but displayed no obvious reaction and no new waypoints were added to the GPS. In fact, he started to find other things to study instead. Ari took to watching the undersheriff as he piloted the boat. When the boat would turn, he'd turn to watch the twin motors.

The undersheriff finally asked with an edge of concern, "Why is your dog staring at me?" I guess being studied by a fairly large

German Shepherd can be a little intimidating, although my boy was as gentle as they come.

"Ari is very observant, and likes to understand how things work." I knew they wouldn't believe me, although I was quite serious. Ken responded in a light, almost joking voice. He directed it at my dog, but I knew he was humoring me.

"This lever accelerates the boat, or makes us slow down. This key turns it on, or off when we get back. This gauge tells us how fast we're going, and of course this wheel is how we steer the boat..."

Even as he spoke, we all watched the dog rear up on his back legs, brace his left paw against the console, shove his shoulder into the undersheriff's hip and loop his right paw through the steering wheel. My dog had effectively commandeered the boat. Embarrassed, I quickly grabbed Ari's collar, "Ariel, get off! You can't drive this boat, come away now."

The sheriff stood there a moment and then started to laugh, a rather uncertain sort of laugh, unsure if he really saw what he just saw. If I didn't know my dog, I'd have been wondering myself, but in reality, he comprehended more than most people gave him credit for. I suspect he truly understood that the steering wheel made the boat turn having watched Ken all morning, and wanted to test it himself. Ken himself took back control of the boat from my dog, but I somehow knew they had forged a bond in that moment.

A short time later the boat turned slowly back toward anchorage. The island we had searched was now off to our left. As I looked, I felt a chill run up my back and goose bumps stand up on my arms. What looked like a pack of wolves was racing across the water-tossed sand bar from the mainland to the island. I blinked and yet they were still there; over and over they ran.

Logic told me it was the wind whipping the waves, that I was just seeing things in the water like people see things in the clouds.

And then Karen bumped me and pointed; she saw them too which made me feel very unnerved and the chill shivered out beyond just my back. We both watched the wolves running wild and free over and over until they slid slowly out of our sight.

The boat continued on, leaving the protection of the island and I once again found my hand frozen on the pole as we turned towards home. The wind that created such an illusion moments before wasn't quite as imaginary as it sent waves of water washing over us again. I nudged Karen and pointed at my dog, leaning happily against the undersheriff as we were piloted to safety. Ken had one hand on the steering and one on my dog's head, neither one appearing to be concerned of the conditions that made me so nervous.

I had dressed warmly for this boat trip; from inside out I was wearing at least 6 layers, and yet I was still shaking. I didn't realize how cold I was until we stopped moving and my adrenaline began to drop off. As we clambered off the boat, my appendages all felt like blocks of quivering wood. Looking around I saw the same symptoms on everyone else. All of us struggled to lift our feet up over the gunwale to the dock. I also knew my soaking at the island was taking its toll.

Walking toward my truck, I was thankful to see it was running. I had left my truck keys at base as normal and at Karen's suggestion we had radioed ahead to ask someone to start it for me. Ari was starting to shake as well and I wanted to put him in a warm vehicle if I could. The walk seemed to take forever, although it was only about 50 yards from dock to truck.

Unclipping the icy wet PFD off of my dog proved more difficult than I expected. Feeling frustration that I couldn't do

250

something normally easy to do, I pulled my gloves off and could see my fingertips were white and had almost no feeling.

"Let me get that for you," Al took Ari's leash and I watched him easily and quickly disconnect Ari's vest and pull a towel from my truck. Rubbing him gently down, he checked Ari's ears for frostbite, ran his hands over his legs and paws, double checking for ice between his pads. Finding none, he helped him into my Yukon. "He's pretty sore Rebekkah, do you have some pain meds at home for him?"

It was obvious I wasn't the only one who was stiff. Lillian's comments before we left rang back in my ears. I should have thought about that before keeping him working so long. Al loved my dogs almost as much as I did and his concern was valid.

"Yes, we keep it stocked now because of Gus. I've got some Rymadil in my pack there, red bag. Can you give him one for me?"

Turning my focus on myself, I found I was unable to unclip my own vest. While my fingers were cold and shaking, looking down I realized there was more to it than just my hands. The vest was layered in ice. Two trucks away I saw Karen banging on her chest with her wrists and realized that was apparently the only way to get myself free. Two cracks and the ice broke off. I shakily unclipped and unzipped the life vest.

Looking at Ari, tucked warmly in my truck with a towel around him, I said softly, "Old boy, you are so lucky you had help with your vest."

Matt and Ken led us into a warm lakeside restaurant that had opened its back meeting room for us. The Port Side appeared to be quiet, although it was large and likely a busy place on a Saturday night. The room was dark, but I could see pots of steaming liquids scattered around the tables that were set up for us.

At that point, anything would have been fine with me, as long as it was hot and in my hands, but I was happy to be handed a cup of coffee. The heat actually hurt and I was reminded my hands would never be the same after my fall through the ice.

I sipped at it and waited to pull off my coat until the internal shaking diminished. Of course that was a mistake because then I felt hot, overly hot as my body finally caught up and the hot liquid seared down my throat. My fingers soon were burning and swollen like little cooked sausages.

I had nothing to report really, just the alerts on the island and the vague checks on the boat that could hardly be interpreted for any kind of location. Worse, we discovered that the GPS had glitched out several times and didn't reflect all the points Karen had tried to record. Likely the batteries had gotten too cold, just like my camera's had. Chris waited while the waypoints and track log were dumped onto her computer, knowing it wasn't complete.

"What did you see? Anything I can include in the map?" Chris had learned to handle the computer and produce maps like a professional cartographer; much better than I ever could or wanted to actually.

"Not much – Ari's alert on the island was fascinating – that old boy took off across the island as if there was a magnet drawing him. Then he just stood and stared out – like an old sailor looking out to sea." Fanciful as it sounded, I saw the others nod their heads.

The other handlers who had searched the mainland were in already. I looked around and saw two handlers from a unit several hours south of us had come up as well as a handler who was connected with an agency in Michigan. Returning my attention to the computer, I checked the mapping of their searches from the shoreline. They appeared consistent with what we had on water, although because my GPS waypoints were lost, I could only go by my watery memory of what the shoreline looked like from the boat.

I hated to admit that I didn't think the work the dogs had done today would make any difference for the underwater equipment coming in the next day.

Shrugging it off, I followed my own nose and saw a waitress bring in fresh hot caramel rolls for us. I wasn't shy; I knew I had burned a lot of energy just shaking with cold. I dove into the pan, and settling at a table, began carefully separating the layers of the roll. I pushed butter down between each layer and let it melt before eating it. While not quite up to McCaffrey House standards, it was still amazingly enjoyable.

As I ate, I listened to the chatter around me from the handlers, careful not to smile when I heard the out of state handler ask how the Sheriff's name was pronounced. Tvrdik, a fairly common name around our area of Minnesota, was not so common elsewhere. Chris softly responded with the correct pronunciation of "Twerdik" and the conversation moved on to the search conditions.

I knew that Chris and Karen, and I'm sure Lillian, were all anticipating the day they could be one of the cadaver dog handlers who sat here talking about what their dogs had done. Their dogs were certified for live find air scent and were training to add human remains detection to their certifications.

I wasn't sure about Karen's dog Chief as he was the most ADHD dog I had ever met, but that made him also one of the best air scent dogs I had seen. He just never quit, working fast and

253

working hard. But to slow him down enough to focus on small details that cadaver work often required I wasn't sure was going to happen. Onyx on the other hand, I knew could do it and likely would in the not too distant future. Chris had started the internal unit sign-offs needed before requesting outside testing and I believed it wouldn't be too much longer for her.

Lillian's dog Cyrus I knew could do it and quickly. The only problem I saw was her attitude. Even now, I could see her whispering and talking with the handler she had supported in the field, and feeling a bit paranoid, I worried it was about me.

I didn't have long to wait to find out. Finishing his caramel roll, the handler came over and sat down.

"How did it go on the boat? I was hoping to talk to you before you deployed out. I had a search like this once, a couple of years ago. I was going to suggest you only stay out an hour or so, but you were already gone when I got here."

I nodded, not sure if the statement was a criticism for staying out in those conditions for almost four hours with my dog, or wishing that he gotten the boat assignment himself, or if it was because of Lillian and Frank. Or perhaps it was just a kindly offered suggestion from one handler to another. Or maybe I was just feeling guilty about keeping my aging dog out so long.

"It actually went alright, more nerve wracking for me than the dog I guess. He seemed to handle it quite well, although I never dreamed we'd be out that long, It took nearly an hour just to get into the search area, so it was best to get as much done as we could while we were out there." I licked my fingertips and savored the sugary caramel for a moment before continuing, "Did you feel your alerts were coming in from a distance or close up?"

"I only had two where the dog showed active interest, and we weren't that close to the shoreline, but I'd say they were getting blown in from further north. You?"

"Yes, said the same thing to the Sheriff. The island was crazy, he went straight across it, didn't veer left or right, got to the other side and just stood there, huffing air from the north."

Dennis nodded and we both silently considered the other. I had met him only a few times, respected his dog, his training and his long years of experience. "Before I leave today, can I talk to you privately?"

Nodding, I turned as Chris brought the newly printed maps over and all the dog handlers came around to study them. Some Sheriffs don't understand that handlers can read a lot by seeing a map with the track logs and waypoints of all the other K-9 teams. We can see what the wind was doing, what impact the terrain and vegetation had on scent movement, and by seeing other dogs alerts in the field, a pattern can be plotted. This Sheriff understood and wanted our input. We all looked at the teepee shaped cone that Chris had plotted by triangulating the different dog's points of interest with the direction of the wind.

Dennis spoke first; pointing out the waypoints marked by the handlers on shore all appeared to be from the wind blowing in from the north. He glanced up at me and I knew that was my cue to speak for the only dog that worked from a boat.

"I agree, the scent is coming in from the north, we had a couple of points where the dog braved the wind and waves to sniff over the side of the boat, however I can't get it any closer than that."

Sheriff Tvrdik nodded, accepting the conditions weren't favorable for a search, and the results couldn't be conclusive. He glanced at his watch and I knew he had to make some calls if he was going to go forward with the search the next day or call it off. He nodded once more and simply said, "They're already planning to come, we'll have them check offshore where the dogs were showing the most interest."

As we stood there, the waitress came up to see how we were doing for rolls and coffee. Glancing down once at our largest map, she said, quite unexpectedly, "Did you know there is an old Indian burial ground up there?"

Matt glanced at her, then at me. "Can you point to where it is?"

"Sure, it is sacred land; you need to ask the elders before you search there. It is right there." Her finger landed on the point of the teepee.

"Holy cow, really? The dogs were alerting to an old burial mound all day?"

"Would that affect the dogs? Can they pick up something that old? I'm so sorry, I should have asked ahead of time." Matt was frustrated, we all could see it.

"Sheriff, the dogs can detect old burials, yes. But we have to consider that the while dogs were alerting in the general wind line of the burial area, we can't discount that there still might be a body in the water." Dennis spoke up, and we all agreed.

"I had pretty bad conditions on the boat. I could never say conclusively what he was alerting to or from where."

Matt nodded, and I knew he would bring in the equipment while he had the chance. It was also at that moment I realized how stubborn he was. He really wanted to solve this thing.

Chapter 16

For your heavenly Father knows
that you have need of all these things.

D riving home, I prayed they would find Tom, that the weather would be conducive to a search the following day. If they didn't, the search would go on.

My mind drifted back to another water search some years ago. No, it was many years before. I wasn't living in Elk Ridge then, and I wasn't even certified for water recovery with my dog. I was a field support for Bev, just as Karen was for me today. The water and weather were much nicer that day, and I remember how sunny and warm it was, I was actually sweating under my PFD, wishing I could unzip and unbuckle it to let more air in. Micala was working back and forth, bow to stern and back again, her frenetic energy making me feel tired, when suddenly she flung her head and shoulders over the gunwale of the boat and Bev had her own death grip on Micala's leash, preventing the dog from completely going over the side. On Bev's nod, I tossed in a buoy and the boat driver let us know he could see something on his side scan. An hour later, divers recovered the drowned boater at the forty foot depth, hovering just above the lake bottom, within a few feet of the buoy.

Why couldn't all searches be that easy? Lately it seemed like the winds and waves, whether the natural kind such as the ones today, or the human ones, made things so much more difficult than it used to be. Or maybe I was just getting old.

I thought back on the private conversation I'd had with Dennis before we left. He wanted me to know that both Lillian and her husband had been making waves for E.R. SAR, and me specifically. They complained of training issues, consistency, favoritism, and more.

"I don't believe it about your unit Rebekkah. We don't know each other well, but we know each other in a professional way and I'd call your unit to a search, just as you called ours to this one. But I will tell you that something needs to be done to stop that type of thing at a search, or even at training ..." He let the thought trail off, but I knew what he meant.

"Thank you. I had a feeling there was something going on. I'm still not sure what. Why complain to others and not address it to the unit?"

"Maybe they are, but to specific unit members. Do you have any newer members? They'd be the target."

"But why? It doesn't make sense. It won't get them anything."

"Rebekkah, you are being naïve. It could get them the unit."

The gnawing concern in the pit of my stomach grew. As I drove, I knew I had to make a call I likely should have made a long time ago.

"Park K-9, Ted speaking," the voice on the other end sounded friendly enough, although I didn't remember any of the Park K9 member's names.

"Ted, my name is Rebekkah James with Elk Ridge Search and Rescue. I'm hoping you, or perhaps someone in your unit can help me with some former members of yours?"

"Sure, I can try. What are the names?"

"Lillian and Frank Weber," Silence met my request. "Is there a problem? Do you recall them? They moved here to our area and joined our unit. I'm just trying to do some background on them."

"Yes, I'm sorry, I understand. I think you should talk to our president however. Joe Ringstad. Can I have him call you back?"

"Sure, he has our number. Thanks!" Curiouser and curiouser, as they say. Ted knew the names, I could tell. He just didn't want to talk about it.

I arrived home and had fully unloaded my gear from the search when the call finally came. Sitting in the living room next to the fireplace, I found I was still trying to get warm.

"Rebekkah? We haven't actually spoken before, but I'm Joe Ringstad with Park K-9. Ted said you had a question on some former members of ours?"

"Yes, I do, but could you help me – is it PAR K-9 or PARK K-9?" He laughed and explained it was Park K-9, as the forming members were all retired park rangers.

"Thanks, I've sort of said it wrong all this time. It isn't an acronym at all then."

"Nope. Now, what can I do for you?"

"I need some background on Lillian and Frank Weber. They joined our unit and, well, I had a complaint about them at a search recently. I'm trying to find out if this is a consistent problem or just something recent."

"Let me guess, the complaint was they were complaining about your unit?"

"Well, yes. That is the case. So there is some history there?"

"I'll give you the short version. Proceed cautiously. They are a force to be reckoned with. Their goal is to either take over your unit or split it and build their own. I will tell you they were asked to leave our unit. But the unit prior to that split and they took half the people – the newer members without as much experience and over-awed by their knowledge – with them."

"So, what happened to this unit they made?" As soon as the question left my mouth, I knew the answer, but I let Joe answer anyway.

"Broke up. The handlers couldn't get certified with anyone that mattered. They tried doing the self-certification thing, but no one would call them for a search. Sounds like they are trying again. Elk Ridge has a good unit from what I hear. Good reputation. Don't let them ruin it for you. They almost took us down. We still lost two members, but in the long run, we got off easy."

Disconnecting, I wondered what to do with the information. One person's story is all I had so far. I would need more than that to confront the charming and knowledgeable Webers.

It is Benjamin who solved the problem for me. A few days later he called. It seems that a neighboring sheriff had met a member of Elk Ridge SAR at a social event and was wondering if there were problems. Apparently, he was led to believe there were issues with leadership.

"Good grief. Can I tell you the whole story? I've not known what to do with the information I have, maybe you are the person to talk to."

"Are you sure you don't want to talk to Bill about it?" I could hear the hesitancy.

"No, it has to do with SAR, I think you're the best one to ask." Slowly, taking my time, I told him what had been going on. I mentioned my conversation with Dennis and Joe, and even the moment on the ice with Lillian.

"I kind of wondered if they were the problem. Al has not been comfortable around them, especially the husband. Vibes he calls it. I haven't been around him enough to know, but I trust Al. He did a county-wide check and they came back clean."

"Wow, I didn't know that. Their FBI fingerprint check came back clean. So what they are doing isn't illegal, it is just not... right."

"My suggestion is have a meeting, tell them that you have heard these things and ask for their side. Give them the opportunity to answer the charges. Don't get in their face however. If you want, I can be there."

"No, I think it is a unit problem. But I like your suggestion. I hate confrontation however, so this is going to be very hard for me to do."

"Have Al do it, he won't have a problem, believe me. Nor will Marge, she doesn't like them period."

"You seem to know more about it than I do. What about Karen or Chris?" I was joking, but he answered quite seriously, "My guess is Karen won't think anything bad about them unless confronted with it. She's incredibly diplomatic and kind. Chris... Not sure about. Rumors have it she really likes Frank and Lillian."

"Frank and Lillian? You said that oddly. Lillian is the charmer and the K-9 handler," I flinched as he answered, "Okay, she appears to like Frank. The odd thing is, Al thinks Lillian likes it."

"I didn't need to know that...yuck." Benjamin just laughed. Again, I was being naïve. As I started to answer him, I heard Gus in the background. My blood ran cold as I heard Jael enter the fray.

261

"Rebekkah, what on earth is that?"

"Gus, I've got to go, he's attacked Ari again."

Hanging up, I dashed out and found Ari cowering by one of the chairs as Gus literally lashed out at him. Jael was snapping at both of them, apparently not sure which side to take. Grabbing Jael, I pulled her off only to have her swing and land a nip into Gus. With Gus's attention distracted, Ari tried to move. Gus swung back around and bit Ari in the hip, felling him like a rock. As Ari hit the floor, the fall broke Gus's hold and Ari screamed in pain. In the second it took for Gus to hit the floor, he was Gus again. Ari, in pain, tried to crawl away while Gus was trying to lick his face and comfort him.

I turned to see my mom, toppling by the counter. "SIT MOM" and shoved a chair toward her. She barely made it into the chair. I sat breathing, hard. I couldn't take this anymore. Jael was still in overdrive as I tried to hold onto her, Ari was slowly trying to stand again, and Gus was wagging his tail and trying to figure out why everyone was so distressed.

I managed to kennel Jael while mom held Gus, although carefully. I then attended to Ari. The tooth had hit perilously close to his spinal column above his hip. The hole was there, the pain was there. Cleaning it up, I knew I couldn't let it go on. As I cleaned the bites on my stoic dog, I felt my resolve crumble as Gus came and licked my hands.

"Mom, what do I do?" I put my hand around Gus, pressing my forehead to his, tears running down my cheeks. He merely snuggled closer and licked the tears.

"Rebekkah, this isn't fair to the other dogs. Gus has become dangerous. I know right now he's being sweet and loving, but a moment ago, he was, well, Cujo. He would have killed Ari if he could have."

"I know. I'll call Dr. Mikkelson in the morning."

And I did. All day I could hardly function, knowing it was our last day. Getting home, I gave Gus his favorite treats, let him rip a stuffed animal apart, something we never let him do but he enjoyed anyway. Then I carefully loaded him up and drove him to the clinic. Mom didn't come with me, and I didn't blame her.

Putting my little golden dog on the table, my hands were amazingly still. My heart was breaking, but I couldn't let him know. He licked my hand, and then the good doctor's. Turning his face up to me, the last thing I saw, deep in those dark brown eyes, was the dog Gus once was. The happy cadaver dog; his joy unbounded and unreserved. And then he was gone.

I held it together until I went to the front and Nancy asked if I wanted his remains. Taking a deep breath, I told her no, that I would always remember my dogs as they were in life. She nodded and said simply, "There is no fee. It was taken care of for you."

The sound I heard next actually came from me, but I didn't realize it for a moment. I was sobbing, deeply and horribly. That single act of kindness ripped my self-control completely away. Apologizing through my weeping, I felt Nancy take my arm and help me into the bathroom. There she quietly left me to mourn. As Bev had said, somewhere out there pieces of my heart lay with Gus, never to be retrieved.

It took a few days, but life without Gus went on. Ari actually stopped creeping around corners, his fear of another unprovoked attack slowly diminishing. We all breathed easier, however there was something missing. Something undefinable was lost. Gus had brought a spark, a 'joie de vivre' into our household that left with him. My little comic dog had a lived such a short life, but it was memorable. He would be missed for a long time to come, I knew.

I wasn't allowed to wallow in my own pain for long. I learned a few days after losing Gus that the Weber's had struck again.

While my heart still felt the deep lacerations of losing Gus, I couldn't leave my unit so exposed. With Al's help, we notified the members we would be having a meeting. I talked to Al and he agreed to bring up the concerns. I think he actually sounded pleased to do it.

I have always hated meetings. They either drag on with nothing accomplished, or they are fast and you find yourself saddled with all the tasks for the next month. I prayed fervently this meeting wouldn't be like that.

I chose a café for the meeting for a reason. I wanted it in a public place to keep tempers from flaring. I had a feeling tempers would flare.

Opening it, we did the mundane tasks of approving minutes and the treasurer's report. We had little old business, although we did discuss the search and I turned in the funds given to me for the surgery for Gus that never happened. The unit agreed to keep it for an emergency vet fund for certified dogs.

"Well, that dog shouldn't have been in search and rescue as aggressive as he was." Lillian looked at her husband who nodded.

Barely controlling the flood of tears, I knew the moment had come, "Al, I believe you have some new business that didn't make it onto the agenda?"

"Yes. It has to do with comments that are being made in the SAR community, at searches, and even at social events about our unit. Those comments are all coming from the same source. Because of that, we made some calls,"

"Who made some calls?" Lillian arched her eyebrows at Al, then looked full at me.

"I made some, Rebekkah made some. Some were made to us. Can I continue?" Not looking at me, Al went on to describe some of the comments that had been made to others about the unit. I watched Karen's face first. It was news to her, but as I flicked a glance to Chris, I knew she already had heard it. She at least had the grace to look chagrined.

"Additionally, we had some complaints from other units and law enforcement that a member or members of Elk Ridge SAR are making unprofessional comments at searches. As a member of law enforcement myself, I can tell you the comments only make it harder for civilians. It makes them all look like a bunch of sniveling whiners. At this time, I'd like those members who are doing this to explain and bring it to light within the entire unit so it can be discussed in a professional and adult manner."

Had we been by ourselves, I'm sure you could have heard a pin drop. Instead, we just heard the kitchen staff clinking dishes and chattering. Finally, Karen spoke up.

"Do we know who is doing this?" She glanced uneasily around the table. It made me think of how the disciples must have felt during the last supper with Jesus – who was the one who would betray?

"Yes, we do. It is Lillian Weber who has made the majority of the comments, although apparently Frank and Chris have also been noted as making similar, although less inflammatory statements."

I looked up, hard and fast, at Chris. That she was enthralled with the Webers I knew, but to actually participate; after her experiences with her previous unit? She refused to look at me, but I saw the embarrassment. It was the person who spoke next, sitting to my right, which nearly had me walk out.

"I think what Lillian and Frank are saying make a great deal of sense. There does seem to be an elitist attitude among the members of this unit. Lillian told me if she were running the unit, why, I'd be a field support person by now, not still in training." Evelyn glanced around the table, and I knew she was lost to us as surely as if she had handed in her resignation right then and there.

"May I ask, Evelyn, how they would have done that when you haven't taken your first aid class yet, although we've notified you of two different classes in the past three months? Would they have you deploy without knowing how to perform CPR?"

"How often is that really used in the real world on a search anyway? And we don't have any medical directive. I've heard you say over and over, Rebekkah, that on a search we are searchers, not medical responders. So we can't perform that stuff in the field anyway."

"I completely agree with Evelyn. In the many years I've been in SAR, I've never yet heard of a time when a K-9 handler or field support has had to use CPR in the field. It shouldn't be required. There are many things that you have on your list of requirements that aren't needed. Like mantracking… For heaven's sake, that is why we have the dogs!" Lillian sat up and self-righteous was the only words I could come up with in my head at her body language.

266

"Well, as much as I'd like to say you have a point, I can't. Al wouldn't be here if it weren't for the person who gave him CPR in the field. Had it been, as you suggest Lillian, not required, he would have died. And as for mantracking, that is one amazing thing to learn because it teaches a searcher to be observant. I've seen it many times in the field, a mantracker gets a direction of travel and the dog finishes the trail – or vice versa." Amos spoke and I wanted to hug him for not actually naming me. It would have only been another attack point.

"Well, that is unusual, but perhaps it is because this unit isn't all it likes to vaunt itself to be, that it needs mantrackers instead of dogs, and that its members aren't physically fit enough they have to be rescued by others," As Lillian said 'rescued' she looked directly at me.

Al took back control by standing and saying very calmly, "There is more I'd like to address. So far, I haven't heard anything said that I can bring back to those who complained except self-righteous mumbo jumbo."

Sitting back down, he flipped open a folder and held up a sheet of paper. "I have had calls from several members of SAR units, as well as individuals speaking in their own name, not a unit's. Lillian, is it true that while a member of Go-Find SAR, you were asked to leave? Can you explain why?"

"For a very similar reason to why we are sitting here today. Because Go-Find is also an exclusive club that really isn't about getting dogs and people certified but about making themselves look good."

"Can you also explain why you quit Park K-9?"

"Whatever is this all about? Park K-9 has no idea what it takes to certify a dog. I had to go outside of the unit to get Cyrus certified. They thought I needed more control on him, but he's perfectly fine. You seem to think he's fine." She glanced around at the others and I watched Evelyn and Chris nod. Amos, Marge and Karen didn't flinch. The lines were drawn.

"The reason I ask is, they forwarded me a copy of the letter given to you; you were asked to leave because of unprofessional conduct, which was detailed in the letter."

The table actually tipped as Frank stood up. For a moment, I seriously thought he was going to grab Al by the throat. By only chance, I happened to see Lillian's face as she watched her husband's violent reaction. With a feeling of revulsion and disgust, I knew she was getting a charge out of it. It made her excited.

Al didn't move. I wondered if he almost wished Frank had grabbed him. It would have been one more nail for their coffin as members of E.R. SAR. But Frank, livid and trembling, forced himself to sit back down.

"I also have other letters, as I mentioned, from people who followed these two, quitting legitimate units to join a unit they created, which later collapsed. The people who joined them are not finding a ready welcome in established and reputable units." With a significant glance at both Chris and Evelyn, Al sat back and tucked the documents back into a folder.

"Are you asking us to quit?" Lillian finally responded. Her arrogant attitude was subdued, but not gone.

"Unless you can refute what was just said and what we have printed in here, yes. However, just about every word out of your mouth, and the behavior of your husband, confirm everything in here." He tapped the folder. "And this folder will be placed in your files for future reference if another unit should request references or information. I say this in front of witnesses."

Frank stood again and, as if realizing this time it might be serious, Al stood as well. Advancing so he was nearly nose to nose with Al, Frank hesitated, then turned and walked away, Lillian trailing behind him.

After they left, I was shaking. With some concern, I looked at Chris first. She was a good K-9 handler, she had advanced so rapidly in all the other search training beyond being a handler. I would hate to lose her.

"Is it true, Al?" She looked at him, not at me.

"Yes, it is Chris. They have been building a reputation across the state, and most reputable units won't work with them. We made a mistake not following up on their references, just taking them on face value. It won't happen again."

Evelyn sat for a long moment before standing. "I think what you guys did here was wrong. They didn't deserve that kind of attack. They haven't done anything wrong, you said so. I like them, they are very knowledgeable. And if they start a unit, I'd be glad to join them." Picking up her coat and purse, she left.

"Chris, do you feel the same?" I finally asked her flat out. I needed to know not only if she'd stay, but if she could still work with me.

"I need to think about it. Some of the things they said made sense, but then, I didn't ask for a second opinion." Chris gathered her coat and purse, and a moment later, she, too had left.

"Why does all this have to be so hard?" Karen put her arms around me and I hugged her back. I didn't know the answer.

There were times when I wondered why I kept trying, today was one of them.

Our next training was subdued, with both Chris and Evelyn missing. I hoped I'd see them back, but didn't expect to. This was the first split I had ever experienced, but I knew nearly every handler in SAR would eventually go through one. It was a fact of life. Some are amicable, others, not.

Returning to work the next morning, I found the sisters in the kitchen, doing their normal work, but something was different. The spirit in the room was lighter. As I moved food from the kitchen to the buffet table, I could hear them bantering back and forth. Stopping to look at them from the doorway, I realized Margaret had blossomed. She glowed as I had never seen before. Martha, having accepted her sister's joy, was actually living it with her.

Winter arrived again, yet no one minded. We were all wrapped up in wedding plans. Margaret wanted simple, Martha extravagant. Jack merely wanted it over with. All the while, the knowledge his son was still missing hung over us all.

And still hanging over my own head was my relationship with Bill. I wanted so much for it to work. He seemed to want to marry me, although the word had never been used. I made two more weekend trips to visit with him in his world. We went to restaurants that cost more than I paid for food in a day. We went to shows and sat in the best seats. We drove around in his expensive car. We held hands and kissed in private. The only problem was the only time I felt comfortable was at his church. Even in his arms, I questioned why I was in that place. Not his arms, but in the city. I couldn't wait to get home and walk through the woods.

During the second visit, we sat before a beautiful fireplace enjoying the warmth and glow of the fire. Bill tossed a few pine cones on the fire and the smell of pine filled the room.

"Bill, do you miss that smell?"

"What do you mean? What smell?"

"The pine, the woods. Have you ever stood in the woods after a rainfall and listen to the pine cones start to pop open?"

"They pop open? Really?"

Pulling away from his arm, I leaned back against the leather love seat, "Yes, they do. As they dry out, they pop open and it sounds like that crispy rice cereal in milk. And the smell of the wet woods is unbeatable. Of course, I also love it in winter when I can snowshoe with the dogs and listen to the sounds – more hushed than in summer. When you come next time, we'll go snowshoeing." I leaned back into him and felt his arm return around me, but slowly, as if he were deep in thought.

"I've never been snowshoeing before. I'm really not an outdoorsman you know. I like working on the houses, the carpentry and stuff, but a walk through a wet woods, or snowshoeing..." He paused and I felt that sensation hit me again, wondering what I was doing here. If I could transplant us to Elk Ridge, I'd have been perfectly happy.

Wondering what was wrong, I returned home with the feeling I was carrying the weight of the world. That night, I had a nightmare. I hadn't had one for many months now, and I woke up soaked in sweat. It wasn't Kenny or the woman this time. It was a shadowy figure, unnamed, unknown, but I knew it wasn't them.

After I finished the morning chores at McCaffrey, I asked Megan if I could use the office for a while, hoping to call Pastor

271

Dave to talk. Instead, as I picked up the phone to dial, he walked in.

"Rebekkah, I need to talk, is this a good time?" He looked distressed and I couldn't say no.

"Good. I know that you know I've been emailing with your friend Connie. I had hoped, well, that someday, maybe she'd consider me."

"I know Dave. I haven't heard from Connie lately though. I hate to say it, but I've been so wrapped up in my own issues, I haven't realized it until now. What have you heard?" Connie, my friend and mentor for many years, made it easier for me to stay in SAR back then. During her infrequent visits, she and Pastor Dave had become friends, and it appeared, even closer than friends.

"I finally got hold of her last night. Rebekkah, things aren't going well for her. She, well she didn't say it, but her daughter emailed me. She got tangled up with another loser. I hate using that term, but he's been leaching off of her for the past year. She lost her job and doesn't know what to do next. She didn't ask, but do you think, maybe you could find a place here for her?"

"Wow, I'm sorry to hear that – that really... if I had kept in touch... I haven't talked to her very much. I do miss her. She was always straight with me. Listen, I don't know if this would work, but... when Margaret marries Jack, I know they intend to move into the old Patrick place. Martha is afraid to be alone. Perhaps we could ask her if Connie could move in with her. The kids are on their own now. It might give her some breather space. She could help around here, but the budget is pretty tight so I wouldn't be able to afford to pay her anything. I'll ask Martha today and if she agrees, I'll call Connie tonight."

"Thank you. Even if it doesn't work out for us, I want her to have a fresh start. This might be it."

"Dave, can I talk to you now? About me, I mean. I had another nightmare last night, only it wasn't Kenny or the woman – it was, well, a shrouded figure this time, but I knew it wasn't the woman. It felt like it was the end of something. I was moving away from it."

"I'm not a dream specialist, but were you terrified? Could you get back to sleep?"

"I was at first, very afraid Dave. I wondered who was under the shroud. But after I woke up, it seemed to be okay. I was able to fall back to sleep."

"Did you have a bad weekend? You were visiting Bill, did you have a fight? It may not be my business, but it might have bearing on it."

"Not a fight. Dave, I really need to talk to someone, and you're the best friend I have right now. Can we take a walk?"

Dave had fun learning to strap on snowshoes, and after a few missteps and falls, he suddenly got the stride and we walked through the woods together. It felt good to finally tell someone my growing concerns about my relationship with Bill. I talked about my feelings as I usually wasn't able to. Perhaps it was the surroundings, perhaps it was the person, but by the time I was done, I knew I had said it all.

"In all the things you said, you never said you loved Bill. Do you?"

"I don't know if I know what it means Dave. Do you?"

"This is something that movies talk about like it is either an easy or unanswerable question, depending on the movie. I think the best answer I recall came from a movie however. It was really talking about sex, but it still counts. It isn't sleeping with a man that means you love him, it is waking up with a man and facing the drab, everyday wonderful world with him that really matters. Do you want to face that everyday world that Bill lives in and loves?"

"No. I don't. I care about Bill, I really do. But every time I go visit with him, I learn more about what I'm not. This last visit, he talked about Jane and the parties she used to host at the house. He talked about being able to host them again. I think because of my work at McCaffrey, he thinks of me as some super-hostess. I'm not. My mom played hostess, now Megan does. I never did. I managed them. I can't imagine hosting a stuffy party!"

I stopped and pointed about fifty yards to our right and Dave looked for a moment and then whispered, "Is that a snowy owl? I've never seen one live before, although Connie took some great photos of one the last time she was here."

We continued on before Dave finally remembered to respond to my last comment.

"Rebekkah, did you tell Bill that?" This time it was Dave that stopped and pointed. Some deer were pawing through snow in a field just on the other side of the woods.

"I did, he only laughed and said of course I could, I'd be good at it. I gave up arguing. He always manages to say something that sounds like a compliment, but I realize later doesn't really apply to me. I think he means it as a compliment. I don't think he sees the real me."

I paused and just let the stillness around me soak in. I loved being out here, I loved it more than I could ever express. Some days I didn't want to put on my snowshoes or hiking boots and

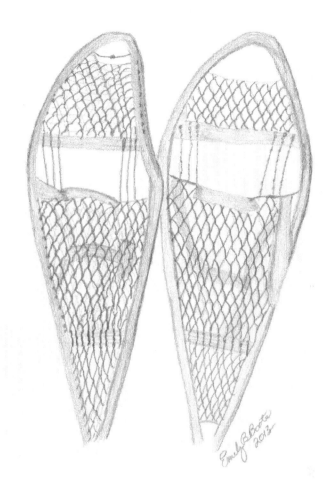

make the effort. But every time I did, it calmed me. It reminded me of who I was and how much God was in control, that I had nothing to fear.

"Rebekkah, is there someone else?" Dave was watching me, I could feel it, but I didn't care. Here I was home; my world was at peace for the moment.

"No. Not really and truly someone else. I can't deny that sometimes, well, I've wondered what life would be like with someone else. But there isn't any living, breathing person. I hope that makes sense."

"I had to ask. If there is no one else, and yet you still don't feel right about Bill, you need to tell him everything you've told me. Talk to him. Perhaps he truly doesn't understand your feelings."

"Dave, how come things can't remain the same. Why do they have to change all the time?" He knew I didn't want an answer. It wasn't a real question, more a reflection of how I felt. Walking in companionable silence, we returned to McCaffrey House.

Going in, I found the sisters in their apartment, sitting with the ever present cups of tea. Pouring myself a cup, I sat with them, wondering how to broach the subject of a roomy for Martha.

"Rebekkah, you look flushed, did you get chilled out there?" Margaret patted my arm and offered me a plate with cookies on it. Looking over the selection, I picked up a cinnamon chunk cookie.

"No, but Pastor Dave and I had a good walk. I needed to talk to him about some things. And he had a problem he's hoping I can help with."

"He's a good man. I like him. Can you help him?" Martha took a sugar cookie, which would have been my second choice.

"Yes he is, and it is possible I can help him. But it sort of depends on you. After Margaret gets married next month, would you be interested in a roommate?" Martha glanced at Margaret, then back at me.

"I guess it depends. I don't want to share it with some rickety old lady. But I also don't want to have some young chick here that would bring down the tone of the place. Is it a friend of Dave's?

"And my friend too... do you remember Connie? She came a few times now, took lots of pictures? She lost her job and needs a place to restart her life. She'd pitch in here at McCaffrey for her room and board. I think she'd enjoy learning to cook at your sides. What do you think?"

"Well, we could give it a try. I liked her when she visited. Her children were well behaved – they won't be coming too, will they? Of course not, they are old enough to be on their own. It would be nice to know I won't be alone. If it doesn't work out, can I make that decision?"

I nodded and gave her a hug. Margaret was all smiles and for the first time I noticed she had put on a little weight. She no longer looked twig-thin. It must be love.

Chapter 17
But seek first the kingdom of God, and his righteousness

A week later, Connie moved in with me where she would stay until after Margaret's wedding. I was saddened to see that her health had deteriorated and I knew she came saddled with debts made by the man Dave had mentioned. I only hoped giving her a fresh start here would actually work.

Margaret's wedding day dawned bright and clear. They had chosen Valentine's Day and, not surprisingly, red was the color of the day. Red roses were brought in for bouquets. Martha, who loved the color herself, bought a new dress for the occasion. Jack, his son's disappearance momentarily forgotten, glowed as much as Margaret did. As I watched them together, I knew I didn't look at Bill like that. I had come to accept that what I felt for Bill wasn't about marriage. Perhaps it was companionship, the need to feel loved and needed. I wasn't sure, but I knew he deserved more than I could give him. I wondered when, if ever, God would put the right man in my life.

The church was overflowing with people who loved the sisters. I knew Jack had no family with him, and while I knew a few of the people who came were his friends, they were swallowed up by the community of Elk Ridge. It really was a celebration by everyone. Margaret had asked Martha and me to stand up for her, which we both were honored to do. For Jack, it was Adam and a gentleman who had come in from Colorado.

As I walked through the people, someone touched my arm. Turning, I found myself facing Chris. I had no idea what to say or do. I wanted her back in the unit so badly, but not at the expense of unity.

"Rebekkah, I'm sorry. I've spent the last month or so realizing just how sorry. I tried to go with the Weber's, but in all honesty, I was better trained than either of them. They really don't understand what it takes, but they charm and smile and people just believe them. And I guess the scary part is they don't realize how much they don't know."

"Do you want to come back to the unit?" I waited, holding my breath. I had always considered her my friend; I wanted her to come back.

"If you'll have me, I'd like to come back. Do you think I can?" I answered her with a hug. The lost sheep had come home. It felt good.

"Rebekkah, Evelyn won't come back. I talked to her and she is starting to sound just like Lillian, except without the charm."

"It's okay. I'm just glad to have you back. Chris, you're my friend. Losing you was like losing a member of my family."

"Thank you – sister. Listen, I know you have a wedding you need to participate in, so I'll go and find a spot to sit. Give my best to the bride!"

Standing in the front of the church, I saw Chris sitting with Al and his wife Paula; together with the rest of the Elk Ridge SAR family. Smiling, I scanned the rest of the faces; so many who meant so much to me, who had impacted my life in so many ways. Then I saw Bill.

The moment our eyes met, I knew he knew. I don't know how, but it was there. Blinking back tears, I wondered if our friendship could withstand this new assault.

After the service, after the photos, after the reception at McCaffrey House, we saw the newlyweds off. I knew they were going to Grand Marais for their honeymoon. I wondered what they'd find to do there in February, but then again, they were newlyweds.

Bill patiently waited while I talked to some friends of Jack's. Excusing myself, I asked Bill if he'd like to come to my little office.

As soon as we were alone, I started to talk, "Bill, I don't know..." Bill put his hand up, and took mine in his.

"It isn't you, it isn't me. During your last visit, I talked about parties and you actually looked sick. I watched you today, how easily you would quietly clean up plates and chat with people at the same time. How you would disappear and suddenly food was on the table. How when it was time for the couple to leave, you managed to get people to the right place... All without people realizing it," He hesitated and thought a moment before continuing.

"I know Rebekkah you could have played my lady of the manor. But I know now, you would have hated it. You would have longed to be in the kitchen helping there, not standing at the door greeting. To be clearing plates and making sure people had what they needed, not chatting nonsense. The person I envisioned you to be isn't who you are."

"Bill, I care so much for you, but your life is not my life. I actually need the woods, the dogs, the searches, and the ability to serve people doing what I'm good at. Playing the lady of the manor, as you put it, isn't it. Getting muddy, bloody and tired, that is what keeps me ticking. I can't explain it."

"I know. I know now anyway. I can't say it helps, it still hurts. I don't know how to go forward from here, I really don't."

Holding out my other hand, he took it and held it. "Bill, I don't either. I would like to think of you as my friend, and be able

281

to call and talk like I used to. I will understand if it would be too hard."

He nodded, squeezed my hands and let go. Walking away, he paused a moment and said, "We'll just see how things go then." Moments later, he was gone.

Drawing in a deep breath, I looked up to see Martha, quietly waiting outside the door. She didn't say a word, just wrapped me into her arms and squeezed me tight. After she let go, we walked arm in arm into their little apartment.

"How are you doing Martha?" I sat her at the table and I made tea. Moments later, Connie joined us.

"I'll miss her, I really will. But I saw how happy she is now. He'll take care of her too. Rebekkah, I'm sorry about Bill, I really am. I couldn't help overhearing. Was it too hard to leave your mom? Like it was hard for Margaret to part with me?"

"No, actually my mom encouraged me to accept Bill if he ever asked. I just wasn't meant for the life he lives, and he wasn't meant for the life I live. Thankfully we both realized it. Martha, do you ever regret not getting married?"

"Not usually. I have lived a very good life. There are times of course when I wonder what it would have been like. I had dreams and I know you think I haven't had any chances, but there was once. Mr. Pophrey lived with sister and me for several years. He asked me to marry him. I said no. I didn't have the heart to leave Margie. I think however, I just wanted to be single. Mr. Pophrey didn't need me, but Margie did. And now, Jack needed Margie. He had no one else you know."

She stopped and studied me for a moment and with a gentle hand on mine, gave me yet another pearl of wisdom, "Rebekkah, embrace your singleness and you will find yourself with so much to give to others. Being single isn't something to be ashamed of or a reason to be lonely. It gives us so much more freedom. Freedom to serve, to love, to give. Embrace it."

She got up and went into her bedroom. Connie, her face drawn and tired, said softly, "I wish someone had told me that years ago. Maybe I wouldn't have made so many mistakes."

"Oh Connie, we all make mistakes, they just aren't the same ones. I have made plenty. You know, for years I dreamed of finding someone like Bill. Someone to give me all the things I think I needed in life. Guess what? I learned that a man couldn't fulfill my life. I have a purpose in what I do now, here. I truly believe if God wants me to marry, He'll provide me the right man at the right time. Now isn't the time, Bill wasn't the man. Does that make sense?"

With a nod, she, too, left to go to her new room. I sat quietly for a bit, wondering if I should head home or wait a while. My mom had gotten a ride from some friends who lived by us. She would have let the dogs out and fed them. I just wanted to sit. I was feeling strangely peaceful considering my life had just taken a dramatic U-turn.

As if someone out there knew I couldn't possibly have a moment of calm, my cell phone rang.

"Elk Ridge SAR, Rebekkah speaking." I yawned, and realized I was exhausted.

"Rebekkah? That you?"

"Yes Matt, it is. Why are you calling so late? Do you have a search?"

"Late? It is only 8:30!" Glancing at my watch, I realized he was right. It had been a long day.

"Sorry, so it is. We had a big wedding in town today, and I guess I'm more tired than I thought. What can we help you with?"

"We have another lead. I know Mr. Hedstrom got married today – oh, I guess that was the wedding you were talking about. Well, I didn't want to contact him right now anyway. We need to check this out first. We've had so many false hopes, I don't want to do that to him again, especially today. I'm ready to quit, honestly. I just can't though."

"I know. I feel the same. So you need a dog? I have Jael. She's a good dog."

"Yes, I heard about Gus, and I'm so sorry. What we have is another person who claims they saw someone out by one of the old mines. It isn't the safest place to search, but we hoped perhaps a dog could sniff without getting too close? Most of the old mines are posted because they are dangerous, but they are a perfect place to dump a body."

I silently nodded my head, too tired to say anything. Or I was falling asleep. I actually jumped when he spoke again, "Can you come tomorrow?"

"Well, there isn't much snow this year, so I guess we'd be able to see where it is safe to walk?"

"That's what I'm hoping. If you want to wait until spring, I guess we can, but I'd prefer to get this over with."

"Sure, I would too. I don't have anything planned at this point, why don't we go ahead. Matt, if we find anything it would interrupt a perfectly good honeymoon you know."

"I know, but I think they would understand. I should show you the stacks of ring binders I have for this case."

I could imagine. Every lead, every clue, every call had to be followed up on and documented. Two years of records.

I met the Sheriff at his office and true to his word, he had two stacks of two inch thick ring binders, each stuffed with papers.

"Every time someone calls, we log it and someone has to follow it up. Thankfully Mr. Hedstrom hasn't hired his own searchers. I hear that happens and then everything goes into cross-purposes. I know sometimes it works, but just as often you end up with more lost information and clues. Or you spend every resource you have following up on things that have nothing to do with the case. Did you know I had four psychics call within days of each other?"

He paused, flipped open one of the binders and fingered through several pages before stopping. Holding an inch of paperwork between his thumb and forefinger, he continued, "This is for those four calls. We followed up what we could."

Shoving the book closed, he sat back in his chair, and I wondered how many pages the dog searches took up in his notebooks.

"I'll be honest with you Rebekkah. I actually had hopes on the last psychic. She seemed normal. She was rational to talk to, and had more specifics than I expected. I won't bore you with details, but the day she walked in and said "I didn't know your deputy smokes" is the day I realized she was pulling us along. If she couldn't sense a man smokes by standing next to him for five minutes, does she really have powers?"

I couldn't help but laugh, but answered honestly, "I don't know – I've never dealt with them before. There are those that say the dogs are black magic. They aren't, but it sure looks that way sometimes."

"Well, I can tell you that there are those that think I'm wasting my time bringing dogs in. They tell me the dogs haven't found a thing to help us. We have witnesses, we have leads, and we have persons of interest. Those are the things to follow. But every time I've worked with the dogs, I see the professionalism of all of the handlers. What your dog did in the impound lot that day. It did look like magic, but I've learned what you put into your training."

"May I ask, do you still believe it is a criminal case?" I watched as Matt paused before carefully putting all the binders in a filing cabinet and locking it.

"Part of me does. Things don't make sense to be honest. Why would an adult man take off without telling his father? Knowing his father is reliant on him? Then that kid that found the coat – was it really found? His story is dodgy at best."

Walking toward the door, he continued with his side of the story. I don't always hear law enforcement's side of a case, so I was glad he was willing to share.

"He claims he found the coat in the woods. I just so doubt that. We executed a search warrant on his apartment and found a few more items that belonged to Tom Hedstrom. Found a few things that belonged to other people who had their cars broken into over the past year or so. But this kid isn't a killer. I just can't imagine him murdering a man pounds heavier and about seven inches taller."

Leaving the office, we drove out to a wooded area clearly marked with "No Trespassing" all over. I didn't see any mine notices, but perhaps they had fallen down.

"As you likely noticed, this is over an hour drive from where the Jeep was found; not exactly walking distance. Why would

286

someone see him here? Went back and sure enough, this was one of the waypoints on the rental's GPS log. In fact, we checked every apparent stop at the beginning of the case. We only called the dogs for that spot off of I-35 you checked. It was the only one that looked promising to dispose of a body."

He paused again and swept a look around the entire area, "you know, we actually line-searched this area as well as another location; came up with nothing. Now we're re-interviewing everyone in the area and bringing a dog in."

After taking my dog out to stretch and take care of her business, I looked over the map Matt had given me and compared it to the landscape. It showed an old mine on the map, but I still saw no actual physical signs of one.

"Rebekkah, the mine is there, you just can't see it. The head-frame was removed long ago. All that is left are the shafts below ground."

Nodding, I pulled Jael's little blue vest over her head and buckled it on. One thing I had learned quickly with a sable-colored German Shepherd is they look an awful lot like a coyote running through the woods. There was no way I would risk a person taking a pot shot at her.

Putting a long line on her and with Matt at my side, we started Jael on her cadaver command. As she worked into the wind, I saw her head bounce twice, up high, then down low. Then I heard her distinctive "HUFF". She was in odor, I knew it. But where was it coming from?

"Matt, I know a lot of men died in these old mines. Is there the possibility that any of their remains are still there?"

"I don't know. They could be. I'd hope they'd get everyone out, but...wait –why do you ask?"

"She's in odor – she has very distinctive changes of behavior when she smells human remains. Did you hear that huff? And watch her head."

Even as I spoke, she huffed again, and began pulling me toward an area lightly covered with a dusting of snow, but no vegetation. I let line out, wondering if what was under the snow was actually the mine.

Hearing creaking and feeling the ground under my feet give, I stopped. I was standing on the boarded over mine shaft. Jael was still pulling forward, but her head was much too high for smelling a body under the ground beneath her. She was pulling scent in from the air. I backed up and walked around the boarded area.

Once out of the concern of the mine shaft, I released her from the long line and let her work the wind. Matt walked along beside me, not saying much which I appreciated. Jael would disappear periodically, but then reappear. The bear bell on her vest ringing fast as she ran, and then slowing as she slowed. She worked steadily, always to the west.

Almost an hour into the search, I could see she was no longer in odor. She had started to come back and look at me, a sure sign she wanted me to assist her. Also a sure sign she no longer smelled human remains.

"Matt, we've passed whatever it was. I'd like to go back, but turn toward the north. The wind has switched as we've worked, perhaps we can pick something up."

He nodded, and I noted again that he was in better shape than I was. While I walked every day, apparently it isn't the same as working out. Turning, I angled our direction back toward where we had come from so the search pattern would end up more like a giant circle. Jael, once again finding the wind in her face, went to work with renewed focus.

Another half an hour and Matt finally spoke, "Did she huff again?"

"Yes, she did. She's back in odor. I only wish I knew where it was coming from. It's like it is all over in here." I watched as my dog swept left and right, head up, and then head down. Feeling a bit out of sorts with the behavior, I felt my blood run cold as she suddenly stopped short and snorted into the ground. All I could see were pine needles, but a moment later, Jael gave me her very best Egyptian cat sit.

"Matt, she's just given her final trained response. I don't see a thing that would indicate a burial there. She didn't check up the trees around it, she seemed intent on the ground, but didn't scratch at all."

"I hope you'll explain all that so I can understand. Do you think she's found something?"

"In all honesty, I think she's in a lot of odor and finally picked this spot to tell me about it. I do not believe she is sitting on a burial. Does that help?"

"A little. What do we do next?" I wondered myself. I had always hated that part of a search. What do you do next.

"I'd like to take a look at a map if we can, see what is around this area. I've marked my GPS. If odor is settling here – you can see we are in a low spot – then it is coming from someplace else. The dog can only tell me where the odor is strongest right now."

"Head back?" Nodding, we returned to the mine and I let Jael take her tennis ball to play with on the walk back. As we entered back into the area of the mine however, I watched my dog once again react to odor. Calling her over, I took the ball and gave her the command again.

Jael after twice trying to steal the ball from my hand, turned and darted off toward the mine. With a "holy cow" under my breath, I realized I should have put the long line back on her. She headed straight to the weak boards that covered the mine shaft area, and I held my breath as she crossed over it. If she broke through, I'd never be able to stop her.

She slowed part way across and I watched her sniff into the boards, but then leave them. Once again, she turned and headed westerly. Calling her back, I pulled her vest off. I praised her and tossed the ball for her before loading her into the truck.

Returning to Matt's office, he located a large map of the area around the mine with help from his Geographic Information Systems, or GIS, department. Leaning over it, I used a ruler to define the wind we had today.

"Matt, does anyone know anything about the mines below ground?" I pointed at a marker on the map some distance northwest of the mine we had checked.

With a phone call, Matt soon had someone who confirmed the marker indicated another mine shaft. I was happy at moments like this to be able to respond to searches on weekdays. When I first started in SAR, I worked a full time, Monday through Friday job. We usually ended up doing cadaver searches on a weekend, and the counties tended to be understaffed and key people unavailable.

"It would be dark by the time we drive back out there Matt. Do you want to try that shaft tomorrow?"

Agreeing to meet in the morning, I went home, wondering if I was on another wild goose chase. Was she really in odor or was it just an anomaly. I was still learning to read this dog. I missed Gus more in that moment than I had before. He was so solid; Jael could still be flighty sometimes.

No one in the unit had been able to come with me the day before, but I hoped that someone could today. I needed the moral support. Calling around, Chris was the only one available. Knowing this was the moment of truth for us both, I asked her to field tech for me.

Meeting Matt at a crossroads, I followed him to an ATV trail. He stopped and asked if I wanted to proceed in my truck or not. The trail narrowed and had lots of twists and turns, but it was wide enough. Agreeing, he got in with Chris and me and I drove on until we reached a point where the trail split, leaving no alternative but to leave my truck.

Jael was happy to get out and run, her blue vest standing out in the stark grays, browns and whites of the winter woods. Working our way north east, I was happy we had wind from a different direction this time.

Chris came prepared and I was glad to have her at my side. Any reservations I had were gone within half an hour in the field. And when Jael alerted, she saw it almost as fast as I did.

"She's in odor, strong odor. How far are we away from the mine?" Before Chris could answer, I saw an old head-frame ahead of us, its rusty metal still marring the beauty of the woods. Surprised it was still there, I lost sight of my dog for a moment until I heard the cracking of wood.

Racing forward, I saw my dog do a flying Frisbee-dog leap and land safely as debris disappeared beneath her feet. Instead of any type of panic, she wheeled around and peered into the hole she had created and then reeled backward.

"Rebekkah – get her back, there might still be poisonous gases down there!" Matt was running with me as I caught up to my dog. Pulling her away, I faced her into the wind and hoped she'd suck in good air.

Instead, she yanked away and went back toward the hole, huffing the entire time. Circling around it several times, I'm not sure why I just stood there, but I guess I instinctively knew she was doing what she was trained to do. Find human remains and I didn't want to stop her.

A moment later, she ran to the southeast, away from the head-frame and then wheeled back. Her energy was almost frenetic and she never once looked at me. She was trying hard to locate the source of the odor.

Watching, I felt Chris and Matt beside me, staring too. Jael, with a determined look instead of her normally quizzical expression, suddenly began snuffing along the ground, away from the hole.

I waited, wondering what she was doing. Dead men don't walk. She couldn't possibly be trailing him. We followed as she worked. With some trepidation, as I wasn't sure where it was truly safe to walk. Old mines were notorious for having cave-ins even now, a hundred years later.

We passed through some low scrub when my dog stopped, turned and bounded over a small knoll. A moment later, she was barking as she flew back to me and snapped at my right hip. Her old live find training, saying she had found a real person.

I followed her back over the knoll at a dead run, and nearly went through a giant hole in the ground. Giant being relative, it was really only about ten feet across, but it looked gigantic as I tried to back pedal away. It was a cave-in.

Jael excitedly barked at the hole, looking expectantly at me. Walking to the edge, I could see nothing. Turning on my flashlight that hung on my pack, I looked again as Matt and Chris joined me.

There was still nothing in the darkness below. But Jael was sure as she yanked at my right hip, actually ripping the pocket of my pants.

"Okay, okay Jael, I believe you." Tossing her ball, she dashed into the woods after it. I only looked blankly at Matt. I had no idea what was going on. What my dog believed she had found. If I had any doubts however, she dispelled them by happily dropping her ball into the hole and looking down, as if expecting someone to throw the ball back.

"That tears it. Matt, she's convinced there is a body or something human down there. What do we do?" I fished out her reserve tennis ball and tossed it again, this time stopping her before she threw it down the hole too.

293

Lying on the ground, he put his head into the hole and shined his own flashlight around. A moment later, all I heard was "There is the tennis ball but I don't see anything else. Wait, I see...it looks like maybe a pack? Pull me back."

Pulling him away from the hole, I glanced at Chris and saw her as wide-eyed as I'd ever seen anyone. Jael had found someone. I didn't doubt my dog, even if Matt couldn't see a body. We just didn't know who it was yet.

Chapter 18
And all these things shall be added unto you.

Matt made the calls to get the equipment necessary to enter an old mine shaft. It requires exceptional safety precautions and specialized tools to access these old sites. In addition, while we didn't know who was down there, it was still a potential crime scene. Matt had to stay. As we had ridden together, Chris and I stayed as well. Truth be told, I wanted to stay anyway. Too much time had been spent on this search. I really wanted to know if it was Tom and what had happened to him.

While we waited, I played fetch with Jael. She periodically would run over to the hole and peek in, which solidified my belief there was a body below us. It reminded me of her returning to the mannequin and repeatedly placing her ball on it. She wanted the person down there to play with her.

Jael had no idea that what lay below us was something humans would consider morbid, sad, or even frightening. She only knew she had found what she was trained to find. And that meant a game of fetch with her tennis ball.

There is no way to explain to more rational human beings what I was doing. That playing with your dog practically over a dead body is normal in our world. Chris understood and periodically would participate. Still, I wondered if the rest of the world were watching, what they would think of us.

The equipment came sooner than I expected, but Matt explained he had put them on standby. I put Jael back into the truck and with Chris at my side, simply watched.

Ventilation fans were brought out, along with what looked like steel girders, ladders, and even self-contained breathing apparatus, or SCBA, equipment. Someone with a high power light crawled to the edge and rechecked the hole. Slowly but surely they began the work to enter the old shaft. I knew Matt had seen what appeared to be a backpack, but beyond that his light didn't reveal anything in the darkness below.

The mine specialists arrived next and with maps and gadgets, prepared to enter the mine. I had no idea if they had a scientific name like cavers did, or maybe it was the same. Either way, I was glad they were going down and not me.

It seemed like hours that we waited, but looking at my watch I realized it was only an hour and a half when the backpack was brought up. Matt waved me over and I looked at what could have been an expensive pack at one time. It was now dirty, chewed on and appeared to have been soaked and dried more than once.

"Found this where you saw it from the surface. We're not finding a body there, but in all honesty, I'd like to bring that dog down below and have it work again – maybe it can give us a direction. There are many levels on this one, more than I expected. It might be faster if the dog really can find human remains." Both men looked at me.

"I don't have all that gear...is it safe?" I looked at all the people around me, all wearing helmets and harnesses and I didn't know what all.

"I'd recommend you put the dog on a leash down there. You never know when you'd cross over a winze that will break through. If we could find an adit, it would make it easier to get you in, but so far, there aren't any close by."

The words alone were enough to warrant a solid no, but once again, my desire to help solve the mystery overrode my caution. I agreed.

In short order, I was geared up like everyone else and Jael put into Ari's old trailing harness. Getting her into the dark cavern was another story however. I went down first with the idea they would lower her to me. Instead, she refused to go. Her claws dug into the board along the edge and she wouldn't be budged.

Going back up the ladder, I wrapped my arms around her and slowly took one step down at a time. Chris unglued my dog's front toenails from the board and the next thing I felt was her back paw try to find a toe hold on my neck. Reaching my collarbone, she held fast and stopped struggling. I could feel blood trickling down into my shirt from her claw, but kept moving.

Reaching the solid floor of the tunnel, I put the dog down and dabbed up the gash with my shirt. Jael, now back on terra firma, immediately huffed. Hard and strong.

Quickly hooking the long line onto her harness, I whispered "go get caddy sweetheart" and let out line. They had the fans running, but thankfully all going one way. Jael circled her head up and sniffing, then turned and headed toward the fans. I let out more line and continued to wait for her to commit.

She committed with a passion. With a hard yank that nearly pulled me off my feet, she put her shoulders into the harness. I followed with the unknown man behind me. We swept past a fan and she hesitated only a moment before moving on. We passed two tunnels off to our right that she barely glanced at, and then swung left. I found myself in a darker tunnel with no fans and no lights.

I nearly yelped when a hand suddenly reached out of the dark, but then the tunnel flooded with light from my headlamp. The man behind me had switched it on, and then switched his own on. Feeling only a bit silly, I followed the dog, who was still huffing and moving steadily.

"We didn't go down this way yet – please be careful." I nodded, which caused my light to bounce up and down. I made a mental note to myself to verbally answer, not nod. It made me dizzy to have the light dance around.

"What's an adit?" Curiosity and the silence were getting to me.

"An outside entrance – often used to help with ventilation and drainage of a mine."

The tunnel ahead made a turn and my dog disappeared around the corner. Almost without warning, my long line went taught. It nearly flew out of my hand except the loop had caught around my wrist. I know I froze. The line felt odd, not like the dog was pulling, but like she was swaying.

A millisecond later I heard Jael whine, then bark and whine. "Something happened up there. I'm afraid to move – I think my dog is dangling. Please help…"

The man slipped past me, dropped to the ground on his stomach and slithered forward. I could only see his feet when he stopped.

"Can you walk up the line? Don't let the line out please, walk up it." He sounded so calm, I didn't panic. Maybe my dog was just fine, although her whining was increasing.

I slowly took a step forward and at the same time pulled in line; another step, another pull on the line. Each step brought me closer to the corner and each section of line kept my dog from going any further than where she was when we stopped.

Turning the corner, I nearly let go. There was my new friend, still on the ground and helping to hold my orange long line. My dog was nowhere to be seen, because she had fallen through a hole in the floor.

"A winze. Please don't panic; just keep pulling if you can. Up to now you've only been supporting her weight. Now you actually have to pull her up. Can you do it?"

"Yes, I think so." Bracing my shoulder against the wall, I began to pull my sixty five pound dog up. I knew the man was trying to keep her from spinning, but I really wished he'd help pull. As I saw the beautiful pointy ears come up out of the hole, the man grabbed her harness and lifted her clear. It was then I realized we had an audience behind us as cheers filled the cavern.

Taking several deep, but shaky breaths, I wrapped my arms around my dog and held her close. She, on the other hand, was still in search mode. She pulled away and went straight back to the hole, peeked down, then turned and gave her Egyptian cat sit.

"Good girl, come here, I'll hand you your ball – no fetch down here tootsie roly." Glancing at the man, I only said "Check down inside – can you see anything?"

Moments later, as I played a modified game of tug with a tennis ball, I heard the "Dear God." I knew they had found Tom.

Returning to the Sheriff's office, I made a running commentary to Chris about what had happened below ground. They had heard the cheers, but didn't know why. They couldn't imagine people cheering to find a dead body.

Entering the office, I was surprised to see Special Agent Paul Mason there. Nodding, he said simply, "Thank you."

"It was Matt. Not many sheriffs would have put this much effort into it. I just trained the dog to do what she does for people like Matt. Has anyone called Mr. Hedstrom?"

"They only told him a body was found, but they haven't confirmed it is him. We really believe it is him of course. All the gear matches, and between you and me, his wallet was still in his pocket. But of course, it could have been stolen. Matt got the dental records a while ago, so it should be an easy check."

"I just don't understand – what really happened? What was he doing up here without a word to his dad? It makes no sense."

"We may never know. From what Matt and the geologists think, it looks like he went exploring and fell down a hole – they called it something else, but it was the same hole your dog went through in the dark. Or he broke through. It appears he was still alive, I hate to say. His cell phone wasn't far from him, but there is no service down there. The bones in his legs were clearly broken in the fall. He must have left his pack right where you guys saw it."

"How on earth did he get there? His Jeep was miles away?"

"Ah, well, while you were out there, Matt had me do some checking. Remember our young man who found that jacket? Yes, well, a few well worded questions and guess what? He stole the Jeep. Took it for a joy ride and decided to park it at the Powwow Trail parking area. Figured it would blend in there longer. A buddy picked him up, helped him clean out what they could to hock later."

"So he found the Jeep over by the mines?"

"By the first one you saw yesterday. Our guess is, Tom couldn't get into that one, so he went to the next one. Overland, it is only about a two hour hike. He was in good shape from what his dad said. He could have made it there and back in a day if he hadn't made the mistake of trying to explore."

"Unless you guys need me, I think Chris and I will head home." Paul started to speak, but I interrupted him, "I know, until they've notified Jack, we won't say anything."

"Correct. Although I hear the media already knows a body was found, so everyone will know about it soon enough." He walked with us to the door, and shaking my hand, he said the nicest thing he could have to me.

"Rebekkah, thank you again. Matt was getting some heat to quit calling for the dogs. I'm glad he didn't. We never would have found Tom without them."

301

Chris gave my arm a squeeze, no words were necessary. It was what we all worked so hard for; to bring the missing home.

I returned home and went back to work the next day at McCaffrey House. My mom knew we had found a body, and I enjoyed telling her about what would likely be a permanent scar on my collarbone because of it.

Several people at the House asked and they, too, were regaled with my bloody shoulder story. I made it as amusing as I could, and people forgot to pursue if I knew who the person was we found. Some still asked what the body looked like. I thankfully could say I never saw it, so could offer no input, and people accepted that.

Several hours later, Matt called to let me know the identity was confirmed. Tom was officially found. Jack had taken it well, and seemed happy that it was a friend who had found him. It seemed to make him feel better about it somehow. I knew from Martha, however, that he didn't understand why his son had left him as he did. What had he done wrong? Was Tom mad at him in the end?

All things no one could answer anymore. Elk Ridge as a whole took on a feeling of mourning, although no one had ever met Tom. Their connection came through the sisters who loved the Hedstroms.

As expected, Jack and Margaret returned early from their honeymoon. Martha, my mom, and I together set up the old Patrick place for them, making sure the heat was up, the bed made and food in the kitchen. As we surveyed our handiwork, Dave and Benjamin came in, carrying wood and a basket of kindling for the fireplace. A moment later, Amy and Adam came in carrying a bundle which presented itself to be a beautiful wedding ring patterned quilt that she had made. In a steady stream, members of the Elk Ridge community came by with offerings for the new couple; including Bill.

Turning, I know I froze a moment, and then was wrapped in a hug by Bill.

"Rebekkah, I couldn't stay home when I heard. I brought some things too for them. And, well, when Terry called to tell me what happened, I found myself wondering if I had my way, if you would have been there to help find Tom. Rebekkah, I really am proud of you."

"Thank you. Friends?" He nodded and rejoined the men. I knew while we would never be as close as we were before, our friendship would continue.

"He's a good man, but apparently not the right good man?" Amy slid her arm around my waist and squeezed.

"No, but I pray he will find the right one, he is a lonely man."

"And you're not, are you." It was a statement. Amy understood as many didn't. I wasn't lonely, I wasn't alone. I squeezed her back. As we stood there in companionable silence, the door opened and Jack and Margaret came in.

After a moment of quiet that no one seemed to know how to break, Dave came forward and welcomed them home.

"Everyone wanted to help get the house ready for you. I hope you don't mind. There is food in the kitchen, the heat is on, and I see Benjamin is getting a fire going for you. Jack, I know this is a really hard time for you, but if you need me, let me know."

We all left, giving hugs as we left. Jack clung to me for a long moment, and finally in a cracking voice, thanked me for returning Tom to him.

I hadn't often had to deal with families after their loved one was found, and usually I had a dog to draw attention away from me. This time however, I just hugged him back and told him how sorry I was. I had no idea what else to say. He drew back and said heartbreakingly, "I don't know why he would do that, leave like that. Not call. I'm so sorry, whatever I said or did…"

"Jack, I'm sure it wasn't you, dear. Likely Tom just wanted to get a head start on your trip. Don't blame yourself." Margaret put her arm through his and led him to one of the chairs by the fire. She nodded at us and we slipped out the door.

After the autopsy, the body was released for the funeral. Margaret was a rock for her new husband. She managed most of the arrangements, and I wondered where that woman had been hiding for so many years.

The funeral, unlike the wedding, didn't fill the church. Those who attended the wedding couldn't make a second trip so soon, but Tom had many friends who came. I helped in the kitchen, wishing the ending had been different for everyone.

Sometimes, we wonder why God allows bad things to happen. We question where God was when someone like Tom is lost, in pain and dying. Yet, as I watched the family that had gathered around Jack in this moment of tragedy, I knew God was there as surely as He had been with Tom. God doesn't force us to be safe, I knew that from experience. He will help guide our footsteps if we let Him, but so often, we don't.

As I contemplated these deep thoughts, I saw Sheriff Matt walk quietly into the room. Smiling, I went to him. I shouldn't have been surprised when he gave me a hug instead of a handshake.

"How is he holding up?"

"Pretty well, considering. I think Jack has more friends now than he's had in many years. He once told me Tom was all he had left to him. Look around the room – everyone here is his family now."

Matt nodded, and gently took my arm, saying softly, "Can we talk?"

Bringing him into the little office down from the kitchen, I waited, wondering what was wrong now.

"We have some information for Jack – I can't call him Mr. Hedstrom anymore either. It's like he's family. I wonder if you could maybe quietly bring them in here."

"Sure, but maybe you can use the apartment there. Connie and Martha are in the front room helping serve, so you should have some privacy for a while."

I went back into the grand front room of McCaffrey and as requested, quietly asked Jack and Margaret to go into the apartment; that Sheriff Matt hoped to speak with them.

Returning to the front, my mom hugged me and informed me the Turner's would be happy to run her home so I could stay as long as I wanted. She was tired. Smiling, I hugged her back and said "thank you for everything mom."

Patting my arm, she only said, "You worked hard Rebekkah, what you did for Jack Hedstrom, well, maybe someone else could have done, but I like to believe that God intended a friend and a family member to find him."

Smiling, I watched her leave, and returned to helping tidy up and making sure everyone felt comfortable. As I went around picking up empty cups and plates, Martha called to me.

305

"Rebekkah, Margaret would like us both to come to the apartment. Connie says she'll be fine out here. You know, she'd make a wonderful front of the house person."

"Martha, you've been watching too many of those cooking shows. But you are right, she was blessed with the skills of a hostess like I never was."

Entering the apartment, I saw Jack holding tightly to some pieces of paper. Glancing at Matt, the sheriff just gave me another hug and left. Margaret took our hands and sat us down before speaking.

"Rebekkah, Jack wanted you and Martha to hear this. Sheriff Tvrdik came as soon as he received these. I don't know if – well, Rebekkah, can you read them for us?"

Jack held two yellowing and rather crumpled pieces of paper to me, along with a very pristine typed letter on heavy ivory colored paper. I could see it was from a ritzy hotel in St Paul and addressed to the sheriff.

"This is the hotel we were staying at, well before Tom went missing. I kept paying for his room for quite a while, hoping he'd show back up there." Jack's explanation helped, but reading the letter, I realized what a blessing God had placed in their hands. As asked, I read them aloud.

Dear Sheriff M. Tvrdik;

During a recent remodeling of our rooms, our staff came across this note behind a dresser. It was found in the Suite that was used by Mr. Thomas Hedstrom and Mr. Jeremiah Hedstrom. We were unable to reach Mr. Jeremiah Hedstrom at his Colorado home, and hoped you will be able to pass this along to him.

I opened the recently crumpled and slightly yellowed note. It was hand-written and I felt my stomach flip around for a moment as I read what was likely the last thing Jack's son had written to him.

> *Dad – decided while you were busy with all that legal stuff I'd pick up some gear and take a quick road trip toward the Boundary Waters – not sure where I'll stop, but I'll give you a call. I want to make arrangements for our trip so after you're done with your business we can go right away. You know how I hate sitting around. Love you! Tom*

Glancing up, I felt the tears welling in my eyes. All was well when he left. Jack had nothing to ask forgiveness for, nothing to regret. He silently pushed the last piece of paper to me. Touching it, I knew this paper was found in the mine. It had the feeling of something old, crackling with having been wet and dry.

"The sheriff said they found it when they... when they prepared him for autopsy." Jack's voice failed at that point, and with blurry vision, I tried to focus on the pencil-written note.

> *Dad – I have no idea what to write, if you'll ever see this. I've tried to call and even text, but nothing happens. Remember the notepad you gave me for Christmas? I'm so glad you did, so I can write to you, to tell you I love you. You were the best dad a boy – and a man – could have. I wish I had listened to you about my marriage, but please tell Sonia I'm sorry too. I leave whatever I have to her, except the camping gear, if it survives. I want you to have it, to use it someday if you can. As a memory for both of us. I'm tired dad, and I can't even see to write anymore. Goodbye, and I love you. Tom*

"He must have been in a great deal of pain, but he thought to write to me. He loved me."

Feeling suddenly more like an intruder, I gently touched each shoulder in turn, and left. Jack could mourn his son properly now. Not everyone we searched for spoke to their family from the grave, but I was so very grateful Tom did.

Arriving home, I walked in and stopped at the front door as I heard my mom's voice. Wondering who she was talking to so gently; I walked quietly into the kitchen.

My mom sat on a chair facing the big sliding glass doors, watching birds at the bird feeder we had put up for her. On either side my dogs sat, watching out the door with her. Her hands were running down their sides, periodically returning up to rub their ears.

"There, Jael, did you see that? That's a Blue Jay – they can be pretty mean to the smaller birds. I hope you are never mean to a smaller dog. Ari, do you know what that was? A Nuthatch. Aren't they pretty and graceful as they dart about? Not like your sister here. She's a bull in a china shop. But you are a prince, Ari, I just know you have royal blood in you. So regal..."

I stood quietly and felt that wonderful, warm and happy feeling of being home.

About the Author

Sharolyn Sievert, An engineering coordinator by trade, has been active in search and rescue since 2003. She lives near Garfield, MN with her mother and her German Shepherd search dogs Ariel and Jael.

Author with K-9 Gus

Sharolyn is an Air Force brat, her father having spent 20 years serving in the U.S. military. She was born on Mother's Day in Tachikowa, Japan. Her dad was an avid outdoorsman and hunter, however Sharolyn ended up going into hunting of a different type – using her K-9 partners to help find missing people.

Search and rescue gives her the ability to be outdoors, work with dogs and give something back to her community. Sharolyn over the years has trained and certified 3 search and rescue dogs in several different disciplines. She also has served as an instructor at national seminars, as an evaluator for K-9 teams and maintains certification in a number of areas related to SAR beyond the K-9 work she loves. Besides her time volunteering as a K-9 handler, she is also a medical First Responder in her community.

K-9 Search: Journey Through the Storm is her second novel.

Printed in the United States of America

Made in the USA
Charleston, SC
20 March 2013